The Yōkai Hunter

I thought I understood this world. I thought I'd seen everything there was to see. I thought nothing else would surprise me. I was wrong.

There is so much in this world that humanity doesn't truly understand. The world is a terrifying place filled with horrific yōkai and demonic creatures that most are blissfully unaware of. They are everywhere. The movements in the corner of your eyes, the shadows that flicker in the darkness, the unending feeling of dread when you know something is wrong but can't tell what.

Against these otherworldly horrors there are but a few humans who know the dreadful truth of such monstrosities. These are the yōkai hunters. My life changed the day I met one of these such people. I was thrown into a terrifying world I knew nothing about yet the encounters I had alongside this lone hunter opened my eyes to the truth. Humanity is but inches away from utter chaos yet there are those who would protect us.

This journal of mine documents the first year I spent with a yōkai hunter. It details the horrific beings we encountered, how we avoided death each time and how ultimately I was able to survive. Since writing this diary I have come to understand that these creatures, and their hunters, are present everywhere. Sometimes they go by different names or have minor evolutionary differences but all are frightful beings that exist only to cause suffering and pain.

If you're reading this then I implore you to remember the details of how to defeat such beings. I hope for your sake that you never encounter one but if you're unlucky then maybe the notes made in this journal will provide you with a chance of survival. I wish I could give you more but despite all of my research and experiences my knowledge barely scratches the surface of this nightmarish world.

A great person once told me not to go looking for these beings. I repeat that warning to you now. To face a yōkai is to face death yet it is through knowledge that we can give ourselves a chance.

Live safe dear reader and know this, when your hair stands on end, when you're alone and feel like someone is watching you, when you hear something you can't explain, run and never look back.

Best of luck.

The Price of Beauty

January 1st

Happy New Year! At least that's what you're meant to say isn't it? What do I have to be happy about? I haven't managed to sell an article for months now, money for the rent is going to dry up pretty soon and, as usual, my New Year's celebration was spent alone. The perfect start to the year.

They say the New Year is a time to be positive though so here goes, this year will be better than last, frankly it'll be difficult to be any worse. Anyway here's to the New Year. Let's hope it's a good one.

I bought this dairy on a bit of a whim. I'm hoping it might come in handy to jot down any leads I find. I can't say I'll stick with it throughout the year though and I certainly won't find time to write everyday but I'll get down what I can, hopefully enough to make it worth the cost of buying the thing. Who knows, maybe one day I'll be able to look back at this year as the one that changed my life.

The year isn't even a week old yet and already I hate it. I always knew freelance journalism was a difficult life but it feels like I'll never be able to sell anything. The big stories have experienced journalists crawling all over them whilst nobody is interested in the small stuff I can get exclusives on. Even the feel-good stories that I've been writing recently aren't getting picked up. It's getting pretty bad. My agency is talking about dropping me unless I can get a piece sold soon. I've maybe got ten weeks of rent left so I need something soon or else.

Tomorrow I have another happy story to write up, some hero dog that should make for a heart-warming tale. I can't say it's the sort of stuff I want to be reporting on but needs must and right now I desperately need something to sell. Hopefully some local paper will want to run it.

That dog story was a non-starter from the get-go. Barely enough story there to cover a paragraph. What a waste of a day! I was told about another event tomorrow though, that might have a bit more promise although it's writing a story for a local dog magazine. How am I meant to get anywhere writing articles like that? I'll do it for the money but still, why can't I stumble across something good to write about?

Take this, for example, I overheard a rumour today of a murder near my neighbourhood that wasn't reported. I couldn't find out anything else about it from anywhere so I can't be certain it even occurred but if it did then I could get top billing on it. If I could break a story like that then I might be able to get somewhere, people always love a good murder piece. Unfortunately without even the name of the victim there's not much I can investigate. Chalk it up as another story that got away. Probably just a rumour anyway.

Turns out that the article for the local dog magazine paid less than my travel expenses. I knew it wasn't proper journalism anyway. Still, if I don't get someone to buy a 'proper' story from me soon I'm really going to have to think about getting a different job, or living on the street.

I did at least hear one interesting thing today. A second murder in our area, similar to the other unreported one. I did a bit of research and discovered four murders in the same district in the last few weeks that somehow haven't been reported by the press. If I get the scoop on them then I'll be back in the game. It makes no sense that nobody has picked up on this, possibly oversight, hopefully a cover-up. That would really make for a juicy piece. I'll look into them tomorrow, see if I can get the police to tell me anything. I don't know why but I'm getting the impression that this might just be my big break.

What a day! I almost don't know where to begin, I could've died! My hands are still shaking. Of course I've seen things doing this job before that have scared me but nothing like this. It sounds so crazy just thinking about it. Hopefully writing it down will help me organise my thoughts, if that's even possible.

It all started this morning when I followed that lead about the murders and, incredibly, it appears to be true, four apparently unconnected deaths over a period of three weeks, two of them just outside their own homes and bizarrely they don't seem to have been reported on. It's just not normal, this is an affluent district of Kyoto I'm talking about. Four murders don't just happen especially in such a short time period. It sounded like the work of a serial killer, if that was the case then that would be the story of the year.

Anyway following up on the lead I visited the local police station and asked around about the deaths. They were especially cagey today, they often are around journalists and I rarely get a straight answer but they refused to even acknowledge that the murders had taken place! It was odd, almost as if they were hiding something. Their evasiveness got me interested about the possibility of a cover up so I questioned some locals about the deaths. They too were surprisingly quiet on the matter although an elderly gentleman was able to inform me that the attacks had all happened at night. It wasn't much to go on but I was also able to confirm with him the locations of the murders.

With that in mind I began a circuit of the four sites after darkness had fallen. It only took half an hour to get between them on foot, all of them being in the same district and a couple on adjoining streets. Unfortunately even though a couple were very recent there were no signs of any murders at the scenes and the streets were surprisingly empty. It was almost as if the police had scrubbed the area clean, desperate to hide that the murders had ever taken place. Each of the locations was an odd choice for a murder site too. I'd expected alleyways and blind spots where the killer could strike at their victims unseen but these sites were all out in the open. A couple on the doorsteps of apartment blocks, one in a busy street with plenty of overlooking windows and the final one at the entrance to a park. That was the only one that resembled a stereotypical murder site yet even that was well lit and near a busy road. It seemed impossible that nobody could have witnessed at least one of the murders. With nothing useful at the scenes I was soon heading home desperate to follow up with any neighbours tomorrow in the hope of finding a big cover up. That was when things took a turn for the worse.

The darkness of the evening seemed to come in surprisingly quickly and the lights of the streets all seemed to flicker far more than usual and I noticed that a thick fog had rolled in. I was just outside my front door fumbling with my keys, looking forward to getting inside before the oncoming rainstorm hit when a woman approached me. I'll admit she kind of spooked me as I hadn't seen or heard her but when I turned she was standing right next to me and staring at me with an intense gaze. She seemed out of place with her long dark hair, piercing eyes and designer coat. The rest of her face was covered by a mask preventing me seeing her nose or mouth. I thought she might have been looking for some sort of event and become lost but before I could say anything she asked me a peculiar question, "Am I pretty?" It was an odd thing to ask at night from a complete stranger but I stopped to look at her wondering if she was drunk or simply going through a rough breakup. Even through the darkness I could tell that she was, long perfectly styled dark hair with fair unblemished skin, she was the stereotype of attractiveness. Trying to be nice, yet wanting to back away slightly as she had moved uncomfortably close to me, I stumbled out an answer to the positive. Well, that seemed to set her off. Instantly she removed her face mask to reveal what was underneath whilst yelling "What about now?" at me. I'll admit, I've seen some awful things searching for stories, even seen a few corpses but never anything as grotesque as what was under her mask. Her face was split ear to ear in a horrific permanent smile that showed all of her teeth and great blood-encrusted scars that ran across her cheeks. I'm ashamed to say that I screamed at the sight which in hindsight probably wasn't the kindest thing to do but in the darkness she looked positively ghoulish. Apparently my reaction enraged her as she immediately drew a knife from her inside coat pocket and lunged at me.

I would've been dead if not for what happened next. The woman's blade was halted just inches from my face by another knife, this one serrated and in the hand of a different woman. This woman was almost the exact opposite of the first, quite tall and well-toned, she wore her hair in a ponytail and carried a look of disgust on her face yet her eyes burned with a hatred I have rarely seen before. Anyway she calmly stated "I think you're only so so" as if she was answering the question the scarred woman had put to me. Incredibly the first woman turned her attention away from me to this second woman and stared blankly at her although their blades remained dangerously close to my face. Before I could move away the second woman drew an additional knife from her waist and stabbed the first in the guts but, here's the incredible part, the first woman simply vanished, disappearing into the air as if she'd never been there. Unsure of what I'd just witnessed I spoke to my saviour but she wouldn't tell me anything only saying that the woman had gone and I should rest. I kept asking her questions though and eventually she did say that if I was interested in having answers about my attacker I should meet her at the local morgue tomorrow morning. I'll head there first thing. I can sense a story here that might get me back in the game, especially if it's linked to that murder cover-up.

It's taken me quite some time to calm down after I closed my front door. I didn't bother calling the police as, without evidence, they'd think my story crazy. Honestly, I'm not even sure myself if any of it was real. Attacked by a crazy woman in my own doorway, it sounds preposterous yet that's how two of the murder victims were found. Could I have been attacked by their killer? Why did she attack me? Why was her face like that? How come she simply vanished? That's why I have to meet that strange second woman tomorrow, I have to find out whether or not any of this really happened.

I'm definitely onto something with these murder cases although it's not something I can truly claim to understand nor really believe. If anything today was even more bewildering than yesterday if that's even possible.

It all started as soon as I woke and headed to the morgue in the hope of getting some answers. The night had felt long and sleepless yet the questions raised by my encounter last night were still burning brightly. Fortunately, I was in luck, and my saviour from last night turned up only a moment after I did. It was only when I saw her again that I realised how little I knew of her, and that what I had seen suggested she was to be avoided. Yes, she had undoubtedly saved my life from the other woman yet she had then stabbed her without hesitation. It dawned on me that she might not be the safest person to be meeting although there were others milling about that gave me confidence that she wouldn't attack me.

The woman was dressed in the same outfit as before, a practical pure black number which did little to hide the fact that she appeared in peak physical condition, and in the light of day I could see that she had a hard face and carried great wisdom in her eyes. On her waist hung the two knives which she'd so gracefully used the night before. It was noticeable that she felt no need to hide them despite being on a busy street yet nobody seemed to pay her any attention, then again, why would they? With the exception of her knives she didn't look out of the ordinary. She hardly paid any attention to me but before she went into the morgue I had to take the opportunity to ask her a few questions desperate for answers. She told me that her name was Shiho but refused to give a family name, or any other information about herself, leaving her something of an enigma. She did however have some incredible information about the woman who attacked me last night. Firstly, she claims that, despite stabbing the woman before my own eyes, she's not actually killed her. In fact, she claims that she can't kill her and that whoever that woman was she's not even human anymore! It sounds ridiculous but Shiho claimed that the woman was an onryō, a vengeful spirit, specifically a Kuchisake-onna. I couldn't believe what she was saying but the way Shiho spoke it was clear that she believed it, or worse, knew it to be true. Of course I've heard ghost stories before, growing up who doesn't, but I'd never taken them seriously. I wouldn't have taken Shiho seriously either had I not seen that woman disappear without a trace last night. Still the notion that it could've been a spirit that attacked me seemed preposterous.

Shiho claims to be an expert in this sort of thing, although I'm not sure if one can be an expert in children's stories, and stated that she'd dealt with other Kuchisake-onna before. That's how she knew how to drive the spirit away. Willing to play along I asked her to explain what she knew. She claims that Kuchisake-onna can be created in a number of different ways but are all caused by death after, or due to, mutilation. Thinking about it, those slits in that woman's face were probably what caused her to die! At least that is if Shiho is telling the truth about all this. She also claims that Kuchisake-onna are quite simple creatures driven by vanity and the desire to be beautiful although, worryingly she also claims that it's set its sights on me after I screamed at it last night. Apparently I've offended the spirit and it's looking to take revenge. I was ready to walk away at that point thinking it all rubbish and Shiho to be crazy but she simply stated "stay with me if you want to live" and how can you say no to that? I don't believe in the supernatural but having researched those murders and seen that woman, I guess I had doubts in my mind. Not wanting to take any risk I asked what I needed to do to rid myself of this onryō. Naturally Shiho had an answer to that too. She says the creature needs to be banished, as if that was an everyday occurrence and simple to achieve. Apparently the thing with Kuchisake-onna is that their vanity drives them to seek revenge on the one who mutilated them. Bringing them to justice should be enough to sooth the spirit and banish it. Shiho claims that unless this is done it will continue to haunt the city targeting any who walk alone at night. More than that Shiho claims that as it kills more the spirit will become emboldened and start targeting groups. She's worried that it could kill hundreds if left unchecked. It still sounded ridiculous to me but there was something oddly terrifying about that woman last night and the way Shiho spoke that was making me question myself. I still wasn't sure whether or not she was insane but I was willing to take that risk, if only to see where it led.

Agreeing with Shiho's theories about the creature I decided to stick with her and asked why we were at the morgue. The answer was quite obvious really, she too had been investigating the recent murders and wanted to examine the victims herself. That at least proved something to me, there was a chance that my story could be linked to Shiho's Kuchisake-onna. If that was the case then imagine how big that story would be. The first person to accurately report on a ghost, it would be worth millions, provided I don't come across as crazy. With that in mind I set about trying to get all the information on the case.

The two of us managed to get into the morgue without a fuss. I don't know if Shiho paid them off or if she knew the people there but they didn't even question her presence and led us straight to the victims. They had all four in there, remarkable given that the police denied the existence of the crimes, and the sight was pretty horrible although Shiho seemed relatively pleased, almost as if she was expecting it. I asked her why and she replied that their injuries were all consistent with Kuchisake-onna attacks and that she was glad "it wasn't something worse" leaving me to wonder what could possibly be worse than a vengeful spirit stalking the night. From the way Shiho had spoken it was clear that she didn't believe that Kuchisake-onna were as terrifying as they seemed to me yet I can't imagine a more horrifying monster. Getting back to the corpses, they were all similar, pale white with large cuts to their faces as if the creature was trying to make them like her, an observation Shiho confirmed. It was pretty grotesque but fortunately we didn't stay long. After confirming that the Kuchisake-onna was the cause of the deaths Shiho was quick to leave heading straight for the police station barely giving me enough time to even consider the implications of what she had said and whether it could be true.

I asked her why we'd go to the police, you can't exactly lodge a complaint against a spirit, but she claimed that she needed further information and the police would be most likely to have what she needed. When I asked what she was looking for she explained that this particular Kuchisake-onna was relatively new, likely created just before the first attack. She also explained that it was therefore likely that the poor soul who had become it would either be a recent murder victim or a missing persons case with the police. I was still unsure what information she wanted other than to tell them that she'd found their killer, or suspected it to be a vengeful spirit, but she told me she was after the identity of the Kuchisake-onna and didn't expect the police to assist in stopping the creature in the slightest. Apparently her plan is to find out who the Kuchisake-onna was in life and from that work out what happened to her. From there she should be able to work out why she's feeling so vengeful. Apparently my suggestion that it could be because she's dead didn't go down well. For a woman who believes in ghost stories, Shiho doesn't seem to have a sense of humour. Her plan seems a long shot to me but, fearful of running into the creature again without her having seen the victims, I followed her to the police station expecting little better than I'd received the day before.

Bizarrely at the police station, similar to the morgue, they appeared to have no trouble at all with Shiho's arrival and didn't particularly question her when she demanded to see their recent murder and missing people cases. In fact they seemed quite pleased that she was there. Perhaps she'd helped them out previously, which would explain why they quickly answered her questions and didn't mine. It raised a troubling thought, if the police knew Shiho and she had worked with them before did that mean that her claims about onryō are real? If so that would explain why the police were so cagey yesterday, if the public knew these things existed it would cause mass panic. Extrapolating threw up a worrying thought, could every unsolved murder in the city be caused by these spirits and the police just refuse to acknowledge them? The officers there told us that there had been no other reported murders in the area over the past few months but a few suicides and a handful of missing people. Shiho immediately discounted the suicides, apparently a Kuchisake-onna is too vain to commit suicide and nobody could mistake her wounds as being self-harm. I asked about the possibility of her killing herself after what had been done to her but Shiho shook her head saying they simply wouldn't commit suicide, no matter what. Discarding them as possibilities she moved onto the missing persons cases and swiftly scanned them for any females aged between twenty and forty guessing that was the age range for our onryō. That was quite a range but Shiho was correct when she asked if I could be more precise about my attacker. It had been dark and with a face drained of blood, it was difficult to place her age. Mercifully there were few that fit the profile and between the two of us we managed to narrow it down to three possible subjects based on the photos provided. Unfortunately each of them were quite similar in size and with the distorted face of the spirit it was impossible to precisely state which it could be. There wasn't much the police could add, each had been last seen less than a week before the first murder and each lived relatively nearby. Shiho quickly made a note of the home addresses and then we were on our way again in search of the identity of our Kuchisake-onna.

The first two places turned up very little in the way of evidence, a distraught family in the first and a hungry yet unhelpful cat in the second. Shiho was keen to give the cat some food and called a local shelter for reasons I cannot imagine but it couldn't provide us any help. There was a boyfriend from the first who may have been a person of interest but the family suggested that they had been in a loving relationship and he appeared pretty shook up about it all. Shiho seemed to suggest that it wouldn't have just been a random attack to slit someone's face ear to ear, unless someone was actively trying to create a monster which is something I hope has never happened, so instead we focused on the final missing person.

By the time we reached the third house, it had become quite late and the sun had set. I could tell that this was worrying Shiho as she kept glancing over her shoulder at the growing darkness. It was only when we arrived at the locked ground floor flat that I realized what she was worried about. At the end of the street, the very same woman from the previous night stood waiting, her face once again obscured by her mask but she was clearly looking directly at us, her knife this time was already in her hand and she was showing no signs of the wound inflicted on her last night. Somehow the Kuchisake-onna was tracking us! "She's here for you" was all Shiho would say before we heard the odd call of the Kuchisake-onna, "do you think I'm pretty?" Having learnt from last night I replied "so so" but the creature continued its advance no longer bemused by the vague answer. At that point I saw Shiho draw her blade and the creature remove its mask showing its horrendous face. "That won't work anymore" stated Shiho as if I was an idiot for saying it and demanded that I pick the lock. Now I've never picked a lock to steal anything before but it is a useful skill for helping sniff out stories so I was able to. Unfortunately the creature was fast and it was quickly next to us. I thought we were going to die but again Shiho was able to save us. She threw something at the spirit which momentarily distracted it, allowing us the time to slip inside and bolt the door. I asked what she'd thrown at it and she said it was boiled sweets! How she knew that would work is beyond me but she claims that it learns from each distraction and those are two of the three she knows. The final method is to simply tell the creature that you're late for a meeting and it may apologise if it believes you. Why that would work, or who found that out I have no idea but it's true that Shiho appears to understand this creature. Unfortunately she explained that the third method rarely works and since we've already encountered it, it wouldn't work for us. If we meet the creature again, she won't be able to stop it.

Inside the flat was similar to what you'd expect, small but well looked after. Searching for clues as to whether it was the home of the monster I found plenty of other designer clothes and bags in the wardrobe that would match the designer coat the Kuchisake-onna wore but Shiho found something even better, a leaflet for a plastic surgeon that had been left in the kitchen. That could've been where she got her scars! That surgery will be where we pick up the trail tomorrow but right now we're trapped in here until the morning. Shiho claims that there's never been an instance of a Kuchisake-onna setting foot inside a building that she's aware of and that it'll vanish in the light of the morning. I must admit, I'm not too sure I believe her but as she sleeps peacefully next to me I write this looking out of the window at the dead eyes of the Kuchisake-onna which keeps us prisoner, I can only pray that she's right and that we survive the night.

How did I end up here? Twenty-four hours ago I was searching for a news story and now I'm here, trapped in a small apartment with a woman I've just met by a spirit that's trying to kill us. I'm beginning to think that I've stumbled into more than I can manage.

I can't sleep. That thing just stares at me showing off its horrendous scars in the moonlight. It's stood right next to the window repeatedly asking if I find it pretty. The apartment is small and there's nowhere I can go to escape its gaze. It can't be more than four feet away from me. I woke Shiho but she just went back to sleep telling me to ignore it. I'm scared.

It's all true isn't it? Everything Shiho said. In the back of mind I thought it all might just be some wild prank but there's no way that thing out there is teenagers messing around. Those scars aren't fake and it leaves no breath on the window. I think it genuinely could be real. If that's the case then what else is out there lurking in the darkness? I don't think I can sleep with that thing watching me.

January 16th (Entry 2)

We survived. I don't know how but we survived. As Shiho had said the Kuchisake-onna just stood there all night watching us and as morning broke it vanished, fading away with the first rays of the sun. Shiho woke maybe an hour before the sun rose and went to stand at the window looking at it. I think she feels sorry for it but I didn't ask questions. The Kuchisake-onna did enough of that, forever pestering Shiho for an answer to its question. Shiho never spoke instead she just stood facing it for an hour, their hands pressed on opposite sides of the glass. I think she's telling the truth when she says she's encountered one before, maybe someone she knew. That would explain why she knows so much about them.

With the Kuchisake-onna gone we were finally free from our prison and Shiho was keen to immediately head to the surgery mentioned on the leaflet we'd found. She stated that she wanted to find out what had happened to the woman as soon as possible because although the Kuchisake-onna was currently interested in us, it wouldn't be long before somebody else stumbled across her and gave her an answer she didn't like.

It didn't take long for us to get to the surgery and in truth it was quite a small one, only a couple of operating rooms and a handful of staff. Despite that it was clean and professional looking, certainly not the backstreet illegal surgery I first thought it would be. It was possible that they could've made a medical mistake but it was licensed and a quick look online suggested no bad reviews. If it wasn't for the fact that Shiho was convinced we had the right woman I would've said we were in the wrong place entirely. The receptionist was surprisingly helpful when Shiho showed her a picture of the missing woman. It didn't take much to gain her trust, Shiho simply posed as a worried relation trying to track her down and the receptionist easily bought her story, it's worrying how easily she lied. The receptionist stated that our missing woman had visited the clinic around a month ago and had been seen by Dr Yamaoka. Why she'd come to the clinic in the first place she wouldn't tell us but she assured us the doctor could be of more assistance. Trying to help us further she even told us that Dr Yamaoka was in today but we'd have to wait until he'd finished his appointments for the day if we wanted to see him. I expected Shiho to object but oddly she appeared happy to wait even though it would take most of the day and the night would inevitably bring the return of the Kuchisake-onna. A return which Shiho claimed to be powerless to prevent. She seemed strangely confident though that this Dr Yamaoka would provide the details she needed as she was already certain that we had successfully identified our Kuchisake-onna. She says that finding out what had happened to her would be key to defeating her and to defeat her we'd actually need her to be there hence the wait was necessary regardless of what we found.

The wait wasn't entirely boring though, it gave me a chance to learn more about Shiho and the strange world within which she seems to operate. She claims that she's been doing this for a while now and that there are all sorts of creatures out there that she deals with on a regular basis. She says that Kuchisake-onna aren't the only type of onryō and that there are plenty of different types of creatures too. In all honesty she seemed slightly dismissive about the threat of Kuchisake-onna compared to some of the other creatures she mentioned which she listed rapidly without any real explanation. Where these beings come from or what their purposes are she wouldn't say although she politely suggested that after we'd dealt with the Kuchisake-onna I shouldn't go looking for them, not that I'd ever want to encounter such beings again, especially those she considers worse than the masked killer stalking me. Quite how Shiho had come to know of these creatures she wouldn't say, nor would she tell me why she had chosen to study them let alone face them. The only thing that she would confirm about herself was that she was indeed investigating the same four murders I had been and was only doing so because the police had come to her for assistance. She calls herself a yōkai hunter, a private investigator for this sort of thing and she often gets work from the police. Whenever they can't solve a case and suspect the supernatural they call in Shiho. The whole thing seems odd to me, if it truly is real then how come this isn't reported on? Surely if these creatures were as common as Shiho claims then more people would know about them. Then again, it's so crazy that I wouldn't have believed it myself if I hadn't seen the Kuchisake-onna with my own eyes. Imagine the stories I could sell if I could get Shiho to tell me more. It could be the break I need provided I don't just come across as insane.

Anyway it must've been getting on towards four in the afternoon when Dr Yamaoka finally decided to speak with us. We were led to his room to meet him and I'll admit on first impression alone, I wouldn't want to be treated by him. His hair was a mess, his beard unkempt and his eyes bloodshot as if he hadn't slept for days. My first thoughts were that he was on drugs but it turned out to be far worse. Initially when Shiho showed him the photo of the missing woman he denied knowing her but he quickly broke after Shiho stated we'd seen the records of her visit in reception, admitting that she had come to him for some work on her cheeks. I was surprised by how open he was but Shiho appeared to be exerting some unseen pressure on him, seemingly knowing his answers before asking the questions as if she'd lived through this all before. Either that, or he was desperate and already at breaking point. He certainly offered little resistance before telling us everything. Dr Yamaoka claimed that he'd made a mistake during a routine operation on the woman when she'd unexpectedly moved causing him to cut deep into her cheek causing the split which the Kuchisake-onna so hideously wears. He then claimed that she'd bled out before he could get help and that he'd panicked, waiting until everyone else had left and then burying her in a shallow grave nearby under the cover of darkness. The way he spoke seemed genuine to me but Shiho appeared unimpressed by his tale. Dr Yamaoka claimed that he didn't know what she'd become and that he was haunted by the Kuchisake-onna every night since. He claims that he's been unable to sleep and hasn't left his clinic for weeks for fear of encountering the spirit. That at least would explain his appearance. He says he can see it through the windows watching him, waiting for him to go outside. Oddly he even reported seeing it the previous two nights making me wonder whether it had visited him at the clinic before coming after us or somehow had the ability to be in both places at once. Shiho later confirmed that the first was more likely as very few creatures could be in multiple places at once and Kuchisake-onna certainly weren't on that list. Fear of the spirit had clearly broken

Dr Yamaoka though, as he spoke he moaned and cursed his luck and was constantly glancing at the window, but he had enough sense to ask Shiho for help after she'd let slip that she'd encountered other Kuchisake-onna before. She reassured him that now she knew what had caused the spirit to be created she would be able to banish it. All we had to do was wait until nightfall and for the Kuchisake-onna to come out to play.

So wait we did, all three of us, sat in the clinic mostly in silence other than the occasional bursts of fright that took Dr Yamaoka until Shiho declared it to be time. Slowly the three of us approached the door and peered out into the darkened street. It was deserted, no signs of the creature nor anybody else. Dr Yamaoka appeared quite happy confirming that this was the time and place he had seen the spirit on previous days and suggested maybe it was gone but Shiho didn't seem to trust the silence. "It's here somewhere" she kept saying "we just need to draw it out". How you draw out a creature like that was beyond me but Shiho knew of a way. Unbelievably, and without warning, she shoved me out into the street and slammed the door behind me! I will admit I did not appreciate being used as bait for the creature but it worked. No sooner had I stopped banging on the door I heard that now all too familiar question "do you think I'm pretty?" My blood froze when I turned around to see the Kuchisake-onna standing all of five meters away from me, knife in hand. Unlike my first encounter with the creature this time I was too terrified to reply and was just hoping that it wouldn't remove its mask and subject me to seeing its hideous face once more. Whether the spirit was expecting an answer or simply didn't care, it started to approach me and I could feel the air around me grow colder. Truth be told after everything Shiho had told me of Kuchisake-onna, I think having already answered it once there was nothing I could say that would stop it from attacking me.

It was then that Shiho hatched her plan, opening the door and strong arming Dr Yamaoka out in front of her as I scuttled back through the door eager to get away from the Kuchisake-onna. I don't know if it would've entered the clinic but I hoped it wouldn't. Dr Yamaoka appeared even more terrified than I was though and quickly collapsed to his knees as Shiho threw him between me and the spirit. The Kuchisake-onna, seemingly an ever easily distracted spirit, possibly why Shiho thinks so little of them, immediately turned towards the doctor asking her question yet again. "Do you think I'm pretty?" Dr Yamaoka was kneeling in front of her sobbing and refusing to answer until Shiho shouted at him to tell her what he'd told her in life. "No, you can be improved." He replied quietly between sobs and the Kuchisake-onna removed her mask causing the doctor to scream at the sight of the gruesome scars he had caused. "What about now?" Screamed the Kuchisake-onna playing out the same conversation I'd had with it two nights prior proving the answer to the first question makes no difference only Dr Yamaoka didn't answer the second, instead he just looked away and sobbed. I expected Shiho to intervene, to force him to apologise, but she just stood watching as the spirit reached for the doctor and slit his face open ear to ear with one swift motion, matching its own horrendous look. Blood gushed out from the wound covering the pavement and it was clear that he had died almost instantly. Horrified I watched as the creature then turned to us, in one hand the body of Dr Yamaoka, in the other the bloody knife used to kill him. I took a deep breath waiting for the creature to kill me as I too had answered it previously but instead it vanished without a trace, disappearing into the night leaving both Dr Yamaoka and the knife used to kill him behind.

Confused as to where it had gone I turned to Shiho who explained that with its vengeance carried out it no longer had a purpose and therefore was no longer bound to our plane. She seemed quite confident in that and tentatively I stepped back outside thankful that the creature didn't return. Feeling reassured that it had been banished I asked Shiho why she'd let it kill Dr Yamaoka after reassuring him that she'd help but all she'd say was "he only explained one slit, not the other" and didn't want to discuss it further. Quite whether he could've been a murderer I'm not so sure but Shiho appeared convinced. Thinking back I guess it was true that his story did only explain why the Kuchisake-onna had a slit running to one ear and made no mention of the other side of her face. It's also true that he could've reported it or attempted to get help even if she was bleeding out quickly. Whether letting him be killed by such a creature was justice though I can't really say but with the disappearance of the Kuchisake-onna I can't argue that it didn't serve a purpose. I guess in the end though Shiho had kept her promise to me to keep me alive so I owed her the benefit of doubt, I certainly wouldn't have survived being attacked by the creature. I did ask what she would do with the body of the doctor and she explained that the police needed someone to take the blame for the recent four murders and that the doctor would be a fitting candidate. Quite why she wanted to make up such a story for the police I wasn't certain but she seemed to think it was better than telling the world that a Kuchisake-onna was behind the attacks. I get the impression that it's not the first time she's given the police a plausible culprit.

With that she bid me farewell and I returned home, quite amazed by everything that I'd seen. Even sitting here, comfortably back in my apartment, I wonder just how true it all was, odd since I lived through it yet the last forty-eight hours have opened my eyes to what might be possible. It will however make quite the story, perhaps one I'll actually be able to sell. Probably a watered down version in the end cutting back on mentioning spirits or I could at least market it as fiction, I don't think people will go for the true horrifying story of what really stalked the streets of Kyoto this last month. I imagine the police and Shiho wouldn't be too pleased if I blew their cover story too. Perhaps if all else fails then I could break the news of a killer doctor. It's not completely true but it's a story that would sell.

I do wonder if I'll ever see Shiho again, sure her world seemed terrifying and dangerous but I can't help but feel alive after the past few days. Then again, it was actually the closest I've ever come to death. Maybe it would be safer to forget all about onryō, after writing up my article of course.

Oddly, one thought keeps coming back to me about the Kuchisake-onna though, she was already pretty before she went to that surgery.

It's been a few days since my encounter with Shiho and the Kuchisake-onna and the whole thing is still playing on my mind. I still can't quite believe any of it happened but the creature hasn't returned. I did a bit of research online about it all and found a number of websites detailing the Kuchisake-onna. As expected each of them were clear that it was just a story and nothing more but I've seen one and know that to be a lie. There was nothing on those sites to settle my nerves about the spirit although it was clear that nobody would believe these things to be real even if I did write up an article on them.

Speaking of my article, I wrote up a quick piece on Doctor Yamaoka suggesting that he was behind the four recent murders. A few of the local papers were at least decent enough to pick up on the story although they sent their own reporters to question the police and I was paid minimum. At least it's pushed eviction day back by a week or so but I really thought that I might be able to make more from meeting the Kuchisake-onna. If I can't then it won't seem worth risking my life for.

I've done some more research and although the truth behind the Kuchisake-onna would be too extreme for the mainstream press I have found some supernatural publications where it might fit. They accept all kinds of ghost stories, fiction based of course, but I can just tell them that the tale was fantasy. They don't need to know that the story was true. It's not the sort of thing that I'd normally write for but I think it would fit quite nicely with the article I'm writing. There appears to be a decent following for this sort of thing and they pay well provided that you can get in.

I'll put the finishing touches to the story over the coming days and send it to a number of them, see if that will scrape together enough to support myself through the next few months.

So it's finally written up. "The Price of Beauty" as I have called it is the full account of my encounter with the Kuchisake-onna and how with the help of my new yōkai hunter friend we managed to banish it from this world. Of course when I say the full account I mean an embellished version in which I play a far more heroic role than the terrified mess that I actually was. I don't see the problem with that, if they can't face the truth of the Kuchisake-onna then why should they get the truth about my actions? Most of the details remained the same, excluding the names of course, so I still count it as pretty accurate. I even made sure that Shiho got the majority of the credit so even she can't get mad if she ever reads it.

I've submitted it to a few publications, I'll admit the more frequent ones would be better but that's because they pay sooner. Hopefully it'll be in time for the February edition for a couple of them but that might be asking too much. Either way I guess it's out of my hands now. All I can do is wait to see if they get back to me and in the meantime try to sniff out a story that the papers would buy from me although that's still looking pretty tough.

Still no word from the publishers, that rules out anything being released this month. Still it's not all bad, the delay has given me time to write some feel-good stories for a few local papers. I guess they're more feel-good for the readers because I didn't feel good writing them. Pointless pieces that don't matter and don't bring in much cash. Still, each one keeps a roof over my head for a little longer.

The story I broke about Dr Yamaoka being a murderer has completely died now. It seems that the police weren't interested in giving many interviews and the interest of the public fades rapidly when faced with newer exciting stories. It's already old news although the disappointment is it's likely going to be the most exciting thing that'll happen to me this year and I haven't been able to sell it for much yet.

Dark Waters

February 7th

Still waiting to hear back from the publishers on my Kuchisake-onna story. I know that the story is good enough for some of the supernatural journals and the Kuchisake-onna itself was terrifying but I swear the waiting is harder than the actual writing. If they don't get back soon I think I'll lose my mind over this.

Whilst I wait my search for 'real' journalism continues, although due to my poor standing I can't actually get to any of the decent stuff. Any story worth reporting on is already being covered meaning I'm left feeding on scraps. The latest lead I've been given sounds like one of these scraps. It's from a friend of a friend who heard about a young boy drowning recently. The official line was a tragic accident with no foul play but apparently some of the people involved aren't so easily convinced including my source. There wasn't much coverage in the papers and it was recent enough that I should be able to get a simple sympathy story written up quite easily. Who knows I might be able to uncover quite the story if their suspicions are true.

The location isn't far, only a couple of districts away so I'll head there tomorrow and see if it's worth looking into.

February 8th

Well that story was exactly as I expected. The community was quite tight, a group of four flat blocks built around a small garden. The garden space is small but nothing out of the ordinary whilst the flat blocks, all high rise, are thoroughly modern. I was able to speak to the local adults, including the boy's parents, but they all say it was a tragic accident and didn't appear to like me nosing around. Can't say I blame them, what parents want a reporter coming round asking questions about their child's death? I'm not entirely sure where my lead came from because everyone I spoke to all said exactly the same thing. The boy had been playing next to the pond in the garden alone during the evening and fell in. With nobody else nearby he was unable to pull himself out and drowned in the cold water. They're devastated of course but seem to think there's no foul play involved. In all honesty with the garden only having access through the buildings the only suspects would be people within the complex. The chance of it being anything suspicious seemed thin although when I happened to speak with a group of the children playing in the entrance to one of the buildings they told me a different story.

The children claim that the boy in question wasn't a good swimmer and was in fact scared of water. They suggest that he wouldn't have gone near the pond unless absolutely necessary. They say that none of the children living there go near the water so it seems unlikely that he would accidently fall in. They believe that a monster lives in their pond and that was what dragged the boy to his untimely demise. They say it's been living there for months and that they've seen it from their windows creeping around at night. It sounded like a child's story but nevertheless I headed into the garden to examine the pond and hear their tale. I'll admit I didn't believe that a monster could be living in their pond but they seemed so glad that an adult was listening to them that I didn't have the heart to simply walk away.

A couple of them told me the tale of the monster as we walked to the pond. They claim that a creature lives hidden in the depths, human like although it's apparently reptilian in nature. They described it as a human frog, the size of a grown adult but distinctively frog-like in the way it looks. They claim that it likes playing pranks on the residents and has been terrorizing the community when it comes out of the pond at night. Apparently these pranks include a variety of harmless acts such as hiding shoes or dragging mud through the hallways but it's always the kids that end up taking the blame. They say that the adults don't believe them other than one who'd visited them yesterday but then left without saying or doing anything. They did all say that lately the pranks have been getting worse, steadily increasing from minor annoyances to reportable crimes. With the death of one boy they're all worried that the monster now has a taste for human flesh and that they'll be next. Seems unlikely given that the autopsy confirmed the death was by drowning and no attack marks were found on the boy.

I still thought it was a child's story and that they'd imagined it all but I examined the pond anyway to see if there was any tangible proof, which at least seemed to calm the children slightly. The pond wasn't too big, probably no more than fifteen feet across but the water was dark and I couldn't see the bottom. Thinking that it looked deeper than it was I picked up a broken branch from a nearby tree and lowered in into the water. The branch must've been maybe four feet long but it didn't reach the bottom, I'm not even sure if it got near it. If there was something living in there then it would be possible for it to hide out of sight in the depths without anyone knowing. I noticed that while I disturbed the water the kids all hung back and looked terrified so I stopped and went back to them. I told them that if they were scared they should stay away from the pond but that I didn't believe their monster existed and that it was just in their imagination. They were all disappointed and begged that I return that evening to see the monster myself as it only emerges from the pond at night. I had a good mind not to but given that it's near to my home I thought I could go just in case there was something to their stories. I guess there was something about the darkness of the water that drew me back, and the fact that the Kuchisake-onna still haunts my dreams and leaves me knowing that sometimes monsters do exist. With that in mind I gave them my word that I would return to witness their 'monster' in the flesh.

Unsure of exactly what I was expecting to find other than a long night of sitting in a dark garden, I returned that evening and, under the cover of darkness, took up a position in the opposite corner of the garden to the pond eager to see if something did indeed rise from the water. Well I must have waited for a good hour or so watching the lights of the flats flicker out one by one before anything happened. Quite amazingly I saw ripples begin to spread from the centre of the pond which was barely visible in the moonlight and then two webbed hands appeared at the water's edge before the monster pulled itself out into the garden illuminated only by the pale moonlight. Just as the children had described, it was humanoid although I would have said more crocodilian in nature than frog like. It had scales running across its body that shimmered in the pale light but looked to be a brownish colour. Like a frog it had webbed fingers and toes which ended in pads and must have been around four feet tall, slightly shorter than the children had suggested. The creature had wide glowing yellow eyes that darted around the garden yet must've struggled to see as I was simply sat on a tree stump and it didn't appear to notice me although I was motionless, transfixed by the odd creature before me. Oddly on the top of its head it wore what looked like a bowl as some form of hat although I think it was actually attached to the creature as it didn't appear to wobble in the slightest. I watched as the creature pulled itself upright and stretched its limbs giving me a look at its elongated appendages, each one disproportionately long compared to the rest of its body and the odd shell that encased its back like a tortoise. It wasn't quite a shell but it resembled one where the scales had grown much bigger and fused together making its back far more rigid than the front. Suddenly it appeared that the children had been telling the truth after all and that maybe this creature was the cause of the recent death. Of course proof that their monster existed was no evidence that it was behind the death but disregarding the death, a creature like that could easily act as a follow up to my Kuchisake-onna story. Unfortunately after my initial delight at finding a potential follow up I realised that I was faced with a second monster and that I had no idea what it was capable of and although it carried no weapons, I was convinced it was no less dangerous than the Kuchisake-onna.

After stretching, the creature slowly crept towards the tower block next to me making an odd squelching noise as it went which was seemingly caused by its padded toes that acted as suction pads. Noticeably the strange bowl hat it wore didn't wobble at all as it crept across the garden yet there appeared to be liquid inside. It headed towards the door of the building, no doubt eager to start its night of pranks, and was completely oblivious to my presence, although it never reached its destination. Instead, as it crossed the lawn, a second figure emerged from behind the bushes next to the pond and set off after the creature. How long it had been waiting there I had no idea, it certainly hadn't come from the water and I hadn't noticed anything else arrive in the hour or so that I'd been there. Judging from the way it moved and its size, this figure was a human although in the darkness it was difficult to tell. The creature noticed this figure approaching immediately and turned to face them ducking as the figure lunged at it showing unexpected agility for its frog-like appearance. Having dodged the figure, the creature then took up a fighting stance and quite impressively displayed all the makings of a martial arts champion, easily besting the attacker, who was no slouch, in a brief hand to hand duel, successfully knocking the figure to the ground. I had expected it to deliver a fatal blow, especially as it had been blamed for the death of the boy but instead as soon as it gained an advantage over its opponent it turned on its heels and charged back to the pond, diving in and disappearing into the murky water with a large splash. The figure was quickly back on their feet and gave chase but stopped at the edge of the water cursing quite loudly as they stared into the pond. Their voice was female and marked them out to be human meaning I was quite sure that they weren't dangerous to me. They had taken quite a blow from the creature in the brief fight and I decided I would check that they were alright, and to add further details to the story I'm going to write about the monster in the pond.

Unbelievably when I approached the figure, who was bent over catching their breath whilst staring into the murky waters which had almost instantly settled, I was amazed to see that it was someone I knew. Incredibly it was Shiho! The very same Shiho I'd encountered last month and had saved me from the Kuchisake-onna. I guessed she must've been there for the same reason I was and at the sight of her I immediately knew that I'd followed the right lead. If Shiho is involved then there must be a good story behind this creature and just maybe if my first story is picked up I'll have a ready-made sequel in the offing. At first she seemed shocked to see me but as she recovered her breath she backed us away from the pond and started to talk making sure to keep the pond in her line of sight at all times. I wanted to ask her about the creature but she was far more interested in what I was doing there, almost as if I was the odd one when she had just fought a strange frogman in hand to hand combat. I told her that I was investigating the story about the boy's death and had heard the children's tales so wanted to check out the pond at night to see if there was any truth to it. I told her that normally I wouldn't have bothered but if the Kuchisake-onna is real then why couldn't there be a monster living in their pond. I don't think she was too pleased that I was actively looking for more beings like the Kuchisake-onna but in all honesty I'd rather never meet something so horrifying again. Eventually she seemed to accept that our meeting again was a strange coincidence and told me why she was there. She said that the stories the children had told me were true although apparently their tales don't do justice to the creature living in their pond. She also explained how she had been hired to deal with the monster by an elder living in the apartment block who had heard their stories and worried. I asked her what it was that was living there and she looked mournfully at the pond before stating that it was a Kappa and that it wouldn't return again that night since she'd scared it off. She, at least, seemed to believe that was the case as she immediately led me out of the garden to a twenty four hour coffee shop opposite the flats knowing that I'd have a multitude of questions about the creature.

Once we'd sat down with a hot drink my first question was obvious, what was a Kappa? Shiho explained that they are a race of reptilian creatures that are incredibly rare and normally live in lakes or rivers. How this one had ended up living in a garden pond, no matter how deep, was unknown but she theorized that it must've been born there as she says they hardly ever migrate yet it is unusual to find one in an urban environment. Usually they prefer large bodies of water making this one strange. She theorised that it was digging the pond out further to increase its living area explaining why it appeared so deep. She reiterated a few times that they were rare creatures and admitted that she had never dealt with one but she'd heard about them a couple of times. She says that they're often seen as pranksters and her theory was that the one living in the pond was acting more aggressively simply because it had outgrown its living space, hardly a surprise given their normal habitat. Even with her answers I still wanted to know more about the Kappa, I had seen it easily best Shiho in hand to hand combat, a woman who had fought off an angry onryō, and I still couldn't get past its appearance. The Kuchisake-onna was at least human looking other than its scar but this thing was completely alien. How one couldn't have been spotted or caught on camera seemed incredible. Shiho explained that every Kappa is an expert martial artist, she even thinks that it's possible one once taught a human which is where the practice comes from in the first place. She also explained the weird bowl type object on the Kappa's head. As I thought it is actually part of the creature and is used to hold water from the Kappa's home. Shiho claims that should the 'bowl' ever become empty then the Kappa loses its strength and will ultimately die. This is, according to Shiho, the only fail-safe way of getting rid of a Kappa. Apparently this had been her plan tonight, to knock the Kappa over by sneaking up on it and spill the water hence weakening the creature. Unfortunately she had been seen and now doubted that she'd get another chance. Either way, with the creature gone for the night, she declared her intention to return tomorrow night and I'll certainly be there to see what she can do.

Before we left the coffee shop I had to ask her how she knew so much about the Kappa and the Kuchisake-onna, they don't seem like similar creatures at all but Shiho said they all fall under her expertise. She admitted that there was a large difference between them and then explained that the Kuchisake-onna fell under the onryō branch of yōkai whilst the Kappa was considered a beast yet to me both fell under the category 'not-normal'. She says that's her speciality, the not-normal, yōkai in particular. I can't wait to see what she's going to do to that Kappa. I don't know how dangerous it truly is. I don't doubt that it could've killed Shiho this evening if it had wanted to but refrained from doing so. Shiho also classes them as pranksters leaving me to think that returning shouldn't pose too much of a risk to my life. Hopefully it will make a good story for my next piece.

February 9th

As promised, I returned to the flat complex this morning and met Shiho who was already waiting in the garden keeping an eye on the pond for any signs of the Kappa. Truth be told from the dark marks around her eyes I don't think she slept at all last night, it's even possible that she returned to the garden after our coffee and had been there ever since. Her face was dark and solemn making me wonder if something else bad had happened. Shiho informed me that one of the girls living in the complex, who I'd actually spoken to yesterday, had a run in with the creature the previous night, leaving her with a broken arm as she fell down a flight of stairs. I think Shiho blames herself, cursing for not waiting throughout the night. It appears the incident occurred whilst we were having a coffee and that the Kappa had simply waited for us to leave before striking. In hindsight it's possible that Shiho is right and that if she had stayed then the girl would be fine but at least the Kappa didn't kill her this time. Even so Shiho wasn't pleased and reconfirmed her desire to defeat the creature today.

With that in mind I asked what her plan was for dealing with the Kappa and she didn't quite seem to know. I'll admit that her response didn't fill me with confidence but she had at least shown some knowledge of what the creature was including giving it a name which made me think that even without a solid plan she'd still be the best bet for stopping it. When pushed a little further on her knowledge of the Kappa she expressed regret for her failed attack on the creature last night. She explained that Kappa are a peculiar sort of creature, filled with immense honour and unlikely to forget an insult. As her attack had been unprovoked and had, in all honesty, been an attempt to sneak up on it, the Kappa would be unlikely to stand its ground and fight her anymore as it wouldn't have forgotten her slight and would deem a fight against her as beneath it. Shiho reckoned that the second it catches wind of her it'll scarper back into its pond and refuse to come out. I asked why we couldn't simply go into the pond to find it or drain the water but Shiho suggested that would be a horrendous idea. She explained that in water it had a massive advantage over her and that draining the pond would only create the situation of a cornered animal more likely to lash out and that although Kappa are usually relatively safe, an aggressive one could quite easily kill a human. That left only the possibility of catching it off guard once it had emerged from the pond but again that seemed unlikely based on the speed and awareness that it had shown the night before. Although at a distance the Kappa appeared unable to see well it appeared to have an excellent sense of everything nearby. Shiho lamented not having any large trees or balconies overlooking the garden from which she could drop onto the Kappa given that their bowl prevents them from looking upwards and that would give her the advantage.

Knowing that her plan wasn't great, but having no other, I found myself waiting in the same spot as the previous night only this time with Shiho beside me. I wasn't sure that her idea would work, or exactly how dangerous the Kappa could be if her plan failed but I was certain that by sticking with her I'd get another chance to see the creature which I was quite fascinated by both for a potential story and out of pure curiosity.

The wait was long, what with the Kappa choosing to come out at night and us having arrived in the morning. Throughout the day we saw a few of the local children come into the garden but they stayed well clear of the pond and didn't interact with us. None of the adults came in either suggesting that they just stay clear of the place. Whether this is due to the Kappa I couldn't tell and Shiho appeared unaware. After a while, I became bored so started to talk to Shiho and before long my questions had swung back to her and the world she lived in. Much like last time she wouldn't tell me much, keeping herself to herself although she did let on that she'd only been doing this for a few years and used to work with a partner. I still don't know how she'd been introduced to it in the first place, she wouldn't say, and as to why she now works alone I didn't ask. It had taken quite a bit to pry out even that small amount of information and from the way her face tightened up it was clear that it wasn't something she wanted to discuss. About her world she would say very little. She reconfirmed that there are all manner of beings in existence besides the Kuchisake-onna and Kappa that I'd seen but wouldn't tell me anymore for fear that I'd go looking for them. Apparently no amount of denying on my account will change her mind on that matter. Truthfully, she's not a particularly easy person to talk with, saying little with each reply and rarely, if ever, posing a question of her own. With silence an uncomfortable option I took the opportunity to tell her about my article on the Kuchisake-onna and ask if she was happy for me to press on trying to get it published. She was fairly dismissive that anyone would believe it or even that it was an interesting case but she did give her approval so that's a positive. Her response did make me wonder exactly what she would class as interesting however I told her that I plan to market it as fiction and change the names of everyone involved so that it couldn't be traced but she didn't appear bothered. I guess protecting the official police story isn't part of her agreement with them. Either way she admitted I'd get a better response calling it fiction. During our next bout of silence not long later I raised my intention to write this adventure as a further story but she merely shook her head dismissively saying nobody would care about a Kappa. Truthfully I no longer particularly care about her thoughts, if she's approved the first then she can have no complaints about me writing up this one. In addition I believe the Kappa is quite interesting. I'll admit compared to the Kuchisake-onna it appears less frightening but perhaps that's only because the Kuchisake-onna was trying to kill me whereas the Kappa has only ever ignored me. Shiho seems to think both are quite tepid but that's probably because she claims to have seen so much more. Maybe if more people knew about these things, even as stories, then they'd know how to defend themselves if ever they do meet them which could save lives. At least that's how I'm going to justify writing them up despite what Shiho might think.

Anyway quite a while later, after the sun had set and night had fallen, the water in the pond slowly began to ripple and, having been alerted to it by Shiho, we prepared ourselves for the arrival of the Kappa. Much like last night the webbed hands first appeared on the edge of the pond and then the bowl full of water emerged above its bright eyes which carefully scanned the garden, evidently wary after Shiho's intervention yesterday. Not seeing us hiding it slowly pulled itself out of the water and started off towards one of the buildings with its strange lopsided walk clearly intent on causing mischief. Knowing that she couldn't allow it to return to its lair

Shiho waited as it crossed the garden, eager to allow it to put some distance between itself and the water. Once it was near the door of the flat blocks Shiho crept out of our hiding place dragging me with her and signalling that she wanted me to help cut off the Kappa's retreat. Once we'd managed to creep unnoticed between it and the water Shiho attempted to sneak up on the Kappa from behind hoping to push it over and empty the bowl on its head. At first, as she crept silently across the garden, I thought she might succeed in her goal but in truth she was probably still a good ten meters away when the Kappa noticed her and spun round to face her. Realising that her plan was now in ruin and thinking quickly she desperately tried to appeal to its sense of honour by immediately straightening up, as if she hadn't been attempting to sneak up on it, and bowed deeply hoping that it would accept her as a challenger. The look of scorn that appeared on its reptilian face suggested she had failed as it remained motionless yet it watched her carefully, weighing up its next move. I saw Shiho snarl slightly, clearly annoyed that her plan had failed and desperately trying to come up with a new one on the fly. With her options thin on the ground she went for the most basic of plans and lunged towards the Kappa. Unfortunately the Kappa was expecting this and, just like before, easily avoided her, darting under her outstretched arms and fleeing towards the pond, and me, without losing a single drop of water from the bowl on its head.

It was at this point that I realized the creature was coming straight for me. Despite its small stature I'd seen it easily best Shiho in combat and knew that it had already killed one child and seriously injured another meaning as the dark figure approached me I suddenly became terrified. At first I thought it was simply going to barrel right through me but it stopped a couple of meters before me and stared directly at me as it weighed up whether or not I was a worthy challenger to its martial art skills. Now I'm no fighter, a couple of misguided lessons at school is as far as I got but I knew this thing was coming at me no matter what. That's when, despite my fear, I had an idea. Following Shiho's example I decided to play up to the Kappa's sense of honour and bowed deeply to it as one would do if starting a duel. Well my hunch was right and the Kappa bowed back, equally as deep, spilling the water from its bowl as it did so instantly weakening it. The look on Shiho's face was something else, she couldn't believe it. Neither could I really, nor the Kappa which fell to the ground desperately reaching out for the pond in the hope of refilling the bowl. I don't think I've ever thought as fast as I did in that moment nor been so delighted to prove myself correct.

With the Kappa subdued Shiho walked over drawing one of her knives. Lying on the floor reaching out for the pond the Kappa looked so hopeless and pathetic, a far cry from the expert fighter that it had been last night. It was clear that the water in the bowl must possess remarkable power over the Kappa as its scales immediately became paler and it almost shrivelled up becoming very frail looking. Taking pity on the creature I asked Shiho if it was possible to send it somewhere else instead of killing it but she replied in the negative stating that her job was to get rid of it not to find it a new home. Doing so would cost her both time and money. I did protest, saying it would be cruel to kill such a rare and odd creature but she explained that it was already dying. Without water in its bowl, it was slowly suffocating. Slitting its throat would be the kinder thing to do.

She was about to end its life when we were disturbed by the scream of a young girl. An odd thing to hear in the middle of the night and it definitely caught our attention but there was nothing sinister about this one. One of the girls from the flats, the same one who'd broken her arm had come out to see the creature and looked horrified at what Shiho was about to do. She'd evidently been watching from one of the windows eager to see the creature which had caused her such harm. Coming from the building closest to the pond I tried to stop her as she ran toward us but she managed to slip past my outstretched arms, drawing water from the pond using her cupped hands and carrying it over to the Kappa which stared at her with untrusting eyes. Shiho watched the whole situation carefully, I thought she would try to stop her as the girl poured the water into the bowl, the majority running straight out as the creature lay prone on the floor. Some however remained in the very bottom and the Kappa slowly managed to pull itself into a seated position. It was clearly still very weak and, as in its current state offered no threat to us, Shiho felt comfortable enough to sheath her blade and watch as the young girl went back to the pond and scooped up more water which she again poured into the Kappa's bowl. This time, in its seated position the majority of the water remained in the bowl and colour started to return to the Kappa's scales. With more strength now, the Kappa reached out a hand towards the young girl which she nervously took and it bowed again, this time in thanks and a lot more carefully than it had moments before so that it didn't spill a precious drop of the water she had offered it. I wasn't sure what was happening but Shiho tapped me on the shoulder and led me away from the creature as other children came out of the flat blocks each scooping up some water and adding it to the Kappa's growing supply. I guess they had all been watching after seeing us hanging around throughout the day but pretty quickly there was a crowd of at least twenty children in the garden all giving water to the Kappa until its bowl was full.

I asked Shiho why she wasn't stopping them as the Kappa was gaining strength with each drop and I doubted we'd be able to trick it again but her answer was quick and simple, bushido code. The young girl had saved its life and, as a being of honour, it would now be willing to do the same for her. I wasn't entirely convinced that such creatures honour such arrangements and asked if the children would be safe with the Kappa around but she replied that they couldn't ask for a better guardian given the Kappa's innate fighting ability. The Kappa would go out of its way to make sure they were safe and as I looked back into the garden and watched them playing and laughing with the creature, I suddenly knew that she was right. It seems odd that in the end something that they thought of as a nuisance could turn out to be their most valuable ally but I guess that's the power of an act of compassion. As for the Kappa, well it was an odd creature but as I watched it playfully squirt water up into the air to amuse the children I realised that maybe it was less of a beast than I first thought. Maybe sometimes even monsters can have a good side, maybe they just need someone to show it to them first.

We departed not long after, Shiho suggesting to the children that they expand the pond slightly before we left and yet again she bade me farewell. I do wonder if I'll see her again, there's no doubt that our meetings provide excellent inspiration for articles. I'll get this one written up as quickly as possible, I'm sure it'll be a good follow up to the last one provided one of the publishers take me up on them. I do wonder what the future holds for Shiho, no doubt some new horror will emerge that the world will know nothing about. Still, I may hardly know her but I get the feeling that she'll be alright.

Still waiting on feedback from the Kuchisake-onna story, it's taking forever for them to come to a decision. I know the deadline for this month's editions has passed but do they really have to take so long?

I have been busy though. The write up of my experience with the Kappa is now complete. Much like the previous one I've edited a few details, notably the location and the outcome. Although personally I am glad that the Kappa has the chance to live out the rest of its days with the children as friends I felt it best to keep that out of the tale. After all I don't think they'd want people turning up out of the blue hunting for the creature if I actually manage to get the stories published.

I haven't sent it off to any journals yet, I think I'm better waiting for the outcome of the Kuchisake-onna story first but it's a useful follow up if they like that and request a second. Honestly I think that might be my bank account talking though. Things are getting a little close to the bone now. I should have charged Shiho for my help, given that I was the one that tricked the Kappa.

I can't believe it! They actually accepted my story! They're going to publish it at the start of next month. It's a local quarterly focusing on the occult but it's a sale and a decent one at that. If nothing else it'll keep the bills paid for a little longer. They said that they really liked it. I shouldn't be too surprised because I know how terrifying the Kuchisake-onna was but even so I can't believe it's going to be published.

Truthfully the publication is probably the best one too, ok it only covers Kyoto but they do occasionally get some stories reprinted in nationals. If that happens then being almost killed will be worth it. Hopefully it goes down well and I can sell them my Kappa follow up.

March 8th

The article came out today and I was first in line to buy a copy. They've really spruced it up too, adding an artist's interpretation of the Kuchisake-onna as described in the piece. They've done a good job but have chosen to leave the mask on, possibly a good idea. I don't think any artist would be able to truly capture the horror of her scars. Reading through the tale again it appears so odd especially when looking back on what really happened but such is the way it has to be. Even if I was to be taken seriously, telling people that this thing really existed could cause panic. Far safer to let it be a simple tale.

The early responses I've received have been mostly positive with people getting in touch to congratulate me and to ask about the inspiration behind it. I can't tell them that it's based on the truth but it's nice to know they're reading it.

It seems odd to think that this is the first significant piece in a publication under my name given the frightening nature of it and it certainly wasn't something I would normally have considered writing. Still, I'll admit to feeling a sense of pride seeing it there in black and white.

March 14th

I've been getting loads of emails about the Kuchisake-onna story, more than I've ever had before and it's only been out six days! Everybody wants to know more about the onryō, maybe there's something about this sort of creature that people find fascinating? If I had a way of contacting Shiho I would ask her to fill in some gaps in my own knowledge so that I could respond to each question. Even without, my social media is blowing up. Loads of people have taken an interest, way more than I expected. This is exactly what I'd hoped when I first wrote the article.

The magazine editor wants to talk to me tomorrow too. Given that I've only ever spoken with them via phone and email as a freelancer I wonder what he wants.

March 15th

The meeting went well I think, much better than I could've hoped for last week when the story was first published. The editor was keen to stress just how much they loved the article. Apparently it's generated some of the most feedback they've ever had. Not bad for almost getting killed. The reason they wanted to meet was to ask me about writing another story, one to put in their next edition that releases in June. They even said that if I had more than one they'd consider giving me the extra pages. It's a generous offer so naturally I accepted. The pay is good, they've offered more than the freelance rate so this could prove to be a good earner for me. Of course, now I need the stories to write about.

I have the Kappa story in reserve but I'm not sure that entirely fits what they want. Even if it did I'm not sure I'd give it to them, the idea of people visiting that flat block and trying to see the creature seems too harsh. I've been thinking it would be better for them to be left alone. The trouble is if I don't use that story then I'll need to find another one to match the Kuchisake-onna. I'm not sure that I've got it in me to create one from scratch, the Kuchisake-onna was real which made writing about it easy. I've never been good at writing pure fiction. If only I had a way of contacting Shiho. No doubt she's already found plenty of other stories that are worth telling. If I could spend an afternoon with her then I'd definitely get something to write about.

End of the Line

March 18th

I'm definitely going to need to find Shiho again to get another story to match my last. I've tried scouring the internet for inspiration but the tales I write from my head are plain awful, they'd never be good enough to be published. It's not that much of a surprise, fiction really isn't my thing given I was trained in journalism. Unfortunately she's not that easy to find, I can't reach her via her investigator website, which was difficult to find and provided little information, but I have heard about a few things around the city that might be of interest to her. Maybe if I can find another yōkai I can find Shiho.

A man has reported that his girlfriend is missing, supposedly vanished from her bedroom without a trace. That could be something paranormal, or more likely someone who's chosen to leave. A child said to have been kidnapped after developing an imaginary friend. Maybe there's a way that the imaginary friend could be a yōkai? That would make a good tale. There's also a student who went missing from a subway station at night and hasn't been seen since. Each of those could involve Shiho if there's a supernatural cause although they could all have reasonable explanations. They sound similar to her line of work though. I'll have to investigate them and see if she's involved. Of course, I don't even know if she's still in the city. Finding her might turn out to be tougher than finding another yōkai.

I don't think there's much to those cases I mentioned yesterday, the vanished woman that left no trace most likely just wanted shot of her boyfriend, he was rather clingy and I only spoke to him for twenty minutes. The police appeared to have the same impression of the case. Seemed to take nothing with her but she was probably just desperate to get away.

The kidnapped child also seems a bust. There's no doubt that he's missing but it appears to be a standard police case. His friends apparently saw him talking to a tall woman before he was taken so that sounds like a kidnapping. Police have no leads on that one either with the woman proving impossible to track down so the chance of me being able to find anything on my own is slim.

As for the missing student, the police found his body on the rail tracks. Apparently he fell off the platform drunk whilst waiting for the train. Grim but not what I'm looking for.

Nobody at any of the places I visited had heard of Shiho either so my search for her and stories will continue.

Curious development today, another person has gone missing from the same station as that student. They were also found dead on the tracks this morning. According to the official statement, this one was drunk too and fell off the platform resulting in the same fate as the first.

Two deaths in a few days at the same station though? That's either suspicious or one hell of a coincidence. Either way it's probably worth investigating. I'll head there tomorrow evening and wait until it gets dark, that's when both have gone missing and should give me the best chance to snoop around.

What a night! I've definitely got a follow up story for the magazine editor now. This one will be right up his street.

It all started when I went to investigate that station where a couple of people have gone missing although at the time I couldn't imagine the true reason why. It was all good to begin with, I managed to duck through the police tape that they'd left, the station having been closed due to the recent accidents. They hadn't even bothered to leave anyone on guard suggesting the police thought nothing of the deaths meaning I found myself alone on the station. It's kind of creepy being on a platform at night, especially with the darkness of the tunnels closing in on you but other than the regular jitters, there was nothing out of the ordinary that alarmed me. Even so I waited for a good few hours but still nothing happened. There wasn't even a single train that went by although I could hear some in the distance, the unmistakable clacking of the rails signifying that the service was still operational. The station is towards the end of the line though so it was likely that they'd just closed off the last few stops whilst they investigated the deaths.

After a couple of hours waiting I was thoroughly bored of the whole affair and decided to search the tunnels, after all it was in the tunnels that the bodies had been found not on the platform. Turns out its surprisingly easy to get into the tunnels from the platforms despite the obvious danger involved, not that I'd ever tried it before. As I mentioned, there hadn't been a train all night so I figured it was safe for me to poke around so long as I was careful. If possible the tunnels were even darker than the platform and the light from my phone barely reached more than a couple of meters ahead of me as I stumbled along the track trying not to be electrocuted. I couldn't have travelled more than fifty meters before I reached the site of the first body, a large blood stain coating the ground around the tracks where his body had been found. There was so much blood, way more than had been previously reported, so much that I started to think that the poor guy had actually lost limbs, almost as if a train had hit him and sliced him in two. No matter what, it was clear that there was some kind of cover up going on here. Details like that should've been mentioned somewhere in the police reports.

Continuing down the tunnel, after a few more meters I noticed something large and stationary looming up out of the darkness. At first I wasn't sure what it was but it was blocking the tracks and was, in all likelihood, why there hadn't been any signs of a train other than the clacking noise in the distance. As I got closer, the light from my phone caught on its metallic walls and I realised that it was a carriage, the type used to transport freight on trains. It appeared unconnected to any engine and was facing down into the tunnel away from the platform so I carefully squeezed myself along the side between it and the wall until I reached the front. I had hoped that its interior would alleviate my confusion but instead I was even more alarmed to discover that the sole item within the carriage, whose door had been left open, was a pair of mannequin legs propped up against the back wall. I'd had to go quite far in to notice them leaving me trapped and, alarmed by how weird it was to find an abandoned carriage, I spun round to try to escape but almost had a heart attack. Stood at the door, staring at me with a look of pure confusion was Shiho, her mouth agape. Somehow I'd found her again!

Once we'd recovered our breath at the shock of seeing one another we both asked what the other was doing there and, no surprise, it was for similar reasons. Like myself she was also investigating the deaths although, unlike myself, she had been asked to help by the police, similar to her dealings with the Kuchisake-onna. This, along with her very presence, suggested that this was indeed something out of the ordinary and that I might be on the right track for a story. Once we'd established each other's reason for being there I asked about the freight carriage, guessing that it was her doing. She acknowledged that it was but wouldn't explain what its exact purpose was. All she said was that it was a trap, one which she'd almost sprung on myself only to stop when she'd recognised me. I was about to ask what she was wanting a trap for when she held out a hand to silence me and listened, her face stretching into pained concentration. I too listened but all I could hear was the clacking of trains, definitely closer than before but still some way away and unlikely to come towards us given the blockage. Shiho didn't seem so convinced though and quickly beckoned me out of the carriage, pushing me down the side back towards the platform. She joined me and together we waited in the narrow gap between reinforced metal and the tunnel wall.

I wasn't sure what was happening but the sound of the train was getting louder, it's clacking intensifying as it became apparent that it was coming up our tunnel. Frantically I tried to explain to Shiho that if a train hit the carriage we'd both die but she just told me to be quiet and not to move. I could see from her face that she was worried although seemingly not by the train. The clacking got louder and louder as it approached until incredibly I heard a banging within the carriage itself as if the train had somehow managed to enter it although there had been no ramp to allow it access. As soon as that happened Shiho leapt out from our position and slammed the door of the carriage shut quickly latching it to the other side to lock it. The banging from within didn't stop, in fact if anything it got louder and more frantic as if whatever was in there wanted to be out. Cautiously I too followed Shiho and joined her in front of the carriage. She appeared quite pleased with herself, clearly glad that her trap had worked. I still thought that she'd trapped a train so I asked her what it was in there and she said it was a yōkai known as a Teke Teke. I must've had a confused look on my face because she began to explain without me needing to prompt. She explained that a Teke Teke is a type of onryō similar to the Kuchisake-onna we encountered, or at least they belong to the same class of spirits. Unlike the Kuchisake-onna, the Teke Teke is a person killed on the rails and missing their lower half. According to Shiho they pull themselves along the tracks on their elbows making a clacking sound similar to that of a train. Apparently it's also where they get their name from. Shiho claims that they stalk the area they were killed hoping to find a victim whose legs they can steal, slicing them in half with a scythe that they carry. Presumably that's why there was so much blood further down the tunnel. It seems our two dead people were unwitting victims of the creature. Anyway, evidently they always reject the new pair of legs immediately and continue to search for another pair. According to Shiho the only pair they'll ever be happy with are their own and as they will never be able to find them, it makes the Teke Teke exceedingly dangerous as they have no other tangible desire. Evidently this was what the mannequin was for although from the noise coming from inside the carriage it was clear that the onryō had already rejected them. I asked Shiho what she planned on doing with the creature trapped inside a large, and rather unwieldy, prison stuck on the train tracks but before she could answer we both heard a horrible screeching sound coming from the carriage and turned to see the metal slowly shredding as the tip of a scythe appeared, dragging its way down the door as the creature within sought an escape. I had hoped that Shiho would've expected this, or at least planned for such an outcome, but instead her face went white and her eyes wide as she watched the scythe disappear back into the container and then a yellow eye appear in the crack, long knotted black hair partially covering it. The creature was clearly looking at the two of us. There was a split second whilst everything seemed to pause and the three of us stood in silence staring at one another and then I heard something possibly more terrifying than anything I've encountered with Shiho, she simply whispered "run". So we ran.

The two of us fled down the tunnel, virtually unable to see in the near perfect darkness. I had no idea where the Teke Teke was but the second we turned on our heels, the screeching of the metal continued before moments later the door must've burst open as the clacking sound of the creature filled the tunnels behind us as it gave chase. Next to me Shiho offered nothing as she ran, unable to fight the creature and seemingly with no plan to distract it. I fear had it not been for the few seconds head start that we had, the onryō would've caught us easily however we were fortunate in that a maintenance room was just down the tunnel and Shiho barrelled the two of us into it immediately calling for my help to shut and barricade the door. I don't think I've ever worked so hard in my life as I did when the barricades went up in that room. Anything not nailed to the wall was shifted in front of the door in a desperate attempt to prevent the Teke Teke from breaking in. To the creature's credit it really went for it and for the best part of an hour we were subjected to scraping noises as it attempted to break down the door and our barricades with both its hands and scythe.

The two of us sat in silence all that time in that cramped maintenance room listening to the wails of the onryō and the scraping against the door hoping that it wouldn't be able to reach us. Unlike the previous time I'd spend a night trapped in a small room with Shiho this time she didn't sleep, instead she just stared unblinking at the door until the noises stopped. Even when they did the two of us remained silent for a long time, neither of us willing to let the Teke Teke know we were still there. When I eventually did ask if it had given up all Shiho would say was that she hadn't heard any clacking sound of it hauling itself down the tunnel suggesting that it was simply waiting outside the door hoping to lure us out.

Another hour passed in silence, no sound could be heard from the Teke Teke before I spoke to Shiho again. Her eyes never left the door but she was happy to speak whenever I asked a question. I asked her how she was going to deal with it but she simply shook her head, an act which didn't fill me with confidence so I asked if she'd encountered a Teke Teke before hoping that she had some experience with them. She replied that she had once, a couple of months after she'd started doing this sort of thing so I followed up by asking if we could do the same thing as she'd done back then but she replied that her then partner had been the one to banish the Teke Teke and that she herself had done little other than witness the onryō at its murderous best. With a lack of experience with Teke Tekes I asked if we could use the same technique as other onryō and find, and punish, the one responsible for her death hence bringing about the vengeance that the spirit desired. Again Shiho shook her head, she stated that a Teke Teke was not the same as a Kuchisake-onna and as such couldn't be beaten in the same way. It was far more aggressive and wasn't hunting a particular person, instead it was simply searching for its missing legs. She also explained that there didn't necessarily need to be a person responsible for the creation of the Teke Teke, she could've simply fallen on the tracks by accident or it could've been a suicide. If either were the case then there would be nobody to blame. Even so with Shiho having little in the way of suggestions of how to deal with the spirit I believed that it would be worth visiting the police to check the records of any other deaths, accidental or otherwise, around the station over the past few weeks. Of course the trouble with that was we would first have to get out of the maintenance room. A check on my watch told me that it was coming up on 4am, still too early to be light on the surface and even if it was, with no trains running through the station thanks to Shiho's trap and the eternal darkness of the tunnels, there was nothing to suggest that the Teke Teke would vanish during daylight hours. Instead it would likely roam the tracks constantly not needing to rest or eat. Shiho confirmed that this was the case. That left us trapped in a small room with a murderous onryō as our warden.

After another half hour of silence from outside, I asked Shiho again if she thought it would be safe to leave and this time she actually thought about it. I think the tightness of the room was getting to her and she too could see that at one point we would need to make an escape. There was no chance of simply waiting the spirit out. Carefully we dismantled our barricade until only the door separated us from the tunnels beyond, praying that if the onryō was still out there it wouldn't be able to hear as the door was already badly splintered by its earlier assault. With that done, Shiho drew a small hand mirror from one of her pockets and sank to the floor carefully sliding it through the small gap into the tunnel. She slowly tilted it towards the station and, although the darkness meant she could only see a few feet, there was no Teke Teke. She then turned it the other way and immediately jerked back as the mirror was pulled from her grip before she scrambled away from the door as the blade of the Teke Teke's scythe swooped across the floor trying to reach our feet. I asked her if it was ever going to go away and Shiho regrettably informed me that she'd once heard of one which had stalked its prey for three whole days before finally killing them. That unfortunate soul had also had the benefit of not being trapped and had travelled half way across the country. Desperate to think of a way out I asked her if there was any chance of fighting the creature, after all she appeared well skilled in both armed and unarmed combat but she replied that the spirit was too quick and she wasn't armed with much. Regardless we both agreed that we needed to get out and the sooner we attempted it the better it would be.

Together we sat back down to plan our escape. I'm ashamed to say that it wasn't the greatest plan known to mankind but it worked because I'm here writing this. Anyway we decided that the best route out would be back past the carriage and out through the station but for us to have any chance of making it we'd need something to distract the Teke Teke long enough for us to get quite a lead on it. We didn't have much on hand in the maintenance room that would help but eventually we decided on the fire extinguisher. The idea was I'd open the door and Shiho would unload a pile of foam on the spirit to buy us time. We'd both then run as fast as we could to get out of there. It was a poor plan but we figured it would at least give us a chance.

When I opened the door I don't think I've ever felt more terrified in my life as I saw the spirit waiting just outside, including my encounters with the Kuchisake-onna. The split second that I saw it was enough to leave its image implanted on my brain for ever. The spirit looked similar to someone who was lying on their elbows although the lower half of its body was completely missing with what looked like long dried entrails spilling from its torso. They were a putrid green and scab red colour yet no blood flowed from them. The face was terrifying too as all its blood had drained out leaving its skin pure white with yellow eyes and long knotted dark hair. The small scythe that it carried was rusted and the onryō rested her head on it as she stared up at me. It instantly lunged towards me but Shiho was waiting with the fire extinguisher and hit it square in the face. It tossed its scythe around frantically in a rage but somehow we avoided it and both ran as fast as we could. We were next to the reinforced carriage, the front of which looked like it had been hit by a train where the Teke Teke had broken free, before we heard the tell-tale sound of clacking as it gave chase. This spurred us to run even faster and neither of us stopped until we were out of the station and well down the street. Fortunately the spirit didn't follow us and in truth I don't think it left the tunnels but either way we didn't want to find out. A glance at my watch told me it had just gone 5am so, despite everything telling me I wouldn't be able to sleep for days after such an encounter, we decided to head home before meeting up at the police station a few hours later. At first Shiho didn't seem thrilled at the prospect of me joining her but I'm determined to see this through now that I've seen the creature.

As I look as my clock now I realise that I only have an hour left before I'm due to meet Shiho. I really hope that she's wrong and that this thing can be banished as simply as the Kuchisake-onna. One thing is certain, I need to find out how this ends so that I can write a story on it.

Well the police station idea was a total bust. As promised I met Shiho beforehand and she asked that I let her do the talking. Again the officers at this station seemed to be aware of who Shiho was and asked her very few questions about why she was demanding information on cases from them. If I'm honest I get the impression that they'd hired her to look into it for them as the police station wasn't too far from the train station where the Teke Teke lurked. Either way it was clear that they were used to seeing Shiho and were trying to give her whatever she needed.

Anyway, we were swiftly shown all the files for deaths in or near that station this year and thankfully there wasn't too many, only four which included the two who had been killed by the Teke Teke herself. Discounting them that left us with just two candidates and, as only one of them was female, we had found our Teke Teke. A female in her twenties by the name of Miyumi. We asked for more information about her case and I must admit I understand why she's vengeful. It turns out that she was deliberately pushed onto the tracks one night by a madman, who after the train had sliced her in two jumped down himself and began to eat what was left of her. The thought that this is what had happened to her is disgusting and it goes some way to helping explain what causes these onryō to come back. It can't have been a nice way to go. Anyway, the police arrived on the scene to find the man snacking on her leg and shot him on sight bringing a swift form of justice at least. The trouble is that means that Shiho was right, unlike the Kuchisake-onna a couple of months back, this spirit wasn't going to be appeased by simply gaining revenge. We did get her address from the police file but when I asked Shiho about it she said there was little point in investigating it, we knew who she was and how she'd died and there would be nothing physically binding her to this world. The Teke Teke is also less attached to their human self as some other onryō. The way Shiho explained it was that the most a Teke Teke had ever said was to ask about its legs, never anything else. It is solely driven to find them with no desire for anything else. Its very existence before that moment becomes no more than a blur to the point that it's unclear if it would even acknowledge anything to do with its past other than by coincidence. The Kuchisake-onna, on the other hand, at least acknowledges her previous beauty and the one who wronged her showing some regard for their prior life. The person who became a Teke Teke however is more like a host in some sense, a simple shell of their former self. At least that makes it easier not to feel too sorry for it whilst still remembering Miyumi. Shiho claims that there are other types of onryō out there too, ones which are fully aware of their lives before. If that is the case then would it be possible for one to interact with a human without them being aware of its true nature? If so, I hope I never meet one. At least these things that I encounter with Shiho are obviously otherworldly. If I couldn't recognise one as such then I don't think I'd even know I was in danger until it was too late. Anyway the upshot of our visit to the police station was that investigating Miyumi's house would turn up nothing of use so we were back to square one.

As we left the police station I asked Shiho what her plan was now, there was seemingly no way to appease the spirit and the idea of somehow fighting it appeared to be out of the question so I was left wondering just exactly what it was she planned on doing. She replied that she didn't know. The Teke Teke was far stronger than she first believed, explaining why she thought she could trap it in a freight carriage. She was aware that it was unlikely to be appeased meaning she wasn't sure how to deal with it given that she couldn't fight nor banish it. I asked if she was thinking about simply leaving it alone, whether that was even possible. I had thought that if they just close that station, they could run trains through there without stopping and nobody would encounter the Teke Teke but Shiho looked at me with disgust. She said it was a matter of professionalism that she dealt with it and that the main problem with my idea was that the spirit would eventually grow weary of having no prey in that station and move further down the tracks in an attempt to find a suitable pair of legs. There was no way round it, one way or another she was going to have to try to get rid of it.

Claiming that she needed some time to think, Shiho suggested calling it a day and offered to meet the following day at the station when she hoped to have a better idea of what she was going to do. I wasn't entirely sure what she could come up with in that time but I agreed knowing that, despite the obvious risks, this would be a perfect follow up for my next article if she could pull it off.

With no chance I was missing out on the story I went to the train station to meet Shiho as promised, thankful that she was already there waiting for me when I arrived. She sat on the bench outside absently watching the world go by and for probably the first time since I'd met her actually looked as if she could belong in the regular world with a normal mundane job instead of running around fighting yōkai all the time. I wonder if she'd even like that kind of life or whether she'd be too bored by it. It must take a unique kind of person to do what she does day in day out. Not one who'd happily work in an office is my guess. Still she looked calm and peaceful, the sharpness of her face almost vanishing in the morning sunlight and yet again I wondered about asking her how she'd ended up doing this sort of thing in the first place. My nerves got the better of me though and instead I held my tongue.

After a quick greeting, which Shiho offered only a brief nod, she said she had spoken to a colleague of hers on the phone who had more experience dealing with Teke Tekes. She has colleagues now? Who knew? I guess she has mentioned a former partner so it's possible that there are others like her out there but the way she spoke suggested there was some sort of hidden organisation of yōkai hunters. She said that her colleague had advised her not to get involved as Teke Tekes are especially nasty onryō and require significant knowledge to safely best. When that hadn't deterred her, she'd told her that the key to defeating a Teke Teke was to remove and destroy its scythe. Without that the spirit will have no means of killing and will cause it to abandon our plane. Of course the scythe belonging to the Teke Teke is the only possession it has and I doubted that it would be keen to part with it despite its one track mind. Shiho too had doubted this and had asked how best to go about separating one from the other. Her colleague had a multitude of suggestions, including a technique of disarming it through unarmed combat which sounded suicidal to me and offers up the question of what sort of person, or beast, could fight such an onryō like that without being butchered? Fortunately it appeared as if Shiho had chosen a different plan. Something far less likely to bring us face to face with the Teke Teke.

As we headed into the station and down to the platform where the ever dark tunnels waited for us I asked her about the fact that her colleague knew more about Teke Tekes than she did. She explained that there was a slowly dwindling population of yōkai hunters, each one with their own specialism. Some were more naturally inclined to the beasts and creatures that roamed the world whilst others preferred dealing with onryō and other spirits. Even within these groups there were further divisions with some being considered experts in particular species. Shiho stated that she was considered an expert in Kuchisake-onna due to her past dealings with them. When I asked if she'd encountered many of them she simply nodded and stated that she'd also spent a great deal of time studying them but wouldn't tell me more. Of the person she'd called she merely told me that she was an expert in onryō and a constant source of reliable information.

Once we reached the platform Shiho explained her plan to me. It was a crude plan at best and even she wasn't sure that it would work. She'd been to the train operators earlier that day and had explained the situation to them and requested that one of their drivers take a train along the tunnels up to this station and then wait for her signal. At that point she would draw the Teke Teke out onto the tracks and call for the train which would hopefully hit the Teke Teke and, although Shiho claimed this wouldn't kill it outright, it should be enough to make it drop its scythe. At that point Shiho would run in and pick up the weapon. It sounded suicidal standing between a terrifying spirit and a fast moving train but then again everything with Shiho seemed suicidal and she'd so far lived to tell the tale. The first question I had was how the train would be able to make the Teke Teke drop its scythe yet not be enough to kill it. Shiho explained that the Teke Teke isn't a normal onryō, the form that we see, the actual body, is still the partial remains of the corpse of Miyumi hence can be hit. Part spirit, part human, the Teke Teke binds the remains together through sheer force of will meaning that it's virtually impossible to tear one apart. She offered me the chance to leave before it became dangerous but, wanting the story for my article, I steadfastly refused.

After a short wait the train slowly rolled onto the platform, the sole occupant a driver who appeared scared but resolute in his desire to assist after clearly being told what we were up against. Once he was in place, the two of us set off down the tunnel knowing that the Teke Teke would find us before too long. The plan revolved around the train being able to pick up enough speed to harm the creature and as such we needed to get a good way into the tunnel. Of course the flip side of this was the further we went into the tunnel the easier it would be for the Teke Teke to catch us. I even made the mistake of asking Shiho just how quickly one could travel and she replied that she'd heard about one that could move as quickly as 150km an hour at full speed. She says this is why they make the clacking sound, the skin on their elbows has worn down to the bone. Of course she did follow this up by reassuring me that their speed was hypothetical as nobody had ever accurately measured as there was no easy way to do so without the Teke Teke slicing you in half. Needless to say, her words weren't comforting. After that I was silent as we crept through the tunnel further from the platform as the air became staler and the darkness more and more oppressive until eventually we heard the distant clacking of the Teke Teke. I think my blood froze but Shiho urged us onwards saying that it would find us soon enough. I know that I'd chosen to go with her but even so I wished that I'd never come and felt as if the onryō was already watching us ready to strike. A couple of minutes later Shiho stopped and we both waited in the darkness, listening to the clacking sound drawing ever nearer. I asked what we were waiting for and she explained that she needed to know if it was on our track before she called in the train. If we sent the train down the wrong track then we'd be dead. I pressed myself against the tunnel wall just in case the train came anyway knowing that if Shiho was even the slightest bit late in calling it the Teke Teke would kill us.

In the darkness we listened to those sounds for what felt like an eternity before Shiho eventually hit a button on her radio to call in the train. As soon as she did, she pressed herself to the opposite wall and we were caught in the middle of a cacophony of noise as the train approached from one side and the Teke Teke from the other. The two noises intermingled and it became impossible to tell one from the other. The only thing that was noticeable was that they were getting louder. I'll admit I wasn't confident that Shiho had called the train at the correct time and as the lights of the train first penetrated the darkness of the tunnel around us I saw the Teke Teke on the tracks just in front of me holding its scythe before it. With a grace unexpected from such a being, it sprung forward from its elbows leaping at least six feet into the air towards me and must've been mere inches away when the train thundered down the tracks smashing into the Teke Teke carrying it like a bug on the windshield away from us. The next few seconds were a rush as the train thundered by, the rush of wind threatening to pull us down and onto the tracks. As soon as it passed I instantly let out a breath of air that I hadn't realised I'd been holding and looked up in the darkness to see Shiho approaching, her torch frantically scouring the ground. Not too far from where I was she found the scythe, dropped by the Teke Teke as the train collided with it. She carefully picked it up and immediately snapped the blade from the handle before looking at me and smiling clearly thinking the threat was gone.

Together we made our way further down the track to where the train had come to a stop and crept round the front cautiously. There was no sign of the Teke Teke although the dent on the front of the train suggested it had left its mark. Shiho seemed satisfied that it was gone for good although I'll admit stood in the tunnels I could still hear the clacking sound it made as it moved but that could've easily been other trains in the distance. Even with Shiho's confidence I was glad to get out of those tunnels and onto the surface not wanting to ever go back into the darkness again.

I told Shiho that I plan to write this adventure as the follow up for the magazine and she seemed happy enough for me to do so. I even asked her if she had any other stories that I could use. She simply smiled and dropped the subject. Instead she explained that she was planning on leaving the city having spent the past few months there. When I asked why she said that as the temperatures warmed for spring and summer more jobs were to be found in the countryside hence she would begin a tour of the country. Apparently she does this every year, travelling to where the best chance of finding jobs are. Before I bade her farewell though she did say that I had a knack for getting into these situations and that if ever I encountered something else I should give her a call. With that I had her phone number and a way to instantly access a great source for future articles, not that I think she'd appreciate me calling her constantly. Even so, it's a great resource provided that I don't irritate her. Who knows, the way I've been finding these monsters the last few months maybe I'll actually need her help in the future. That's a scary thought. I know I looked for one this time but I think it's safe to say my yōkai hunting days are behind me.

Everything about this strange new world seems terrifying to me yet Shiho faces it all with minimum fuss. It certainly makes good inspiration for my articles though.

56

Perhaps further research would help, maybe research I can do from the safety of my own home and, if not from my home, somewhere I can reach without needing the subway. I fear the Teke Teke has put me off trains for life.

I've had a call with the editor of the magazine today. He wanted to know if I'd had any ideas for my follow-up piece. I gave him a brief overview of the Kappa and the Teke Teke as monsters and he seemed more interested in the Teke Teke. I'm not surprised by that, a second onryō would fit their style more than the Kappa. I'll get a full write up done and submit it as early as possible. Who knows, maybe they'll pay me in advance this time.

The editor was very much on the fence with the Kappa, he prefers onryō to beasts so I reckon I may have to abandon that story. It's a shame but probably best for the creature. The real downside is that if I want that second slot I'll need another story. If I can't come up with something in the next few weeks I might give Shiho a call and see if I can pry a monster out of her, I'm certainly not going looking for one though.

The latest story is all packaged up and has been sent to the magazine editor, hopefully it produces just as much of a buzz as the previous one did. Again I had to change some of the details but it seems as if it's the actual yōkai that cause the biggest interest. There's nothing wrong with that but I can't help feeling as if the amount I've changed would make it impossible for the readers to survive if they encountered one. Mind you, I would never have survived if not for Shiho and I don't think I would if I encountered one again. Thankfully these things are quite rare, even if I have now encountered three of them.

In other news I've been in touch with my parents and they've invited me home for a weekend later this month. I'm going to take the opportunity to visit, it's not like I've got anything else to be doing. It'll be my first time back in about a year so I'm looking forward to it. Maybe the change in scenery will give me the inspiration to write the second article my editor wants.

I received some feedback from the editor on the Teke Teke story. He loved it! Not too surprising I guess, he had expressed a liking for it when I described it to him but it's always nice to get good feedback on a written piece. This time he's actually asked in advance about putting an image within the story to help the visual appeal. I think it's a good idea although he expects me to have an input on the final choice, something about me knowing the creature better than the artist. I can't say I'm looking forward to judging them. I've already seen one Teke Teke and I have no desire to see another. Somehow I doubt anyone will be able to truly capture the grotesqueness of that thing.

A Duel to the Death

Today is the day I finally headed home, first time in what feels like forever. I don't mind the trip to Nagasaki, I never have, but it feels like a long way even if the flight is less than two hours. Still it was nice to see my family again at the airport after all this time. My little sister even came out with my parents to greet me.

They've all read my article, other than my little sister who at ten was deemed too young, and were very complimentary about my imagination. I don't think they'd have been able to handle it if I'd told them that I'd actually encountered the Kuchisake-onna in the flesh. They did admit it was a stretch from what I usually cover but said they were happy I'd finally found some source of income, especially after I told them that the editor had requested a follow up.

Not much has changed here, truth be told it all appears the same as when I left. I've always liked Nagasaki but it's weird how spending time in Kyoto, away from this place, has left me feeling as if it's no longer my home. That, or the fact that my room here is still laid out for my high school life. I'm not complaining though, it's good to be back.

One thing did catch my attention, throughout a constant stream of information about people I hardly recall my parents mentioned that a couple of kids from my sister's school had died recently, both in the school itself. Apparently the two deaths were both in the same girl's bathroom. My parents didn't seem to know the full details but they were certain that they remain unsolved, they'd even had discussions about my sister changing schools. I spoke with my sister later about it, she'd been told the two had simply moved school, presumably some attempt to stop panic and to avoid having to explain death to children, especially the younger ones. She told me that she didn't like either girl and was glad that they'd moved. Apparently they'd been seen as schoolyard bullies. Even so I asked her about the bathroom in question and her answer was very odd. She said that her friend lived in there. When I pressed her about her friend she said that she was another girl who was a similar age who was never in any classes but was always in that bathroom and happy to see her. Something about it intrigued me, a girl in the bathroom where the deaths occurred whom my sister had never seen anywhere else in the school. I asked if anybody else she knew had spoken to this girl and my sister replied that she didn't know, only that her friend was always happy to see her and was very friendly often playing games with her, just the two of them and always in that bathroom.

I don't know if the deaths in that bathroom and my sister's friend are linked. Honestly, I don't even know if it's another of my sister's imaginary friends, she's had plenty of them, but after what I've seen in the past few months and the fact that two children have already died I didn't want to take any risks. I called Shiho just to get her opinion. It was the first time since the Teke Teke incident that I'd spoken to her and at first I thought she'd tell me I was paranoid but as I spoke she listened, more so than usual, occasionally asking questions to which I didn't know the answers, things like how did the children die? What did my sister's friend look like? Where exactly is the bathroom where they were found? All details which I'm sure meant something to her but nothing to me. Anyway after I finished telling her she paused for a moment before she told me that she'd be on the next flight to Nagasaki.

Her reaction was enough to worry me. Everything I knew of Shiho suggested she only acted when she was certain that something was up. I don't know what's going down at that school but I'm sure that Shiho will get to the bottom of it. Even if it's nothing, I have to know that my sister is safe.

As promised Shiho arrived today on one of the earliest flights. She must've set off incredibly early, dropping whatever she'd been doing to come straight away. I went to meet her at the airport and drove her back to our neighbourhood. As expected she repeated her questions from the previous day alongside the details I'd told her. This time I did have an answer to some of her questions having done a bit of research myself. The two victims had died from different causes, one had been strangled and the other stabbed, a horrendous thing to do to a child. Within the bathroom they had both been in locked cubicles which had to have their doors kicked in to gain access to the bodies. When Shiho asked if it could be the same cubicle that they died in I admitted that I didn't know, it was the same bathroom and apparently there were only three stalls so it was possible that it could've been. Why that would make a difference she didn't tell me. On the subject of my sister's friend, all I could add was a brief description given to me by my sister of a young girl in a red dress with long dark hair that she'd never seen outside of the bathroom. It didn't seem much but rather cryptically Shiho whispered the following, 'that wouldn't be her style'. When I asked her about it she dismissed it as nothing but I can't help but worry about my sister's safety and whether her 'friend' is everything she claims to be.

I had planned on just driving Shiho back to my parent's house so she could ask questions about the deaths and whatever it was in the bathroom but instead she insisted on going straight to the school stating that she had no time to waste. It's a weekend so I knew the school would be closed but fortunately there's a live in janitor who met us when we arrived. He seemed shocked to see anybody at a weekend, especially two people asking about the recent deaths but Shiho assured him that we were there to help and insisted on being shown the bathroom. When the janitor refused she claimed to be investigating on behalf of the police. It was a lie, I knew she was simply investigating because I'd asked her to and it dawned on me that I had no way of paying for her services if there really was something supernatural in that bathroom. Shiho's bluff worked and the janitor relented, pointing us in the direction of the bathroom. I guess if there was something there then the police would eventually turn to Shiho, or someone like her, so we weren't particularly tricking him.

As we made our way towards the bathroom I raised the subject of a price with Shiho but she shrugged it off saying that she'd investigate as a favour to me as we were friends. It was odd her saying that, I'd never really considered us to be friends what with so few interactions with one another but I guess looking back on it one doesn't face death multiple times with somebody without a friendship blossoming. I'm glad too, she went on to tell me that if I really insisted her fee is dependent on the yōkai but starts at no fewer than a million yen but if it was what she thought it was the cost could easily be ten times that. Seems like I'd have to sell a lot of articles to be able to afford her services. I don't know if she always charges though, there's no way that community with the Kappa could've paid her that rate so maybe she just charges the police, or simply makes up a price depending on how she feels at the time.

As we approached I asked her what she was expecting to find in the bathroom but she kept her cards close to her chest, not letting on what she thought was in there. Even so I felt sure that it was to do with my sister's 'friend' and that Shiho was just trying to keep me from bad news. She did ask if I trusted her to which I replied in the affirmative, she had saved my life before which made it hard not to trust her especially after she'd rushed here to help. She also asked me to follow her instructions exactly. I agreed and she explained that she first needed to know what it was in there. Only once she knew what we were up against would she be able to formulate a plan for getting rid of it.

The bathroom itself was small, only three cubicles running along one side with three identical basins opposite. The place was dark too, lit only by a single uncovered fitting which buzzed and seemed dim giving the whole place a dank feel. Even so Shiho strode in calmly and began to carefully investigate the basins. She ducked underneath popping back up a moment later with a scowl on her face. When I asked what was up she stated that she'd found dirt under the basins. Other than for hygiene purposes that didn't seem so horrendous but she said that usually that sort of level of filth would attract a creature known as an Akaname but the absence of one suggested that something worse dwelled in there. Apparently Akaname are relatively harmless creatures, generally considered to be a type of vermin. They can spread disease but Shiho seemed to dismiss them as nothing unusual going so far as to suggest that they are fairly prevalent across public bathrooms. The lack of one appeared to be what she found unusual.

With the basins searched she next turned her attention to the cubicles carefully entering each in turn and checking that they were working. When she reappeared she stated quite plainly that the deaths had occurred in the third cubicle. I asked how she knew and she replied that there were tell-tale signs in there. For starters, it was far cleaner than the other two cubicles suggesting that it had been thoroughly cleaned recently whereas the other two had years' worth of grime clinging to them. I asked again if she knew what it was that had killed them but she declined to answer only stating that there were still a number of possibilities. Apparently a large number of yōkai can make their homes in a bathroom.

With her investigation of the premises done, she beckoned me into the middle cubicle and told me to keep quiet. When I asked why she said she was going to talk to my sister's 'friend', whom there was no sign of, and as such it would be better for her to do the talking. Having previously given her my word I reluctantly agreed and watched as she went into the first cubicle and locked it. Oddly she then climbed over the divider between the two cubicles into mine making it very cramped considering this was a school bathroom and we were two grown adults hiding in a child's stall. Shiho wasn't still for long though, sticking her arm out of the cubicle and knocking on the door of the third. She then closed the door to our cubicle and called out 'Hanako-san, are you there?'

This time I really thought she'd lost it as she'd instructed me to kneel on the toilet lid whilst she balanced her feet on it leaning her back against the door in the hope that our feet couldn't be seen from the gap under the door. We remained there in silence for a couple of minutes but just as I was about to deride her for being ridiculous she received an answer. 'Yes, I'm here.' Replied a young girl's voice and we heard the cubicle door next to us slowly creak open. 'But where are you?' The voice was odd, clearly that of a young girl but it was slow and methodical in speech, sounding out each word carefully as if it was speaking in a foreign tongue and desperate to get it right. In our cubicle Shiho slowly raised a finger to her lips and looked me dead in the eye to make sure I wouldn't say anything. I could tell from her expression that whatever she was speaking with wasn't merely a young girl and as such I did as Shiho requested and remained silent. Shiho told the girl that it wasn't important where we were entering into a conversation with whatever was in the cubicle next to us saying that she'd like to talk about the recent deaths. Whatever had taken on the voice of a young girl and was answering to the name Hanako-san seemed annoyed by the suggestion instead replying that if we weren't going to show ourselves she'd find us instead. From our cubicle I froze as I heard the door of the cubicle next to ours open and then the methodical plodding of small feet. I wondered why this thing was so desperate to find us, especially as it had materialised out of nothing given that the cubicle had been empty moments before, but remained silent. Shiho however continued her conversation, asking if Hanako-san had been the one to kill the children. The answer she got was emphatic, 'no, he did it!' At the same time I saw a pair of hands, again belonging to a young girl, reaching under the door grabbing at the air in the hope of locating us before moving onto the next cubicle. The shock of hearing the anger in its response led me to mouth to Shiho the question of was there something else in there to which she nodded slowly and asked Hanako-san if 'he' was something she wanted rid of. Hanako-san replied in the positive, saying that 'he' had invaded her home and was ruining it for her. She claimed that her friends were visiting less and less because of 'him' and that was making her sad. Shiho asked her to describe 'him' to us and the girl said 'he' was a man who wore a red cloak but could offer nothing else. She didn't like showing herself when 'he' was around so couldn't say more. It was the description of a child but it was beginning to dawn on me that might well have been what we were talking to. Even so, her next sentence was terrifying. 'Found you!'

Looking up from our cubicle, peering down from the divider between our cubicle and the third was the face of a young girl, only it was pure white as if bloodless and her long dark hair dangled down until it was only a few inches from my face. Unlike the other yōkai I've encountered, Hanako-san seemingly wore no injures yet was deathly white. Even so I could tell from her eyes that she was other-worldly and something to be afraid of. Slowly she reached one of her small arms towards me and instantly

Shiho screamed at me not to touch it and to run. The scream seemed to temporarily distract Hanako-san who recoiled and dropped back into her cubicle as Shiho desperately fumbled with the lock on ours. All around us we could hear the sound of Hanako-san laughing and then I saw an arm of a little girl appear out of the toilet just as Shiho swung the door open and we tumbled out into the small bathroom. Further arms were coming out of the wash basins, all grabbing towards us but at the entrance of the final cubicle stood the little girl in a red dress just as my sister had described only her face was one of pure anger. 'Bullies' she screamed at us. At the same time Shiho yelled at me to run before Hanako-san charged at us, the plumbing in the room breaking and sending jets of water into the air as the pipes burst. I half ran and was half dragged by Shiho to the door where we just managed to get out before Hanako-san caught us, dropping to our knees on the other side of the corridor watching as water flooded out from below the door to the bathroom. Shiho stated that Hanako-san wouldn't cross the threshold of the bathroom so we'd be safe there but even so I kept my eye on the door as I demanded that she tell me what it was we'd just encountered.

Her explanation was quick and delivered through short sharp breathes as we recovered. She said it was a Hanako-san, the spirit of a girl who died in that bathroom due to suicide. Apparently the most likely cause was bullying which is why it accused us of being bullies. According to Shiho if it reaches its victim it drags them to an equivalent of hell which doesn't sound pleasant, nor plausible yet with everything I'd seen I wasn't going to question it. I asked Shiho how we were going to get rid of it and she looked at me as if I was an idiot before asking if I'd not been listening. She's decided to trust that this Hanako-san was telling the truth and that it wasn't her that killed the two children, although I have my doubts about that, the thing appeared incredibly dangerous and quite insane to me. Shiho instead believes that the description given by Hanako-san sounds like an Aka Manto, a different type of yōkai and one that would match the causes of the deaths. Even so I said that Hanako-san couldn't be trusted and was clearly too dangerous to be left in a school bathroom especially as it appears to have befriended my sister. Bizarrely Shiho disagreed and flat-out refuses to remove it from the bathroom, saying that she's come to stop the murders and that Hanako-san hasn't been responsible for them. She says that if it had wanted to harm my sister it would've done so long ago. She claims it's a lonely spirit who only wants friends and as such is likely to appear to those who want friends too or those being bullied. Apparently it will latch itself onto these friends and protect them from any bullies that try to hurt them in a similar, if more violent, way to a Kappa. I still disagree with Shiho on that but she thinks that my sister and Hanako-san are good for each other just so long as anybody bullying her doesn't follow her into the bathroom. I countered that it can't be healthy to grow up with a dead spirit as your friend but Shiho simply replied that she did and she turned out fine. I think her definition of fine may be different from mine but maybe I ought to speak to my sister about bullying.

Anyway with the Aka Manto yet to be seen but apparently only likely to appear in that same bathroom we left for the day as Hanako-san was so riled that Shiho's convinced she'd kill us immediately if we tried to enter again. Our hope is that she'll calm down overnight and tomorrow we'd be able to try to summon and banish the Aka Manto instead.

I offered Shiho the chance to stay with us that night which she accepted. It only seemed right since she was here at my request and had in all likelihood saved me yet again despite being the one to summon Hanako-san. At first it felt weird introducing her to my family but we made a point not to discuss her line of work, she was simply called a colleague. Even as I write this I can hear her talking to my parents about local events. They're getting on well and Shiho is surprisingly open around them, completely different to how I've seen her interact with people before. She's very polite and asks pertinent questions and they all seem to like her. Sometimes it's difficult to see that it's the same woman who so gracefully disarmed that Kuchisake-onna all those months ago.

This morning, before we headed back to the school, I was able to drag Shiho aside after breakfast to find out more about the Aka Manto, deciding it was better to know about the monster prior to meeting it to save myself from yesterday's failings. Her explanation was detailed and not particularly reassuring. The Aka Manto is a yōkai that haunts bathrooms which, unlike the previous spirits I've encountered with Shiho, has no purpose other than to kill people. It isn't vengeful like the Teke Teke or the Kuchisake-onna and apparently appears to be fully in control of its faculties. Of course Shiho stated that this made it even more dangerous as it was less likely to be distracted. Its hunting method is somewhat alarming but I do now understand some of Shiho's previous questioning. The Aka Manto lurks in bathrooms waiting for people to use the final stall. When they do it offers them a choice of paper, blue or red. Choosing the red results in the spirit brutally stabbing you multiple times until the room is coated red with your blood whilst choosing blue results in it strangling you until your skin turns blue. It sounded like a lovely creature and one I really didn't want to meet. I asked Shiho if there was any way round its question which it seems duty bound to ask and she replied that people have tried different techniques in the past. She says you cannot refuse to answer the spirit, it will simply keep asking and won't allow you to leave until it gets a response but apparently people have tried asking for different colours to varying levels of success, she recalled a tale of one soul who asked for yellow and was found drowned in the toilet bowl. She says from her experience the best chance is to simply decline its offer and say you don't need any. This apparently can give you enough time to escape if one is quick enough to dart out of the bathroom whilst the Aka Manto weighs up whether or not you were lying. It seems to me as if a number of these spirits ask a question to which there is no right answer. I even asked Shiho why they bothered and although she wasn't certain her theory was that they often do it for fun. At least the Kuchisake-onna was driven by vanity but the Aka Manto just sounds plain crazy. Perhaps most crucially when I asked Shiho how she was going to get rid of it, she replied that she was going to talk to it and ask it to leave. When I said that sounded like a dumb idea she replied that some could be quite reasonable if they could be convinced a better hunting spot was available although Shiho added that she wasn't aware if one could be killed. Without a purpose other than killing, it was difficult to find a method of disposing of one. I did ask if it was possible that this one could've been attracted to the bathroom because of Hanako-san but Shiho seemed to doubt this stating that although Hanako-san was evidently aware of the Aka Manto we couldn't be certain that the reverse was true and there had been no previous recorded incident of a Hanako-san attracting other yōkai.

Still unsure of whether her plan would get us killed, after breakfast the two of us went back to the school hoping to summon the Aka Manto for a chat. Again we knocked on the door for the janitor only today he wasn't happy to see us at all. He blamed us for causing a large mess in the bathroom yesterday by flooding it which although technically not our doing was probably on balance our fault. I don't think he liked our explanation that it was done by the spirit of a dead girl any better as he slammed the door in our faces. Not to be deterred, Shiho broke in through a window near the bathroom in question reasoning that if we could get rid of the spirit then the lives of the students were worth more than the cost of the broken window. Truthfully I got the impression that it wasn't her first time breaking into places and after our nights imprisoned by the Kuchisake-onna and the Teke Teke I too was developing a habit for it.

As we made our way to the bathroom I tapped Shiho on the shoulder and asked if we could be sure that Hanako-san wouldn't interfere with her plan, or in fact that she still wouldn't be rampaging around, but Shiho replied that she probably wouldn't appear if the Aka Manto was on the prowl. The fact that the janitor had been in to deal with the flooding proved that she'd clearly gone back to wherever she resides after we'd left.

Even with Shiho's words I was still nervous as we entered the bathroom and found it much as it had been yesterday. There were few signs of the flooding and everything was quiet, almost unnaturally so. Undeterred, Shiho went straight to the third cubicle and entered despite that one being the home of Hanako-san. I was hesitant but Shiho eventually stuck her head back out to ask if I was planning on joining her. Together we waited in the cubicle for five minutes in complete silence, my eyes constantly darting around for any signs of the girl that had attacked us yesterday. Nothing happened and I asked Shiho again if the spirit could've been lying, painfully aware not to speak her name as we stood in her stall and I was fearful of those dreadful arms emerging from the toilet again. Shiho said no but left the cubicle anyway, taking the only roll of paper with her which she dumped in the bin before returning. Again we waited in silence for five minutes and again we were unsuccessful. At one point Shiho even asked for some paper complaining that there was none available but got no answer from the empty bathroom.

I was about to declare the whole thing a bust when she had an idea. Evidently the Aka Manto wasn't interested in attacking two people at once, although the description Shiho gave me of it would suggest that it would certainly be capable of doing so, therefore Shiho suggested that I move to a different cubicle. Quite how the spirit would be aware that there were two of us in there I don't know, I guess it must have been watching on invisible to us or something. Choosing carefully I opted for the first cubicle, the furthest from where Shiho was trying to call the spirit and waited there silently as Shiho moaned about the lack of paper in her cubicle. Incredibly her complaints were answered and a deep voice could be heard asking if she wanted red paper or blue. It certainly wasn't the voice we'd heard yesterday, deep and less plodding than Hanako-san, the voice sounded completely human. Plucking up my courage I peeked round the cubicle door and saw a man standing outside her cubicle dressed in a long flowing red cloak wearing a simple white mask designed to hide his face. Most disturbingly, both of his hands were protruding through the closed cubicle door where I imagined they were offering different colour paper to Shiho. To her credit, Shiho wasn't flustered by the hands magically appearing in front of her and instead of answering the question, asked what the Aka Manto was doing there. Her answer was a somewhat predicable repeat of the original question posed to her and so the conversation continued for a while with both just asking the other the same question on repeat until eventually Shiho realised this was getting her nowhere. From my cubicle I heard the creak of the door as she opened hers to stare at the spirit who remained motionless, blocking her path and asking its cursed question over and over. Finally Shiho answered him, stating that she didn't want any paper but instead wanted to talk. As expected this confused the Aka Manto who backed away slightly giving her the space to leave if she wished. With its question answered it was far more open to answering Shiho and informed her that it was there because it was a good hunting ground. When she asked it to move on it replied that it wouldn't as it saw no purpose to leaving. She then asked if there was anything she could get the spirit to convince it to leave. The answer it gave was hardly inspired, fresh victims, that or chose a colour of paper to take from it.

During the interview of this spirit Shiho had left the cubicle and had backed away towards the exit so that she now stood outside my cubicle and I could see from her expression that she was thinking hard. The Aka Manto clearly had no desire to leave and it seemed like the only way to remove it would be to trick it and I'm not sure if that was possible. Even with it answering her questions I'm not convinced that it wasn't simply toying with her, willing to discuss its life knowing that it would kill Shiho later. Still not to be deterred, Shiho asked the spirit how it had come to be in this particular bathroom but it didn't answer, instead I saw Shiho take a step back and swear as suddenly the Aka Manto was right next to her having clearly lost patience. One of its ghostly hands wrapped around Shiho's neck and lifted her up into the air and slammed her into the wall next to the door. I could see Shiho struggling to breathe and I knew that if it killed her I would be next. Panicking but knowing that I had to do something I ran out of my cubicle and kicked at the Aka Manto. In hindsight it wasn't a great idea, my foot went straight through the yōkai and I ended up kicking Shiho in the shin but I must've caught it by surprise because it instantly dropped Shiho and turned towards me drawing a knife from its cloak. My blood froze but I instantly felt a warm hand grab mine and drag me out of the bathroom whilst the Aka Manto recovered from shock.

Outside of the bathroom both of us collapsed to the floor breathing heavily and watching the door for any signs of pursuit. Once we'd caught our breath I asked Shiho if she'd got what she needed from her conversation with it. She scowled and replied that it had confirmed that it wasn't going to leave of its own free will and that would be an issue. It was going to be impossible to fight the spirit ourselves as my attack had proved that we couldn't physically touch it. When I asked what we were going to do she replied that she had one last play but it was risky and that I really wouldn't like it. She said that she needed to confirm her thoughts with one of her colleagues and that she'd tell me the plan in the morning. We'd let it sleep tonight but tomorrow we'd be back to finally get rid of the killer yōkai.

Shiho was right, I don't like this plan of hers. I don't like it at all. Today is no longer a weekend so the school is open again. That means we're waiting until this evening to go back and hoping that nobody is unfortunate enough to stumble across the Aka Manto today. According to Shiho after our stunt yesterday the spirit will have a personal vendetta against us so will try to harm us and anything to do with us so I've warned my sister to stay away from that bathroom for today. Shiho says that this will help for now but in time the spirit will start visiting other bathrooms in the school in an attempt to find her so that it can get to me.

Shiho was able to speak to her friend last night, apparently the same one who knew of Teke Tekes, and they appear to believe that her plan has potential although I'm not entirely sure that they have any experience of this. Her plan relies on the vendetta of the Aka Manto as Shiho hopes to use my sister to help defeat it. I don't like putting her at risk but evidently by looking into it in the first place I've managed to do so anyway. Failing to act now will mean having to convince my parents to have her move school and even then there's no saying whether the Ako Manto will follow. Although we personally cannot beat the Aka Manto, Shiho believes that there's a chance that Hanako-san may be strong enough especially if she thinks a bully is attacking one of her friends. Unfortunately that's where my sister comes in as the role of her friend. Shiho assures me that she'll be there to protect my sister but I can't say I'm thrilled at the idea of bringing her to a grudge match between two immortal spirits. Also her offer to protect my sister rang a little thin after she'd already declared that she couldn't stop either of them. Our whole plan, including the safety of my sister, rests on her friendship with the very spirit that tried to kill us not two days ago. A spirit which by Shiho's own admission, may simply be swatted away by the Aka Manto. It seems that even people in her profession are unsure which of the two are more powerful.

We're heading there this evening so all I can do till then is wait. I'm very nervous about this.

As planned we waited until the end of the school day and then a little longer to make sure that all the staff had left before we made our move. Getting my sister to agree to come along had been incredibly simple although I still wasn't happy when I lifted her through another window broken by Shiho as we trespassed for the second day in a row. Yet again we were fortunate that the bathroom was located a long way from the janitor's living quarters and he hadn't heard our arrival leaving us free to execute our plan.

As with the previous times, the now familiar bathroom looked perfectly normal when we entered it, no sign of either of the yōkai that called it home. My sister looked round eagerly hoping to find her friend but Shiho had told her not to call for her and although it was apparently capable of appearing at will, it had chosen to remain hidden, either because of our presence or that of the Aka Manto. Carefully Shiho laid out her plan to lure out the Aka Manto. It involved my sister waiting in the third cubicle for it to appear whilst Shiho and I waited in the adjacent cubicle. Again Shiho reminded me that should the spirit appear and attack my sister she would intervene to buy us time to escape. Despite her young age, my sister had listened very carefully to Shiho's instructions although whether or not she actually understood what was happening I wasn't sure. Part of me hoped that she didn't and that she'd forget about it with time. Of the little that I knew of Shiho's world I was already painfully aware that it was dangerous and I wanted my sister to have no part in it after tonight.

As we took up our places in the cubicles my heart was pounding and my throat was dry. Shiho had made sure that there was no paper in the third cubicle and it wasn't long before we heard the signature question of the Aka Manto asking whether my sister wanted red paper or blue. As soon as I heard it I wanted to get her out of there but Shiho held me back hoping that she'd do as she'd been told. Shiho had given her explicit instructions as to what to expect and what to do and reasoned that if she did exactly that she would be fine. So following her instructions my sister remained silent, no doubt entranced by the floating hands in her cubicle but otherwise silent. This caused the Aka Manto to repeat its question slightly more forcefully, evidently the spirit did not enjoy being ignored. It asked a third time in a raised voice and this was when Shiho's plan came into play. As instructed my sister screamed back at it with Shiho's words. 'I don't want any paper you bully.'

What happened next was a bit of a blur but as it had the previous day being shot down from its offering the Aka Manto paused allowing enough time for my sister to run from the cubicle to the door where I joined her with Shiho between the Aka Manto and ourselves. The spirit appeared to recognise us from yesterday and it came at Shiho only to stop a couple of feet short as a sharp scream rang across the bathroom. 'Bullies!' I don't think I'll ever forget that scream, so loud and piercing but it stopped the Aka Manto in its tracks. I took the opportunity to shepherd my sister out of the door and then went back in for Shiho although by the time I had returned, despite only being a few seconds, Hanako-san had materialised standing in the door of her cubicle and looking truly outraged. It was still difficult to get past the fact that she looked like a little girl but the Aka Manto had turned to face her, completely ignoring Shiho who backed towards me knowing that she was insignificant compared to the two yōkai in the room.

Incredibly we watched as the Aka Manto asked Hanako-san his question although I think even he was a little unsure where she had come from suggesting he hadn't been aware of her previously. The two squared off for a moment, the deranged killer and the psychotic little girl, each one capable of inflicting horrors upon humanity yet duking it out for control of a girls bathroom in a small insignificant school. The Aka Manto made the first move lunging at Hanako-san drawing his blade from his cloak as he went. The small girl didn't react and instead we saw arms emerging out of the wash basins and the toilet bowls again. This time they weren't reaching for us instead all grabbing at the Aka Manto as Hanako-san took a blow from his knife as it slid across her cheek, cutting deep yet drawing no blood nor any reaction at all from her. Infuriated the Aka Manto dropped his blade and grabbed her by the neck lifting her off the floor and trying to choke her but her pale face never turned to blue as he'd hoped. Instead, the hand that had emerged from the third cubicle's toilet grabbed his cloak. No bigger than a child's hand I thought there was no way it was going to be able to do anything to the Aka Manto but incredibly it began to drag him back towards the toilet with Hanako-san still in his grip smiling horrifically at him despite the pressure on her neck.

I don't know exactly what happened next as they disappeared into the cubicle but it sounded as if the toilet exploded such was the racket that came from within. Moments later Hanako-san re-emerged from the cubicle staring at us wildly and I noticed that the arms in the basins were now all turned towards us. Shiho nodded once at the spirit and then tapped me on the shoulder saying it was time to leave. We exited immediately and met my sister just outside the bathroom who wanted to go back in to speak to her friend. I suggested it wasn't a good idea but Shiho thought otherwise and I couldn't reach her in time to stop her. Shiho held me back as I tried to follow warning me that although Hanako-san had made friends with my sister, it would not offer me the same privileges. She also swore that it wouldn't harm her. Even so the time waiting for her was the longest of my life.

As we sat waiting for my sister I asked what had happened to the Aka Manto and Shiho reminded me that Hanako-san can drag people to another realm often thought to be Hell although she wasn't sure exactly where it was people taken by her end up. Evidently nobody has ever returned from there but Shiho doubts it's nice. Wherever she takes people, it was where the Aka Manto would be now, trapped forever in an endless void. I asked Shiho if she was satisfied by that outcome, sure one killer spirit had been trapped in another realm but the thing that put it there was still free to haunt the bathroom preying on anyone it deemed to be a bully. I know that the Ako Manto was dangerous but if anything Hanako-san is surely more so given how easily it had dismissed the Aka Manto. In response Shiho shrugged and told me that was as good as we were going to get. Shortly afterwards my sister came back out to join us and said that she'd never seen her friend so happy before. I guess no longer having to share her bathroom with the Aka Manto will have given her a reason to cheer and I had to admit it didn't seem to want to harm my sister so that was a point in its favour. Time will tell if Hanako-san ever grows to be a real problem in that school. I hope not. I fear that if she does, there'll be nobody capable of stopping her. Certainly not Shiho based on what she's told me.

With our work complete we headed home where my sister was all too keen to spend the evening chatting to Shiho. She's really taken a shine to her these past few days, it's strange given how little Shiho says about herself but I swear I caught her smiling.

With the end of the Aka Manto and nothing to be done about Hanako-san Shiho's work is done and she informed me of her plan to leave Nagasaki in search of more jobs. She told me that she was going to rent a car and drive back towards Kyoto stopping along the way at any jobs that she came across. As she was slowly heading back towards Kyoto she asked if I'd like to join her saying that she'd become quite accustomed to having me around and that ultimately I can call it a long ride home.

I'll be honest, based on her line of work and how dangerous it is, it should've taken me longer to answer but I jumped at the chance. I have everything I need to write articles with me and the chance to spend additional time with Shiho might open up a whole world of stories. Who knows, by the time we reach Kyoto I might have enough stories for my editor to last years. It's odd too, just as she's becoming accustomed to having me around, I too am becoming accustomed to her being there.

Today is the day I left my family and Nagasaki behind. It's been great to see them all again and, excluding the encounter with the Aka Manto and Hanako-san, has actually been quite relaxing. Certainly a nice break from life in Kyoto.

Still I'm excited to be hitting the road with Shiho. She says that it'll be a long road back to Kyoto, possibly lasting months depending on how many jobs she finds but truthfully I've got a way out at any time. There's nothing particularly holding me to Kyoto either. All that's there for me at the moment is boring articles that make no money. I've certainly got a better chance of finding better stories by sticking with Shiho.

We had a big feast before we left. Shiho has been off dealing with something else the last few days but returned this morning and ate with my family this evening. They all seem really taken with her, maybe that's more amazing that anything I'll ever see with her. Still, I wonder what we'll find as we explore Kyushu.

A Killer Bargain

April 28th

I've been travelling with Shiho for a few days now. I'll admit it's nowhere near as exciting as I first thought. I honestly thought that she'd be battling yōkai every day but the truth is far from that. She tends to stop at every police station in every town to see if they have any jobs for her and mostly they don't. Indeed we're yet to have even the faintest sniff of a lead. I guess this is why she charges so much each time, she doesn't need that many cases to make a healthy living.

A healthy living she makes too judging by her expenses. Sure the car we're using isn't the best model out there but it's easily big enough for the two of us. It's also big enough to carry the few cases that Shiho has with her. Most of them are full of strange instruments and artefacts that she won't tell me the purpose of but I guess are related to her work. The accommodation isn't too shabby either. Although she can shy away from the finest of establishment, she doesn't scrimp on the cost of accommodation. Of course her route is taking us meandering through Kyushu and there aren't always a lot of options for where to stay. When that is the case she's perfectly happy to take a budget option not that I complain, for the most part she's footing the bill.

She still doesn't tell me much about herself preferring to discuss my life but I think she does enjoy the company. Maybe in time she'll open up and I can learn more about her world.

It's now been two weeks since we left Nagasaki and we're definitely further from Kyoto than when we started. We headed south originally, down towards the southern shores of Kyushu in search of any jobs and just arrived yesterday. There hasn't been much so far but I'm starting to think that this is the way with Shiho's lifestyle. She can't always stumble across these monsters and even when others do the chances of them contacting her are slim given how difficult she is to reach. She frames it as placing herself in areas where she expects to find things but it's not an exact science and she assures me this is pretty standard.

During the last few days Shiho has opened up a bit more. She still doesn't say much about her past but she is at least happy to chat and does answer any questions I have about the yōkai we've already faced together as best she can. I have little doubt that in time I'll be able to find out more about her but until then I'm happy with what little she does feel comfortable to share. I even showed her the article on the Kuchisake-onna and she seemed bemused more than anything after reading it. Still she didn't explicitly say she didn't like it though. She's also been remarkably helpful in answering the questions people have sent in to me about the spirit although not many of her answers are repeatable if I'm to maintain that the story was fiction. I also showed her the Teke Teke story and the draft I've written of the Aka Manto. She suggested a few changes but ultimately declared that these articles were my area of expertise not hers and pointed out that I had changed enough details to merge fact and fiction whereas she liked to deal in facts. Truth be told I think she was rather smug that someone believed her tales worth telling.

Getting back to our search for yōkai and Shiho received an interesting sounding email today through her website from a woman whose husband has disappeared. It may not be supernatural but she suspects foul play and wants Shiho to investigate. It may be nothing, according to the woman the local police force believe that to be the case, but as we're only a few hours' drive away we'll head out tomorrow and see if there is something going on. What I can say is that if this woman has gone so far as to contact Shiho, she must be either certain or very desperate.

I don't think I've ever witnessed such a reaction to someone arriving as when we turned up in that village to start our investigation into the missing husband. For starters, there was a welcoming party waiting for us, and not one that was happy with our arrival. It was a small village, no more than forty buildings dotted around and it appeared that at least half the villagers had turned out in protest. The reason for this was that the woman had previously asked the other residents for help and when they'd failed to produce a satisfactory response she'd turned to Shiho. Some of the residents had taken this to be an insult and were determined not to let an outsider interfere claiming that they were trying to protect the woman from Shiho fleecing her. To her credit, Shiho was relatively respectful and didn't get annoyed with them, continually stating that she was doing a job for the woman and that if they had a problem they should bring it up with her. I have no doubt that they will at a later stage but eventually the two of us were able to make our way past them to the woman's house where she welcomed us and explained what had happened.

It's been four days since her husband went missing during an evening walk by the river. He went on this walk most days and there was nothing to suggest that he'd simply want to abandon her, at least that's what she claimed although given how devoted she was it appeared unlikely she'd be able to think that way. Everything about his life seemed to be going well, she was pregnant and he'd just been given a promotion at work. It was because of this she thought his disappearance was strange and suspected foul play. I must admit, the brief profile we were given seemed to back that theory. Shiho was the one asking the questions whilst I merely listened, trying to gather the details of her story. Even if I had been asking the questions I don't think I'd have been able to follow Shiho's line of thought. As always it seemed to leap from one thing to the next, often without any connection, and focus on tiny details that I certainly wouldn't have picked up on. With little to go on in terms of his disappearance, Shiho asked about his regular route and whether anybody else would've been out for a stroll in the evening that he might've encountered. The woman replied that she wasn't sure but he often mentioned seeing the village elder during his walks and that he'd be a good person to ask. She also said that his route took him past a couple of houses closer to the river that belonged to a pair of brothers who liked to think of themselves as the big shots of the village. They were two of the people who'd offered to help in the aftermath and had been strongly against requesting outside help. No doubt they were part of the crowd that had greeted us, possibly the ringleaders. Shiho also asked plenty of questions about the man's other routines, locations he'd visited recently and his reasons for going on walks every evening. The woman answered them all to the best of her ability but ultimately left us with little to work with.

As we came out of her house the crowd, led by the Fumimoto brothers, were still waiting, wanting to try to drive us away. They told us that they had already looked into it and found that the man had a lover in the city and had simply taken the opportunity to abandon his wife. The villagers had then made a collective decision not to break his wife's heart by telling her whilst she was pregnant choosing that her believing him to be dead was kinder than the truth. Shiho refused to be drawn into their speculation though and told them that she intended to investigate anyway and that if they had information she would be grateful to hear it. I could tell they weren't happy to have her snooping around but after warning her not to interfere a final time they let us be, noticeably not providing any evidence of their claim, and we made our way to the home of the village elder.

He invited us in very cordially and although he shared the brothers' assumption that the man had most likely abandoned his wife he backed it up by saying that disappearances were a common occurrence in the village. For as long as he could remember people would vanish, usually two or three each year and always in the spring. He said it was just the way things were and that nobody ever really bothered trying to find these people as it was obvious that they had moved on, bored with the rural lifestyle. He said at first people had contacted the police but as the years rolled by he'd slowly convinced them that it wasn't worth it and they'd be better off hiring a private investigator in the city instead to track down these individuals although none ever came back to the village. He told us that he personally didn't have a problem with us poking around and even apologised for the brothers' behaviour but did inform us that he thought we were wasting our time and could only bring pain to the woman who'd hired us. Even so after we'd left his house, Shiho led us on the route down to the river so that we could retrace the missing man's steps for any clues.

On the way I asked Shiho what her thoughts were on the case and the people of the village and she admitted that although she didn't appreciate the way they had greeted us she wasn't that surprised. In her experience small villages like to keep things to themselves and portray an idyllic picture to the outside world. She said that few villages she'd been to ever appreciated someone like her snooping around. On the case itself she wasn't sure, there was little reason to believe the theory that he'd run off as he appeared happy although there was also little reason to suggest that anything out of the ordinary had occurred. She stated that the only thing that interested her was the surprising frequency that people went missing from the village. Without that she stated that it could easily be a missing person's case or even a murder investigation but something about the frequency bothered Shiho and she seemed to stop frequently to examine nearby trees and rocks.

The path we were following led all the way down to the river bank where it snaked along the shore for a while before turning back towards the village about a fifteen minute walk away. The river itself was a good seventy meters wide with a sandy beach interlaced with large rocks running down from the path to the water. Not too far from here it flowed out into the sea. It truly was a magnificent view but we hadn't come to admire the scenery. We stood at the edge of the path for at least five minutes as Shiho scanned the beach for anything out of the ordinary although even if there had been any evidence on the sand it would've been washed away by the four high tides since the night the man vanished. Even so she focussed on a rock easily large enough for two adults to sit on roughly half way down the beach and slowly walked over to it holding her hand out to tell me to be careful as I followed her due to the rocks being slippery as opposed to any potential threat.

At the rock, she stopped and examined it carefully, scrutinising every inch of its surface until she eventually turned to me holding what looked like a very thin piece of string. When I asked what it was she told me it was human hair, black and so long that it had to belong to a female. As far as clues go to a missing person case, a hair on a rock a number of days later was hardly proof of anything but Shiho appeared happy with her find. She slowly climbed onto the rock and helped me up too where she pointed to the sand and asked me what I thought about it. I took a look and in the sand there was a clear trail running from the rock to the river where it looked like someone had dragged a log although not straight but in an odd wave pattern. Shiho nodded and pointed out that it was fresh, made that morning and that it was no log that had been dragged through the sand. When I asked what she thought it was she replied that she believed it was a tail. The tail of a Nure-onna. I hadn't heard of one so she explained that a Nure-onna is a half woman half snake creature that's native to the southern shores of Kyushu. Capable of drinking the blood of a human or crushing them with their tail, they tend to be found on river banks during this time of year. When I asked why only this time of year she replied that it was breeding season and that they would spend the rest of the year in the ocean. She even told me that the creature was watching us at that very moment. She'd seen it earlier, probably whilst we were searching the beach and told me to scan the water whilst not looking at the beast directly before she guided my eyes to a black rock just peeping out near the opposite bank. Only this rock wasn't a rock, as my eyes scanned over it I realised that it was in fact dark hair plastered over a forehead and a pair of vile red eyes. I almost flipped out but Shiho assured me that the Nure-onna would remain in the water whilst it thought we hadn't noticed it. If it thought we'd seen it, it would attack. When I asked if she was going to somehow drive it away she replied that the water was its domain and whilst it was in there she wouldn't stand a chance. Instead she claimed that the creature would return to the very rock we stood on in the evening but until then it would remain bobbing just below the surface.

As we slowly returned to the village leaving the Nure-onna behind I pointed out that there was nothing to link the creature in the water to the missing man although its presence was disturbing. There was no corpse to suggest he'd been killed and although the creature wasn't something I wanted to get close to, it didn't appear that dangerous just chilling out in the river. Despite admitting that was true, Shiho disagreed that it wasn't dangerous and stated that Nure-onnas are clean creatures, unlikely to leave a corpse in their nest area after feeding. If it had killed the man it would've dumped his body in the river and let the water carry it away leaving no evidence behind. She planned to inform both the wife and the village elder of the creature so that she wouldn't be disturbed that evening when we went back to confront it.

As expected the wife was devastated to hear that a creature like that could've attacked her husband and wanted it immediately killed so that we could check it's remains for any proof despite Shiho pointing out that it would only drink his blood which would be hard to trace, especially after this length of time. The village elder appeared less concerned, denying that such creatures even existed and even accused Shiho of lying to try and extort money from them. To be honest a few months ago I would've thought the same thing. Despite this Shiho told him to keep everyone away from the river until she could deal with the Nure-onna unwilling to leave such a dangerous creature so close to civilisation.

We waited the rest of the day outside of the village. Shiho thought it best not to antagonise the locals any further so we stayed away until dusk at which point we made our way back to the river bank, a little further along the track. There we found a large bush we could hide behind which gave us a view of the rock we had been on earlier and it was there that we waited for the Nure-onna. I glanced out across the river towards where we'd seen the creature earlier in the day but it had moved leaving me unsure of its whereabouts. Shiho assured me that it would be close by yet it was important that it didn't know we were there explaining why we were hiding so far from the rock.

After what felt like hours, Shiho nudged me with her elbow and pointed to the water which was lightly rippling as something made its way towards our side of the river. I was amazed as I saw the creature pull itself out of the water. It was exactly as Shiho had described, the top half consisted of a woman's body with long glistening black hair yet fierce red eyes that marked it as otherworldly. The creature also had a long forked tongue which hissed into the air before it similar to a snake and appeared to be dripping with some sort of venom. At end of its long arms, its fingers were curled into sharp claws capable of ripping flesh from bone. Incredibly, near the bottom of the torso, its flesh gave way to scales, an oddly simmering dark green which caught in the moonlight. The tail stretched at least three meters before rounding out at a sharp pointed tip. It was like nothing I'd seen before, part human, part snake. The closest I could say would be a horrific version of a mermaid yet somehow disproportionate with the length of its tail. We watched as it pulled itself onto the rock and sat looking out over the river. Despite the horror of what the creature was capable of, it looked somewhat majestic sat on that rock as it started to comb its hair with one clawed hand seemingly oblivious to the rest of the world, its scaly tail coiling around its body.

We watched it for quite a while before I whispered to Shiho asking what she was going to do. Her reply was short but to the point. We were going to observe the Nure-onna and see what it did. She stated that Nure-onna were often known to work with other creatures, namely Ushi-oni or Iso-onna, and Shiho wanted to make sure that this one was working alone so that she didn't walk into a trap. I asked about the two she'd mentioned to which she replied that the Ushi-oni was more of a beast likely to have eaten our missing man whereas an Iso-onna was way more cunning than the other two creatures and would be a problem if one did haunt the area yet she refused to say any more fearing that undue noise might startle the creature. As it was nothing else turned up for at least half an hour and when it did, it wasn't a supernatural creature. Instead we saw a torch approaching from the village and then we saw the owner, one of the two Fumimoto brothers, the older I believe, was slowly making his way out to the beach carrying a basket as if he was readying a picnic despite the time of night. The Nure-onna had seen him too and was watching him carefully as he approached.

I nudged Shiho and pleaded with her to interfere knowing that the man was going to get himself killed if he approached the Nure-onna but instead he stopped just shy of the rock and appeared to speak with it before he placed the basket next to the creature and left. I asked Shiho what was going on but she was just as baffled as me. We watched the Nure-onna hoping that it would show us what was in the basket but it never got the chance. A few minutes after the brother had left we saw another torch approaching, this time much slower and eventually the village elder came into view on the path. The Nure-onna noticed him too and this time, instead of letting him approach as she had the brother, she bared her fang like teeth and hissed at him. The elder was clearly shocked to see such a creature having earlier dismissed them as being stories and we saw his mouth drop open. He attempted to back away and slipped on the sand, dropping to the ground and the Nure-onna was on him in a flash. Her tail wrapped around him quickly dragging him towards her before poking a hole in his neck with her claws, sticking her long forked tongue into the gap and slowly drinking his blood. I appealed to Shiho to help but she just shook her head saying he was already dead and that approaching the creature would simply lead to our deaths too. Honestly, I think that might have been true.

As the slurping sound of the Nure-onna drifted across the night air Shiho turned and walked away back towards the village. There was nothing we could do for the elder but she vowed to get to the bottom of why the creature hadn't attacked the brother in the morning. I asked why we didn't wait to see if we could spot the interior of the basket but Shiho replied that once the Nure-onna had finished feasting it would retreat to the river to clean itself and dispose of the body. When it went it would take the basket with it meaning that staying would provide us nothing more.

It's a strange creature, an odd mix of beauty and danger and completely unlike anything I've seen before. The Kuchisake-onna and the Teke Teke were clearly originally human, the Kappa something else entirely but the Nure-onna was an odd mix of both. I know that it had just killed a man but there was something intoxicating about watching it and part of me wishes we had stayed but Shiho appeared unimpressed. I think she's seen one before.

This was the second time I've seen somebody die right in front of me, and both of them with Shiho alongside me. It's not a pleasant thing to watch and I hope that I don't have to deal with it again yet I fear that Shiho has seen plenty of deaths before and knows she'll see many more.

Following the events of last night, the villagers gathered together to come to terms with the death of the elder. Officially he's classed as missing as few would believe the tale of the Nure-onna but even so the village mourned his loss. We'd given the gathering a miss and we were glad to do so, the wife of the missing man presumed killed by the Nure-onna called to let us know that the Fumimoto brothers had stirred up suspicion against Shiho and myself and had convinced most of the residents that the elder wouldn't have vanished if not for our intervention. I'll admit I don't know if our findings were what brought him to the river last night, I guess we'll never know, but having seen the creature I am certain that we needed to intervene to prevent further deaths and disappearances.

The village meeting did give us a chance to investigate the brothers' houses though and as soon as we saw them leaving, we immediately crept up to their homes and Shiho picked the lock. I know that it wasn't exactly legal but something about the interactions I'd seen between Shiho and the police suggested that we'd be fine even if we were caught. Besides, it's hardly the first time we'd broken into somewhere together, in fact it was becoming a frequent occurrence. The two houses, being set well away from the village and close to the river meant that we were almost certain that nobody would catch us anyway provided that the gathering wasn't a short affair. On the way there I'd scanned the river bank and hadn't seen a trace of the Nure-onna or the elder's body. When I pointed this out to Shiho she assured me that the creature would be about somewhere, probably in the river watching us carefully. She also reconfirmed that it would've dragged the body out into the water to be taken away by the current. A fate which she is now certain befell our missing man.

The first house, belonging to the elder brother, was a good size, two floors and plenty of space for a single occupant. Before we'd gone in I'd asked Shiho what we were looking for and she'd replied anything out of the ordinary or something that could've been in that basket he'd given to the Nure-onna. It couldn't have been food given the creature feeds on human blood so it was unclear what it could've been. She also hoped there'd be some trace of whatever it was that allowed him to get close to the creature without it attacking him, that was what had baffled Shiho the most given her past dealings with Nure-onna. Even with everything I've seen with Shiho and the multitude of things she's seen without me I don't think either of us were expecting what we found in that house. Starting in the kitchen there was a small makeshift incubator, a cardboard box stuffed with straw underneath a heat lamp. In the incubator lay six eggs unlike any I'd seen before. They were a dark green and leathery in texture and I couldn't tell what species they were. Neither could Shiho initially although she had her suspicions.

These suspicions were proven as we went upstairs where we could hear the faint sound of splashing water as we approached the bathroom. Just to be on the safe side Shiho drew her knife as we reached the door and slowly turned the handle. Inside the bathroom was one of the strangest things I've seen in a home. Both the washbasin and bathtub were filled with water and in both swam a multitude of creatures. As they didn't seem able to leave the confines of their respective basins, Shiho sheathed her knife and we were able to investigate in peace. The washbasin contained no less than eight snake like creatures that could've been sea snakes if not for the small baby face protruding from their heads. Each was no longer than five inches and were clearly some form of the Nure-onna only unlike the big one which had clawed arms, these only retained the face of a human, the rest of their form was pure snake. Those in the bathtub were far more similar to the creature we'd seen the previous night. They were about two feet in length and although they lacked arms, the human body was slowly beginning to form on the creatures causing a break between the scaly tail and the head where flesh poked through. There were five of the older ones which added to the eight in the sink and the six eggs downstairs meant we were sharing the house with nineteen Nure-onnas, a fact which wasn't lost on Shiho. She looked horrified at what she was seeing and I asked her how it was even possible. Her response wasn't particularly inspiring. She replied that she'd never known where Nure-onnas came from, she had suspicions and had heard rumours but never seen it in person before. The whole place was undoubtedly a Nure-onna nursery if such a thing existed. I asked Shiho what we were going to do, if we were going to kill them and she looked at me with disgust. She stated that they were innocent creatures, it wasn't their fault what they were or how they'd come to be and that killing them would make her the monster. Although I accept her point I'm not entirely sure that I agree. If these offspring all grow to be similar to their mother then perhaps the world would be better off without them. Even when I pointed this out to Shiho she repeated that she wasn't going to kill them, not unless she absolutely had to. Not being in a position to argue with her I instead asked how they'd even come to be, from what she'd told me Nure-onna were a single gender race. She nodded her reply yet proceeded to theorise that their human characteristics must've come from somewhere originally and she had heard stories of them having some hypnotic abilities. It all pointed to a singular reason as to why it would return to this village every year. Further investigation of the house told us what they were feeding the creatures too as we found a cooler filled with bags of human blood although it was impossible for us to tell exactly where, or whom, it had come from. Either way it was another gruesome discovery. I can only hope they procured it from the local hospital instead of extracting it themselves.

The whole time we were in that house I could see that Shiho was grappling with the question of what she was going to do. She'd already ruled out killing the young creatures but clearly leaving them there was also out of the question. Even if she did remove this batch, the Nure-onna would no doubt return next year and the cycle would begin anew. She needed a way of stopping it permanently. For that to happen, she needed to deal with the big one.

Knowing that we'd been there a while and that the village meeting wouldn't detain the brothers all morning I desperately pleaded with her for a plan and finally she replied. She said that she needed a bargaining position to convince the Nure-onna to leave and that the only thing she thought it would respond to were its children. As such we needed to round them all up and take them hostage. Had they been human it would have been an atrocious suggestion but we were dealing with half human half snake creatures which I'd suggested killing not much earlier so I went along with it with a clear conscience. We quickly found ourselves a large wicker hamper which we thought could take the weight of the young Nure-onnas and set about trying to transfer them across. The eggs were clearly very simple to move and Shiho even built them a little nest to keep them safe. She couldn't add the heat lamp but did place a blanket around them to keep them warm. It was an odd thing to see, her taking care of such a monstrous thing but I guess she felt sorry for them. The small ones in the washbasin were a little tougher but we actually used a pair of chopsticks to pluck them from the water and transfer them to a sealed container filled with water and an air hole. The bigger ones were a nightmare to catch. They were large enough that the chopstick method wouldn't work so we had to use our hands. Let me just say that sticking my hands into a bathtub filled with young Nure-onnas is not something I'd ever like to repeat. We were fortunate that they hadn't grown their claws yet as they were vicious things. Their long forked tongues were constantly after us as they could sense our blood and eventually Shiho had to use one of the packs in the cooler to help calm the creatures. By placing it on the edge of the bathtub we managed to attract a single Nure-onna which we promptly pinned to the edge as soon as it lifted its head from the water. With Shiho on its head and me holding its tail we were able to carry it to the hamper where it promptly curled up once we'd dropped it, hissing at us with clear distain. With a tactic that worked we were able to coax a further two the same way at which point we no longer felt outnumbered trying to tackle them in the water. With all of them successfully transferred to the hamper I did ask if it was safe keeping them all together, they had presumably been separated for a reason, but Shiho simply replied by asking if I often felt the need to eat my younger sister whilst growing up. It was a fair point and together we lugged the hamper down the stairs and out of the house. Shiho waited with it at the front of the house while I went to get the car and fortunately the brothers didn't return until after we'd left. We drove a short way out of the village with the hamper on the back seat constantly hissing before Shiho pulled over. We needed to wait until the evening for the Nure-onna to return to the rocks where Shiho could negotiate with it so we had packed a couple of blood packs to feed the things. My experience of negotiating with the yōkai of Shiho's world suggest she doesn't have a hope of succeeding. Then again if the Nure-onna is smarter than the others, which it might be, most of the others I've encountered being incredibly single-minded, then perhaps it will be open to having a discussion.

That evening we stumbled back to the river bank, desperately trying not to drop the hamper containing the Nure-onnas. Shiho had told me before that if even one of them managed to get out then in the darkness it could become a real threat so we took our time in returning to the hiding spot we used the previous night. Apparently alone, without guidance such creatures can become incredibly aggressive, more so than usual. The hamper was heavy too, especially with the water that Shiho had added to keep the creatures happy. When we did arrive, it wasn't much of a surprise to see the Nure-onna waiting on its rock combing its hair as it had done the previous night. Standing next to the rock were the two brothers watching the creature although it appeared to be taking no notice of them. Seeing no point in waiting Shiho urged us forward and we slowly made our way towards them stopping around thirty meters from the rock. The two brothers had been quite late in seeing us but the creature had spotted us immediately and carefully watched us all the way evidently weighing up whether we were worth attacking. At this distance it was clear that the Nure-onna had the upper hand if it wanted to attack us. I had no idea how quickly it could move but with its long tail and the way it had killed the elder last night I knew it wouldn't have had a problem killing us. Shiho chose her stopping point carefully though, knowing that from this distance she'd have enough time to react and use the lighter she carelessly flicked in her free hand on the hamper killing the Nure-onnas inside before the creature reached us. From her previous statements I presumed that this was a bluff and in reality she had nothing but just needed to convince the Nure-onna otherwise. Still part of me trusted that she had a backup plan in case the Nure-onna saw through her ploy.

The Nure-onna seemed to be aware of her threat, especially after we opened the hamper lid for a moment to let out some of the hissing noise coming from within and it kept to its rock watching us carefully. The creature never spoke to us, I don't know if it can but I was certain that when Shiho spoke it understood. At first she told it exactly what she had in the hamper and what she would do if the Nure-onna didn't agree to her terms. Her terms were, in my opinion, quite reasonable. She wanted the Nure-onna to release the two brothers from her hypnotic spell and then to leave the village and never return. In return she would release the creature's children. At no point did she mention that she was also sparing the creature's life although I began to doubt that she could kill it even if she wanted to. What she was going to do if the Nure-onna was happy for her to burn the hamper I had no idea. I don't think she'd factored in such an occurrence. Fortunately the creature didn't want to test her and, despite hissing intensely, listened to what she had to say. Once Shiho had finished talking a standoff occurred with neither saying anything nor moving from their respective positions. This lasted a good few minutes before Shiho threatened to burn the hamper by moving her lighter towards it prompting the Nure-onna to snap its claws releasing the two brothers from her spell. The two of them fell to the ground spluttering before they saw the creature on the rock and scuttled away backwards from it whilst it kept its eyes firmly on Shiho. I don't know how it had been controlling their actions but it was clear that they were unaware such was their adverse reaction to seeing the Nure-onna. Shiho ignored them as they made a run for it instead choosing to thank the Nure-onna whilst maintaining eye contact with the creature. After another few minutes of the standoff Shiho asked if it accepted her other terms as it became apparent to me that it could simply return the following year and ensnare another unfortunate victim. Very slowly the creature began to lower its head and I worried that it was about to charge before I noticed it slowly bringing it back up. Ever so slowly it dawned on me that it was nodding. Shiho nodded back and signalled for us to place the hamper on the ground. We did so and began to back away constantly keeping our eyes on the Nure-onna in case it decided to attack. Once we had retreated about fifteen feet it made its move, dragging itself off the rock in the blink of an eye and pulling itself towards us. At first I thought we were done for but I quickly realised that it was solely after the hamper which it tore open with its claws. The larger of the creatures immediately slithered out and she quickly freed the others scooping them up in one of her claws as she slowly made her way back towards the river, the others in tow. We watched as the creature entered the river and reappeared on the other bank a few moments later, clearly wanting to put some distance between her family and us before taking stock. I asked Shiho if she thought it would come back the following year and she admitted that she wasn't sure. Instead she said that she hoped that by returning her children this year she would honour her side of the arrangement but there was unfortunately nothing else to bind her to it. For this year however, it would no longer be a problem. Maybe for Shiho that's best, I'm sure if it does return Shiho will be back and perhaps repeat business is good for her.

As we were leaving the brothers stopped us to thank Shiho for freeing them and to apologise for anything they might have said whilst under the control of the Nure-onna. Shiho took their thanks graciously but I could see that she found it uncomfortable and wanted to be away from the area. We also bade our farewell to the wife of the missing man. It was almost certain that he had died at the hands of the Nure-onna and Shiho assured her that the thing that had killed her husband had been dealt with. It wasn't exactly fully dealt with but it seemed to give her the closure she wanted and perhaps that was all she was after when she first contacted Shiho. I did ask Shiho how she felt about unleashing a new brood of Nure-onnas on the world but she didn't answer instead she just got in the car and waited patiently for me to join her.

We must've travelled a good couple of hours despite the time before seeking a bed for the night. I don't think Shiho knows if she did the right thing in sparing those creatures. Sadly I don't think we'll ever know. It's strange though, so often these things I meet with Shiho are terrifying monsters, the Nure-onna included yet unlike the others this one reacted to the most basic of instincts, that of a protective parent. I guess Shiho figured that it would, at least I hope she figured that out in advance. One thing I'm beginning to notice about Shiho is she often sees alternative ways of dealing with these monsters and instead of killing them lets them live, sparing them when she has the chance. I wonder if I'll ever feel that way about them. I will admit my view was that we ought to have killed the Nure-onnas when we had a chance but if we had I don't know how we'd have dealt with the big one. There's so much about this strange world that I'm yet to understand but with the way the Nure-onna reacted, maybe these yōkai all follow the same basic instincts as humans.

I've finished the article on the Aka Manto and sent it to the editor. With luck he'll like it as much as my others and I'll be able to get a second piece in the edition coming out next month. I'll wait for a response but I have high hopes. It's the sort of thing he likes. As usual I changed the details removing mention of my sister and changing the setting from a school to a cinema so that there's absolutely no way of tracing it. I also made no mention of Hanako-san, she's something the world can do without knowing about for the time being. I still have time if this one is pushed back to get a write up of the Nure-onna too although if needs be I can add Hanako-san for that extra boost to the tale. Hopefully it won't come to that.

I finally received an answer from Shiho about how she came to know so much about all these different types of yōkai. It's taken her long enough to tell me but today was the day she decided to open up. She told me that the basis of her knowledge was rooted in a book known as the Gozu. I hadn't heard of it but it sounds terrifying if it includes details of all the beings we've encountered together plus apparently countless others.

She says that the book starts with a long rambling tale about a legendary cow headed creature before branching into the other species and providing detailed information on them including their likely habitat, mannerisms and details on dealing with them although it's apparently relatively dated and some techniques no longer work. She does however say that the information contained within the book comes at a cost. Reading the Gozu isn't for the faint of heart and around ninety-five percent of people who attempt reading it break out in shakes, failing to finish the first tale. Apparently they either die from fright or commit suicide within three days of reading from the book. Those that manage to press on past whatever horrors are on those pages chose whether to forget or to become like Shiho and hunt the very monstrosities contained within.

I don't know what's in that book other than this information I've jotted down here but I could see that reading it had affected Shiho from the way she spoke. She wouldn't mention the titular creature either when I enquired about it saying only that some things shouldn't be known. One can only wonder what caused her to look at those pages in the first place.

Fortunately any minor curiosity I may have had for looking through that book was immediately crushed by Shiho. She informed me that due to the high death rate associated with reading the Gozu, few copies of it remain. Shiho herself does own a copy although she doesn't travel with it. She simply said that she leaves it at home where it's kept under lock and key. It's odd, I never really considered her having a home, I thought she just sort of drifted about. I tried asking her about it but she wouldn't tell me anymore. I think I am slowly breaking down her walls though.

May 18th

The editor got back to me today about the Aka Manto piece. He was delighted with it and told me that he was going to add it to the edition coming out next month. That'll be two of my articles in the same magazine! This has never happened to me before. I'll be certain to pick up a copy when I next get the chance. The money's good too, easily the biggest payday I've had. That ought to keep my apartment going whilst I'm out here with Shiho.

I told Shiho too. I think she was happy for me but it's often hard to tell with her. Either way two stories in the same publication is quite an achievement. He even mentioned that he wanted me to start writing up articles for the following one due for release in September.

Our journey around Kyushu is slowly coming to an end. Still as we turn back northwards our travels brought us to a nice wooded area today. It was a beautiful forest with lush greens that felt very airy but something in it spooked Shiho. All I could place was a slight ringing in my ears but Shiho kept whispering something to herself before she told me to run to the car abandoning the food we'd brought for a picnic.

When we were back I asked her what had spooked her so badly and she replied that she'd spotted a headless corpse lying in the wood. I said we should inform the police but she shook her head instead insisting that we got away from there as quickly as possible.

She says there was a creature known as a Gashadokuro in the woods. Apparently they're ninety foot tall invisible skeletons that enjoy biting the heads off people caught unaware. I have no idea if Shiho was right about it. An invisible giant? It's the sort of thing which one hopes doesn't exist but if they are real and one was in those woods then Shiho saved my life yet again. What one would be doing in those woods I have no idea, it was kilometres from anywhere but as soon as we reached the car the ringing in my ears stopped. I guess things like that really are possible.

Our time in Kyushu will be ending soon with Shiho looking to return to Honshu in the coming weeks. I think she's achieved all that she wanted to, or at least had enough jobs to pay her way for a while. For the time being, with summer now upon us, Shiho claims that the typical breeding season for the yōkai she hunts has died down meaning they'll be harder to find. Instead she plans to rely on people contacting her specifically for jobs.

Most of the things we encountered whilst on Kyushu were small, barely worth mentioning and truth be told I think Shiho is a little disappointed. Still I imagine her pay for the Kuchisake-onna and the Teke Teke is easily enough to cover the costs of our trip. Other than the Nure-onna most yōkai we've encountered have been easily taken care of and, for the most part, harmless.

I've enjoyed my time this last six weeks and I'm not particularly looking forward to parting with Shiho when we get to Kyoto. I guess I'm quite fortunate then that our time together isn't coming to an end just yet. Honshu is a big place and there are many kilometres between us and Kyoto. Plenty of time to squeeze in one or two more adventures, provided they're out there.

The Sands of Time

June 7th

Today we did stumble across a new yōkai, if that's even what it is, one that Shiho herself appeared amazed to see. It all started a couple of days ago when we first heard stories about a village where a number of the locals had suddenly gone insane. At first we passed it off as nothing out of the ordinary, a rumour that spread across the region with little to back up the story but we kept hearing about it in each town and village we stayed. Eventually Shiho decided that we ought to check out the village in question just to see if something was going on. It's barely out of our way and no more than fifty kilometres from the crossing to Honshu so Shiho thought it worth a look.

The village in question was a small place, scarcely more than a hundred residents by my reckoning, clearly a farming community. Rice fields lay on either side of the road for kilometres approaching the village and there was little other business. When we first arrived we were greeted by the sole occupant of what passed for the village square who, although at first looking suspicious, opened up after Shiho informed him that we were there to look into the stories of people going insane. The reason he was happy for us to do so was that he had been personally affected, his sister, Tamiko was one of those who'd gone insane, and, so desperate was he to help her that he immediately told Shiho everything hoping that she might somehow produce a cure. I think they'd had a couple of gawkers arrive before us but straight away he could tell that Shiho wasn't a simple thrill seeker. As always, keen to find out all the information she could, Shiho asked if he could show us to his sister so that she could ask her questions. The man, Suehiro, agreed although warned us that there wouldn't be much she'd be able to help us with.

Suehiro's house, which lay just off the square, was small yet cosy and had clearly been well looked after. He led us through to a back bedroom where he'd been keeping his sister for the last four days and unlocked the door allowing us in. The woman, Tamiko, looked completely normal, other than her wide unblinking eyes and the foam forming at her mouth. The fact that she sat bolt upright on the bed and apparently hadn't moved for days also triggered alarms in my head. She was practically catatonic, seemingly unaware, or unfussed, by our presence which I'll admit, made her one of the creepiest things I've encountered. Shiho did her best to ask questions about what had happened to her, what she'd seen and where she'd been but despite her brother repeating the questions the woman didn't answer. The whole time she just sat there staring straight ahead, unblinking. Suehiro told us that this was now normal, she hadn't said or done anything since she'd been found like that four days prior. He said that her symptoms weren't the worst, some in the village had started screaming incomprehensible babble constantly causing them to be locked in their homes. Indeed Suehiro informed us that seven people within the village had similar or worse symptoms than his sister and that nobody knew how to cure them.

He wanted to know if we thought there was any way his sister could be brought back to the way she was before but I could see from Shiho's face that she didn't think so. She didn't say as much but I knew that was the case from the way she stared at Tamiko, a strange sadness appearing in her face. Instead she wondered out loud what had happened to her and the others all of which had been found in the last few days. Bizarrely Suehiro said he could answer that but first we'd need to take a walk to the edge of village with him.

Confused we followed him out to the edge of the paddy fields where he stopped and pointed to a field next to some woods. I scanned the field but saw nothing out of the ordinary but when I looked back Shiho had gone completely white before she whispered that it wasn't possible. Looking back out into the field I again failed to spot anything unusual but it was clear that the other two could see something. When I asked them what we were looking at Suehiro pointed directly at the centre of the field where I could see what looked like two large sheets of rice paper standing upright tip to tip shimmering and blowing about in the wind. They were incredibly thin, barely visible against the sunlight but appeared to be around eight feet tall. I asked if that was what we were looking at saying it appeared to be rice paper but Suehiro shook his head saying he wasn't sure what it was but it was the cause of the symptoms appearing in the villagers. Shaking my head I pulled out a pair of binoculars to see it better but as I lifted them to my head Shiho slapped them away furiously. I began to protest but her reply was barely audible as she watched the thing in the fields. She said it was no rice paper and that she believed it to be a Kunekune. Again I tried to look through the binoculars at the weird sheets of paper that appeared hazy from a distance but again Shiho stopped me informing me that I'd become like Tamiko if I looked closely at it. I asked her what a Kunekune was still doubting that we were looking at anything more that rice sheets blowing in the wind but her response was quick and odd. She said they were a myth. After all the things we'd seen together I was surprised that she believed anything was a myth but she told me that sometimes monsters are simply just stories and that the Kunekune was one of these such monsters. She says there hasn't been a reported sighting of one for decades and even then the reports were wildly varied due to the fact that anybody who reported seeing one was later classified as insane. It meant that even in her line of work nobody truly believed that the creature existed. Suehiro seemed taken aback that Shiho had a name for the thing that floated about aimlessly in the field never really moving from its spot and he told Shiho that he would gather the other affected families and bring them to her so she could explain everything to all of them. Shiho objected saying there was no explanation she could give but he wouldn't take no for an answer and quickly left us to find the others. Once he'd gone I was quick to talk to Shiho, I'd never seen her this worried before and that in itself was enough cause to be alarmed.

The first thing she said as soon as Suehiro was out of earshot was that we shouldn't have come and that we ought to leave. I was surprised to hear her say such a thing given that she usually searches for such creatures and that it was so out of character for her not to want to get involved. Desperate to understand exactly what it was she was so afraid of I asked about the Kunekune hoping for more information. She explained that it was a being unlike any I'd seen before. One which had existed for centuries if not millennia and that she couldn't believe was actually real. Apparently the legends, and they are just legends, say that a Kunekune causes insanity simply by being in the presence of humans. It's also said that should one look too closely at a Kunekune, they too will be driven insane. Focussing too much on one would spell doom for a human. That would certainly explain what had happened to the locals. Unfortunately, as there was so little belief that they existed Shiho had no information into the sort of distances involved and hence couldn't be certain that we weren't already in danger. The thing that Shiho seemed most confused about however was what the creature was doing there in the first place. She couldn't work out why it would suddenly appear especially if there hadn't been a sighting in decades and they were supposed to live so long. I suggested that it had come to hunt the villagers for food or sport similar to the other yōkai we've encountered but Shiho shook her head and said it wasn't like the others, there was simply nothing else like it. The way she explained it was the others would look at a human like a steak, as such they would attack but to a Kunekune a human is no more than a microbe, impossibly irrelevant, and as such it would have little interest in their comings and goings. That at least explained why it had just stayed in the same rice field since first appearing four days ago. It would also suggest that the Kunekune didn't actively attack people. I'll admit I didn't quite fully appreciate Shiho's explanation so she tried to explain the basic theories about the being to me. She stated that the universe is split into multiple planes all layered on top of one another. Most of the time these are completely separate but occasionally they can meet. The best example of this was how our plane, which I'll describe as the 'living' plane can meet the 'dead' plane allowing the creation of the onryō that we've encountered. She explained that there were many other planes, mostly unknown to humanity who'd never encountered them but could possibly include the concept of afterlives. Somewhere within these planes was the hellish one that Hanako-san drags her victims to where the Aka Manto we encountered now resides. A Kunekune supposedly exists across all of these planes at once, a singular being which was forever trapped between the planes, unable to truly be in any of them but present in all of them. That explains their hazy appearance as they are forever shifting between different planes leaving their actual form unknown as each plane only sees a fraction of the whole. Of course, all of this was based on a legend that Shiho had heard but given that the being was clearly real, we were willing to take any story as fact. I asked if we could get rid of it somehow to prevent the rest of the village succumbing to insanity but her face went blank. She pointed out that she couldn't fight it, she couldn't even get close to it without going insane herself and trying to bargain with the Kunekune seemed unlikely as she doubted it would even acknowledge her presence, especially as she'd have to be at a safe distance with no way of knowing whether the creature was responding. There was simply no way of dealing with it. The best she could think of was building an exclusion zone around it and leaving it be.

When Suehiro returned with a few others from the village whose family members had been affected Shiho explained what a Kunekune was to them too. She didn't tell them that there was no way of dealing with it though and watered down the whole interdimensional immortal being part but they all seemed thrilled that she knew what it was. It gave them hope that she'd be the one to help them although she never claimed that their relatives' sanity could be returned. Trying to at least give them something, Shiho asked a few questions about their interactions with the creature and where it had come from. Their replies were all similar. The Kunekune had first appeared four days prior in the same rice field where it currently resided. Of the people who'd been driven insane by it, all but one had been working in that field at the time it appeared. The final one had ventured into the field the following day and when he stumbled out gibbering later that day they took it as proof that the hazy anomaly was the cause and kept their distance. Since then the creature had neither moved nor had anyone attempted to approach it. Shiho later confirmed to me that they could in fact move although time is strange for a Kunekune, their speed is relative to their lifespan and as such it could take weeks, even months, for it to take a single step closer to the village. Shiho did explain to them that there was nothing that could be done for their relatives. She said that knowledge of Kunekunes was thin and that there were so few prior cases, all dismissed as a Kunekune that she couldn't be certain if they'd ever recovered. In the end she told them that there was always a chance but that they shouldn't get their hopes up. Even so the villagers pleaded with her to look into the Kunekune further and help protect them from it. I could see that Shiho wasn't expecting a good outcome, probably why she made no attempt to charge them but ultimately told them that she'd do whatever she could.

With the basic facts about the appearance of the Kunekune gathered Shiho then started looking for a reason as to why it had appeared. The very nature of a Kunekune would suggest that it shouldn't be affected by anything a human did given that we are inconsequential to an endless being of cosmic proportions yet it must've shown itself for a reason. If she could find that reason she reckoned that she might be able to come up with a plan of how to limit its effect. The residents seemed puzzled but slowly began to explain everything that they each did that day in painstaking detail. Unsurprisingly Shiho disregarded the idea that the Kunekune could've appeared based on what breakfast they'd had or the fact that they'd started work a little late but the villagers were insistent on telling us everything. She was far more interested in what might have been happening in the field in the time before the Kunekune appeared but of course the people that were there at the time could no longer say. The others said they were simply farming at the time and not doing anything that they hadn't done a thousand times previously. Pressing on Shiho asked if anything was going on in the village that was new. There were a few suggestions but the most interesting was the fact that they've recently started logging in the woods just beyond the rice fields where the Kunekune lurks. Afterwards I asked Shiho about it and she suggested that the logging may be to blame as it could've disturbed the Kunekune's home, if such creatures have homes. Even then she doubted it would be the cause given that even the longest lasting tree was a mere footnote in the life of a Kunekune. Not knowing what to expect the two of us set off for the woods to see what we could find.

We took a long way round, eager to stay clear of the Kunekune which forever shimmered in the rice field and when we arrived it was immediately clear what damage the logging had caused. A multitude of trees lay haphazardly around a newly formed clearing not too far from the edge of the wood that joined the rice fields. There was nothing obvious that would suggest the Kunekune lived there however, just a couple of bird's nests in the fallen trees. I asked Shiho if she thought it was possible that it lived in those but she replied that truthfully she doubted it lived anywhere. She wasn't even sure that it could build a home in this plane or even if it was in a Kunekune's nature to attempt such a thing. She added that even if it did have a home in the woods it would've taken centuries for the Kunekune to reach the rice field meaning if it had lived there, whatever had happened would've occurred centuries ago. When I asked why we'd come to the woods if that was the case she replied that it was the only place where something new had been happening around the time of its appearance therefore was the only place worth investigating. The only trouble was there was nothing there that would even suggest it was remotely connected to the Kunekune, just a pile of cut trees on the edge of a wood.

We were about to give up when Shiho tapped me on the shoulder and pointed to a creature emerging from the woods. She whispered to me to keep very still and remain quiet whilst the creature slowly stalked into the clearing. Once it was out of the bushes it became obvious that it was a fox, only not like any fox I'd ever seen before. It was a pure white, similar to the snow foxes that you often see in winter wonderlands but so much purer in its colour, radiant and enchanting. Bizarrely it had multiple tails, five in total that swept across the ground behind it remaining white even as they brushed against the ground. I whispered to Shiho to ask what it was but the words seemed to startle the creature which backed away slightly yet remained in the clearing peering as if it were judging us. Without answering Shiho took three slow steps towards the creature always checking that it wasn't going to bolt before she dropped to her knees and held out her hand. The creature watched her intently but didn't move until she whispered that she wanted to help. Incredibly the animal seemed to understand her and it slowly approached, sniffing her outstretched hand before it nuzzled against it. The creature then stopped and stared at her straight in the eye and it appeared for all the world as if the two of them were communicating silently with one another. A couple of minutes passed and then the creature bowed and walked away, vanishing into the woods from which it came leaving me none the wiser.

Once it was out of sight Shiho turned back to me sensing that I was eager to ask questions. Before I could ask she explained that it was a Kitsune, a legendary fox like creature with impossible wisdom. Everything other than its tail appeared regular to me but Shiho claims that they grow a new tail every century making this one at least four hundred years old. She also said that, as it had looked, the two of them had communicated through touch. She claims this is a trick unique to younger Kitsune. At four hundred years old, I wouldn't have classed it as young myself but she claims that they can live for over a thousand years by which point they've learnt enough to be able to fully shapeshift into a human and converse freely. Apparently this shape-shifting ability isn't unique to them and plenty of yōkai have developed the same trick. I asked if she'd ever encountered one before and she admitted that she had once. She'd discovered two young ones who'd lost their mother and were being hunted. At that stage they only had one tail and looked like regular foxes but she knew what they were after letting them touch her skin. This was the first time she'd seen one with multiple tails however.

I asked her what it had said to her and she explained that it was tasked with guarding the Kunekune, or more precisely, preventing it from doing harm to humans. Despite the wisdom of a Kitsune, it too has no way of communicating with a Kunekune, it's simply too bizarre to communicate with, but the Kitsune could somehow contain it. I asked what I thought was an obvious question of who tasked the Kitsune with doing this but Shiho looked at me blankly, for the first time I'd asked a question which she herself hadn't asked of the creature. When I said I would be curious to know she simply waved it off suggesting that there were some things not worth knowing and that the Kitsune probably wouldn't tell us anyway. She said that in her discussion it had claimed to have been here for over three hundred and fifty years guarding the Kunekune so whatever it was that had placed it there was presumably long gone. Instead the conversation Shiho had with the Kitsune was more concerning the Kunekune and why it had appeared. The Kitsune had explained that the Kunekune was always there, wandering that rice field even beyond the lifespan of the Kitsune but it had been using its powers to keep the Kunekune hidden from the humans. Without being able to perceive the creature, the villagers had been spared their grim fate. The Kitsune managed this by placing itself in a trance like state which it had been in for centuries. That was until a few days ago when the Kitsune was rudely awoken by finding its home disturbed by the logging that had been going on in the area. With the Kitsune now forced to focus on survival it could no longer contain the Kunekune hence causing the issues for the local humans. Shiho appeared quite pleased by all of this as it meant that she didn't have to deal with the Kunekune directly, instead the Kitsune would go back to its task provided that it could have a home to grant safety whilst it entered its trance. This was one of the things that she had discussed with the creature and with a plan now set we headed back to the village, again taking a long way round to avoid the Kunekune which eerily remained where it had always been.

Back at the village we found Suehiro easily and Shiho informed him of the Kitsune. He was surprised but only that it was an actual living creature. He informed us that there was a tale that ran through the generations in that village of a powerful samurai who had ventured across Japan after the death of his master, traveling with his faithful dog. According to the legend this samurai had died in the local area fighting some terrible beast and it was claimed that his spirit lived on holding back the will of the beast. He was certain it was a child's story but it seemed reasonable to believe that if one substituted the Kitsune for the dog and suggested that what it was holding back was the Kunekune, it could sort of make sense. Shiho also explained to him that the creature's home had been destroyed by the logging and that was what had caused the appearance of the Kunekune. Unsurprisingly he appeared appalled by the notion and immediately suggested that they needed to find the Kitsune a new home, one that wouldn't be disturbed. Shiho agreed but pointed out that it would need to be close to the rice field or else the Kitsune would have no power over the Kunekune. It also needed to be sturdy given that the Kitsune could in theory remain there for over six centuries.

In the end Suehiro suggested that they build a temple next to the field where the Kitsune could rest and be looked after. He reasoned that a temple would have the least chance of being destroyed over the years and as such offered the best protection. In the meantime he offered his own home as an alternative until it was built. With few other suggestions, and Shiho seeing no other way to deal with the Kunekune, the three of us headed back towards the woods with the hope of getting the Kitsune to agree.

It was dusk by the time we reached the clearing in the woods, the shimmering entity that was the Kunekune giving off odd glimmering lights as it floated round the adjacent rice field in the growing moonlight. The way the light flickered on its odd form almost made the thing appear enchanting and subconsciously I felt myself drawn towards it despite knowing the dangers. Fortunately we had Shiho to keep us on the right path. I've always found the woods at night to be an eerie place, especially since Shiho introduced me to her world, and the crowing of a bird didn't help ease my nerves as we waited for the Kitsune. We were given very little instruction on the way there from Shiho other than to remain quiet and not to scare the Kitsune with quick movements. She'd explained to Suehiro that he'd have to be the one to communicate with the Kitsune. For our plan to work and the creature to agree to move to his home followed by a specially created temple it would first have to truly believe that he was trying to help it. If it didn't believe that, then it would run. We had no idea where it would go in that circumstance but Shiho informed us that they could cover a surprising amount of ground in a single day and it would probably move hundreds of kilometres away, well beyond the influence of the Kunekune. If it did that, we'd have no way of stopping the Kunekune and it would be back to Shiho's exclusion zone plan. I did ask how come it trusted her so easily but she figured it was to do with the fact that it could sense the touch of another Kitsune on her and knew her to be a friend having scanned her memories.

We waited in the clearing for a long time listening to the breeze and trying not to focus on the Kunekune despite the overwhelming innate desire to see it close up until the Kitsune finally showed itself. I have little doubt that it had been there far longer watching us. Even so it slowly walked out into the clearing watching as Shiho bowed to it before lowering its head in response. As he had been taught, Suehiro took a few steps forward, careful not to frighten the creature, and then knelt and held out a hand exactly as Shiho had done earlier in the day. The Kitsune was far more reticent about approaching him but eventually it began to creep towards him. As with before it eventually nuzzled its head into his hand and we saw his eyes go wide as it opened up its connection to his mind. It took a long time for the two of them to communicate, probably due to him being new to it, but after about an hour the Kitsune moved away and sat on the ground next to him. He stood up, slightly wobbly, and informed us that the Kitsune had accepted his offer and would be returning with us that evening. The relief was clear to see on Shiho's face and together we made our way back out of the woods towards his home. It was noticeable that the Kitsune always made sure that Suehiro was by its side and although it would occasionally allow Shiho on the other, it wouldn't let me walk next to it. I have no idea what it would be like to interface with a Kitsune, judging by the reaction of Suehiro I hardly think it's a pleasant experience but this one seemingly disliked me so I wasn't about to try. Shiho had maintained the link quite easily suggesting that she had prior experience, way more than the two young ones she claimed to have encountered but perhaps she's had experience with other yōkai that communicate similarly.

The journey back to the village was quiet as we weren't wanting to cause a scene. The notion of having all the villagers gawking over the Kitsune wasn't great as they can be timid creatures by nature so we were thankful that the night covered our movements and nobody stopped us. Once we arrived back at Suehiro's house, the Kitsune immediately took off sniffing everything until it began to paw at the door to Tamiko's room. At first Suehiro looked concerned, not wanting to put his sister through anything more but Shiho suggested that it couldn't harm her any further and they needed the creature to be comfortable so he relented and opened the door. It immediately stalked in and leapt up onto the bed nuzzling into Tamiko's lap despite her empty stare and promptly appeared to fall asleep. To our amazement Tamiko instantly blinked, then yawned, then stared at her brother with recognition in her eyes. They greeted one another and she appeared to be perfectly normal, constantly stroking the Kitsune which had curled up on her lap asleep, never once asking about it. Suehiro seemed amazed by her recovery and wondered how it was possible. Although we weren't certain, Shiho theorised that it could be a side effect of the Kitsune suppressing the Kunekune. She couldn't know if the effects were permanent or whether Tamiko would need to remain near the Kitsune to keep her sanity but whilst the creature was there she seemed to be fine. She accepted this surprisingly well considering the restrictions it would put on her but she had taken a liking to the multi-tailed fox. She even offered to run the temple meaning she would always be within reach of the creature. Whereas others may have been saddened by the loss of freedom she appeared grateful just to have any form of life and the Kitsune appeared quite comfortable asleep in her lap. I think that's the best way for her to look at it. Compared to how she was, having any form of life is a bonus.

Bidding them good luck, Shiho and I left, taking one final walk towards the rice field where the Kunekune roamed. It was no longer there, instead we found an empty field with the strange creature having left no trace. Even so, Shiho refused to enter the field reasoning that the Kunekune was still in there only we could no longer see it. When I pointed out that it had been that way for centuries and nobody had ever reported insanity before she still wouldn't enter and I didn't want to push her given that I was also loathed to go near. As we walked back to the car I asked what would happen to the village in the future. Shiho said she wasn't sure, Kitsunes can live up to a thousand years so this particular one, if looked after correctly by the village, would live for another six hundred years. Although she was pretty certain that the Kunekune would still be around at that point, she wasn't worried. It was odd to hear Shiho say it was someone else's problem but I think even she can't be expected to deal with things that far into the future. Who knows, maybe by that time humanity will have progressed to a point where we can communicate with such incomprehensible beings.

As we drove away I was left thinking that this world is far bigger than I realised even from the start of the day. There are creatures that inhabit it that even Shiho doesn't think exist which opens up the possibility of all kinds of things being out there just waiting to be discovered. Despite it all there were also creatures like that Kitsune, willing to assist humans for very little in return. I guess Shiho has shown me some of the worst kinds of creatures but now I realise that for every monster trying to kill us, there's one trying to save us.

These two were certainly odd though, I don't think the Kitsune was a threat to anyone at all. The other friendlier ones I've met had the potential for harm but not the Kitsune. Even the Kunekune, despite it being the cause of the madness, I don't think it was trying to harm people. I think it was just living its life and the villagers were unfortunate to be caught up in something beyond their comprehension. Still, a strange day nonetheless.

We made the crossing back onto Honshu today and I was able to collect a copy of the latest issue of the magazine. It's odd seeing our adventures written out in such a way but it brings in the money. Again I've received a lot of positive feedback from people on the stories and this time I have Shiho to help with any questions they throw at me although at times her answers go beyond what I feel comfortable replying with.

I'm glad to say that Shiho has decided not to head straight to Kyoto. Instead we're going to have a leisurely drive across Southern Honshu first. I'm happy about it. I'll need more adventures for the next edition of the magazine.

On Shiho's Past

Shiho finally told me her story today. I didn't ask, she just started to talk while we were having lunch and I was happy to let her continue. I don't know how long she's been holding it all in but she explained how she'd been introduced to this world, how she'd ended up a yōkai hunter as well as why Kuchisake-onna are classed as her specialty. It was fascinating, if slightly upsetting, to hear her tale and it's safe to say that I definitely feel closer to her now.

It had all started for her years ago. I knew from our previous talks that she'd been acquainted with a Hanako-san at one point growing up and maybe that's what had introduced her to it all. Of course, she was a child at the time so like my sister it's possible that she wasn't aware of the spirit's true nature. I don't know how their unlikely friendship had ended but from the way she spoke it had just been a case of her finishing school and moving on, the one thing a Hanako-san cannot do. I think it might have been years later when she realised what it was. Apparently it was a couple of years later, when taking a ferry that her ship had been attacked by an overly aggressive Umibōzu, a particularly nasty form of sea spirit, that she'd truly been introduced to this strange world of hers. On that ship another woman by the name of Keiko happened to know a number of things about Umibōzu. She saved the ship by confusing the creature, giving them time to escape. Amazed by what she'd seen Shiho had struck up a friendship with Keiko who claimed to be a yōkai hunter and together they'd travelled around Japan taking jobs involving yōkai whilst Keiko taught her about the different creatures they encountered. I guess it must've been somewhat similar to what I'm doing with Shiho right now except Shiho was training all the time whilst I'm simply recording events in my diary. Shiho spent that time working with Keiko to perfect her skills and knowledge of the creatures so that in time she might manage alone. As would be expected Shiho's skills and knowledge of the yōkai in this world improved enough that Keiko gave Shiho her own copy of the infamous Gozu, and after warning her of the potential dangers allowed her to read it opening her mind to the truths of the world. Shiho didn't tell me what happened next between the two of them only saying that after reading the Gozu she left Keiko, venturing far across the continent. She wouldn't say what she was doing during this time only that she felt the need to go but she did mention a number of countries that she visited and it seemed likely she was searching out yōkai leaving me to wonder if there are different species out there native to certain countries.

Anyway for whatever reason Shiho returned to Japan around a year later and six months after that was back with Keiko touring the country, picking up jobs here and there dealing with various yōkai much as they had before. The way she spoke about that time makes me think that Shiho was at her happiest then. Maybe it explains some of the sadness I see in her now. Back then she had someone to rely on, someone who always seemed to know what to do whereas now she bares all the responsibility.

Anyway the two journeyed together for a good while until one day in the city of Sapporo they ended up offending the locals. They were set upon by a gang of men who weren't happy with the work they'd done dealing with a particularly bloodthirsty yōkai. The gang had blamed a local whom they disliked and took issue with Keiko and Shiho clearing them of fault. One thing had led to another and the men had broken into their lodgings that night placing a knife to Keiko's face and slashing it before Shiho could intervene. The whole attack had taken less than two minutes. Having not meant to kill her the men panicked after seeing what they had done and fled leaving Shiho to mourn her friend and mentor. A couple of days later, whilst still trying to arrange a funeral, Shiho was approached about a new contract, one that would easily cover the cost of the funeral. It was for a Kuchisake-onna that had killed a man the night before. It wasn't long into her investigation when she recognised the dead man as one of the gang that had murdered Keiko.

I think that was when the truth dawned on her about what had happened. Desperate, she researched Kuchisake-onna for any way to bring her mentor back but all the while the bodies were mounting up. Eventually, with all the men involved in the murder dead and others not connected being targeted, there was talk about hiring someone else to deal with the spirit and, out of time, Shiho admitted that she should be the one to banish it. The way she talks about that night I think she set out with the intention of letting what was left of Keiko kill her too but for whatever reason it didn't and when morning came she was forced to banish it. She took the knife from the Kuchisake-onna, the same one Keiko had used so many times before, the same one Shiho uses now, and then spent the next year researching even more to see if she could've done anything else. I don't think her research ever found anything and I didn't want to ask. Truth be told I sort of hope that she didn't find anything that she could've done to help her. If she did then I can't imagine the guilt she must feel every day. I don't know how close Shiho and Keiko were but I think she was the closest Shiho's ever had to family. Even talking about it now, it's clear that Shiho still mourns for her. I wish I could do something to make that pain disappear but I doubt it ever will, I think she'll carry it forever.

Since that day she's been doing this by herself. Maybe, just maybe, there's a reason why she wants me to hang about. Maybe she's simply desperate for some company.

It's seems odd to me, Keiko was exactly like Shiho, a little older and wiser perhaps but she led the same lifestyle. She fought countless yōkai and they never once laid a scratch on her yet she was undone by a simple human. Perhaps it's true what they say. Perhaps humans truly are the worst monsters in the world.

We arrived back in Kyoto today. It seems odd being back after such a long trip around Kyushu. Everything in my apartment was exactly as it was two and a half months ago when I left. It's almost a reminder of how stale my life is when I'm not around Shiho. With her everyday has the potential for adventure whereas now my old life just seems dull and mundane. I do at least have framed magazine articles on the wall now.

It's fortunate too that Shiho has offered me the chance to continue with her for a while yet. She says that she plans on travelling abroad later in the summer. Apparently she can get some lucrative contracts overseas so tends to travel there each year. With about a month before she leaves she's planning to spend her time travelling around Honshu as we did Kyushu. Unsurprisingly I jumped at the chance to join her.

We'll spend the next couple of nights in my flat whilst she buys some provisions and then we'll be on the road again. I can't wait.

A Web of Illusion

A curious day to say the least. It all started shortly after we left Kyoto when Shiho received a request for help from a mother worried about her missing son. It sounded like she'd have been better going to the police but instead she'd come directly to Shiho via her website. When questioned, she claimed it was because she thought it was more Shiho's area of expertise. Anyway the location was a village at the foot of the Minami Alps in Yamanashi. We were already winding our way in that direction so we thought we'd check it out.

The mother lives in a small settlement near the foot of the mountains, a rural place with only one long road leading to it and little traffic on that. There was only a scattering of houses and we found the woman in question sat outside the front of hers waiting for us. She immediately told us everything she could, her son Takeyuki, a man in his early twenties, went missing two weeks prior and she's worried for his safety. Again I thought this was more a matter for the police than Shiho but the woman was quick to explain otherwise. She said that her son had taken the path up the mountain from their village despite her warning him not to. She explained that locals believed the path to be guarded by a fearsome creature that preys upon weary travellers. That's why she went to Shiho instead of the police, she's worried that this creature has killed her son. Regardless of whether the stories are true she wants to know what happened to him and wants us to find him and bring him home if possible.

Shiho seemed to take an interest in her words, especially after a couple of other passing residents expressed their same feeling towards the mountain path which we could see winding up the slopes which towered over the village. Bizarrely Shiho stated that we would look into the disappearance but informed the woman that the chance of us finding her son alive after this length of time was slim. Even so, she was delighted and led us to the start of the path where Takeyuki was last seen. It was a narrow track, unsuitable for vehicular usage so we found ourselves abandoning our car and setting out for a hike up the mountain.

The trail was perfectly pleasant to walk along. It started through rolling fields but quickly entered a wooded area as the climb began in earnest. The trees were widely spaced though and offered shade from the sunlight which we were thankful for. Along the way I asked Shiho what it could be that the residents thought guarded the path. She replied that she wasn't certain, there were plenty of yōkai she could name that would live near or on a mountain and most of them would be considered dangerous, although there were plenty of regular animals that could live there too. She was certain that there was something behind the tales though or else they simply wouldn't have lasted throughout the years. Even that thought wasn't enough to diminish what was a delightful hike along the trail. The path slowly meandered up the mountain until it found a small stream that flowed from the top down into the valley where the village lay. It followed that stream for a while before turning sharply and vanishing out of sight of the village. Here the incline increased rapidly for a few kilometres and the trees began to fall away until it levelled out and we took the chance to rest having been walking for several hours.

On this small plateau, the stream was much wider and deeper and the water, having come down a magnificent fifty foot waterfall almost rested there before continuing its journey down the mountain. Across the water from the path stood a thick forest, far denser and darker than those on the lower slopes. The dark green canopy blocked out the sunlight and we could only see the first few rows of trees. Oddly on the far bank, standing in-between the water and the trees was a solitary house. Quaint looking with a water wheel slowly spinning in the stream the house looked like it had stood there for years yet it was immaculately well preserved. The white of the walls shone vibrantly in the sunlight and the wooden timbers on display had been well preserved. In front of the house was a small fenced vegetable garden where we could see all different types of well tendered plants growing. A second to the rear of the house appeared to have been made into a Zen garden and added to the strangely tranquil appearance of the dwelling. Beyond the garden, the trees of the forest moved closer to the water but a clear path remained, only a few feet wide, that ran about thirty meters to a small jetty where a self-use ferry sat, connected to the opposite side of the stream by means of a rope.

It was an odd thing to find half way up a mountain especially as the residents of the village had made no mention of it when describing the route. Whoever resided there would have to come down into their village too as there was only one path and continuing onwards would force them to cross the mountain to find another village for food and supplies. Still we camped out on the opposite side of the stream to the house and feasted on the lunches given to us by the villagers. The hike had been enjoyable and we couldn't work out neither where Takeyuki had gone nor why there were tales of a vicious beast guarding the path. I pondered if it was possible that he'd simply reached the other side of the mountain and chosen to leave. Shiho admitted that was a possibility, one she'd seen many times before, yet the village at the other end of the path hadn't reported seeing him pass through. With our meal done, we packed up and decided that instead of pressing on we should first ask at the house to see if they knew whether Takeyuki had passed.

There had been no movement from inside the house whilst we ate yet we were both certain that there was someone home, the windows overlooking the stream were open and a washing line filled with sheets waved in the wind next to the vegetable garden. Carefully Shiho pulled on the rope to summon the ferry, finding it surprisingly easy to move despite the size of the craft and the thinness of the rope. It was easily large enough for the two of us and probably still had space for another two yet it didn't appear well used, although was, like everything else, immaculately well kept. Once we had made it across we found ourselves on the narrow path of land between the stream and the trees and from this close the difference to the woods further down the mountain was apparent. The density of the trees combined with a thick layer of webbing that hung from most branches blotted out the sun leaving the woods in a state of permanent darkness. I had an uneasy feeling staring into those trees, almost as if something was staring back at me, something that thought of me as food and I could tell that Shiho had the same feeling. It's odd how we were less than twenty meters from where we'd had our lunch yet the atmosphere on this side of the stream felt completely different. I asked Shiho if Takeyuki could've wandered in there and she replied that it was possible, the ferry had been at this side of the stream yet there was seemingly no reason for him to cross and then wander into those woods. He could've tried the house but nobody in their right mind would enter the dark woods. Not wanting to hang about for longer than necessary we made for the house and rapidly knocked on the door.

The door was answered by a young man who surprisingly matched the description of Takeyuki. A quick spot of questioning confirmed that he was indeed the lost son and he invited us in after we explained that his mother had sent us. It was strange finding him there. I think both Shiho and I had written off any chance of finding him alive yet he appeared entirely unharmed. How he had survived for two weeks on the mountain we weren't quite sure. It was clear that he had been living in the house yet it was impossible that he could've built it in the short time he'd been missing. It also didn't appear that he'd been kept there as a prisoner as he moved about freely and was surprisingly open about his identity, clearly not wanting to hide. The interior of the house was, much like the outside, immaculately well-kept with nothing out of position save for a couple of mirrors which had blankets thrown over them to prevent their use. The ceilings were surprisingly high however and the doorways far wider than most but other than those odd quirks, a nice place to live.

Takeyuki, a surprisingly generous host, offered us a drink and took us through to the living room where immediately Shiho asked him about his disappearance. He appeared concerned by the worry that he'd caused his mother and the other residents but confirmed that he was fine and that he hadn't disappeared, he was merely choosing to stay in that house half way up the mountain. It didn't add up though, he hadn't offered any explanation as to why he'd remain nor how the house had come to be there. That was when he told us the story of the day he'd set off on the mountain path.

It wasn't normal for him to take the path over the mountain but that particular day he'd set off with hopes of reaching the village at the other side before nightfall. He had family there which he had planned on visiting and had followed the path much like we did until he came across the house. He claims that he paused there for a drink, much like we did for lunch, but when he did he noticed a beautiful young woman tending the vegetable garden, she appeared to be struggling with her task and, with a gentlemanly demeanour about him, had offered to help. The work in the garden took them longer than he expected and by the time he was finished rain had set in and he no longer had enough light to reach the end of the path before nightfall. To repay his kindness for his work the young woman had invited him to rest there that evening for fear of him falling ill in the rain or getting lost in the dark. Aware of the tales of the mountain he'd accepted her offer and spent the night there with plans to continue onwards the following day. The next morning when he woke he found the woman back tending the garden, a seemingly never ending task and he stated that he didn't think it right to leave her to work on it alone. He'd pitched in again that day, and then the day after and so on until he had been there over a week. During that time he had spent every day working in the garden or on parts of the house with the woman and then the evenings talking to her. He claims that he has fallen in love with her and her with him and that seeing no reason to part ways he has chosen to remain with her in the house. With the vegetable garden outside they can grow their own food and the water wheel provides enough electricity for the single residence. He claims it's an ideal life and that he has no plans to return but asks that we inform his mother of his choice and let her know that he will return for visits when he has less to do around the house.

Idyllic it might be looking out over the stream and down the mountain yet through one of the windows in the living room we could see the dark forest that still gave me the creeps. Asked about that he replied that the woods were not somewhere he ventured seeing no need to part from his lover, the evil feeling emanating from the darkness appeared not to bother him. For all the world it just looked like a young man hopelessly in love but Shiho wasn't convinced that everything was right. She asked him a simple question which proved quite telling, if he was living with this beautiful young woman then where was she? The house was empty other than the three of us and the ferry had been on this side of the stream. That meant for whatever reason, if she existed, she must've gone into the forest that Takeyuki wouldn't set foot in and even Shiho shied away from. At this question he became quite agitated and told us that as we had found him and he had no desire to return with us we ought to be on our way to pass on his message to his mother. Shiho ignored this request and looked behind one of the blanket covered mirrors only to have the young man immediately cover it back up and reiterate that we ought to leave. In response Shiho simply grabbed him and asked if he knew what this woman really was and how much danger he was in. I was taken aback but clearly something about his story and the house worried Shiho. The young man replied that he was in no danger and then changed his attitude saying that we could stay and confirm that for ourselves if we wanted. He said that his love would be back at any moment and once we'd seen her we'd know how safe he was. Shiho shook her head and demanded that he leave with us but again he refused and then we heard an odd noise. There was a loud bang that came from the wall closest to the forest, almost as if something very large had smashed into the side of it. I noticed that Shiho suddenly drew her knife and edged me towards the door as she glanced about the ceiling of the room almost expecting it to collapse.

I expected some large monster to charge in but instead the back door opened and a beautiful woman calmly strolled in. I will admit she was possibly the most attractive woman I've ever seen, long black hair, an exquisitely symmetrical face with porcelain skin and she took to having uninvited guests very easily, bowing deeply and coming to stand next to Takeyuki. Shiho clearly disliked her though as she kept her eyes firmly on her and gripped her knife tightly. The woman didn't seem bothered by this act of hostility and instead asked if we would like anything to eat or drink. I couldn't answer before Shiho interrupted stating that she'd met her kind before and she demanded that she release the three of us or else there'd be trouble for the young woman. The young woman, to her credit, didn't appear fussed about Shiho's attitude, she simply repeated her question and ignored Shiho entirely. Takeyuki, sensing Shiho's hostility, jumped to his partners aid and demanded that we leave again although the woman wrapped herself onto his arm and calmed him saying it was no way to speak to guests. By this point Shiho had clearly had enough of the conversation and simply repeated that she knew what the woman was and demanded that Takeyuki get away from her. For whatever reason, the young woman snapped back at Shiho saying that if Shiho knew what she was then she'd know that she meant no harm to him or us. She claims if that was the case she would've killed all three of us the moment we entered her home.

It was a compelling argument, although as I stood looking at this small woman who appeared unable to hurt a fly I wondered exactly what harm she could do to any of us, Shiho is a natural fighter, Takeyuki himself was well built, a chunk taller and clearly stronger than her and I'd even have backed myself against her if needs be despite my lack of experience. I expressed my confusion and Shiho replied that the woman was a Jorōgumo. The woman smiled slightly at the name but Takeyuki seemed nonplussed as if he was already aware of this fact. Again I expressed my amazement that this young woman could be anything other than what she seemed but Shiho replied that what we were seeing was a lie. Apparently a Jorōgumo is often considered a shapeshifter but in reality release pheromones which alter the perception of those around them making the Jorōgumo appear human. Shiho told me to really concentrate on her if I wanted to see her true form. The other option was to look in a mirror which explained why they had been covered. The woman appeared bemused by Shiho's explanation but could see that I was struggling to concentrate on her. She smiled at me, one of the most attractive things I have ever seen, and then offered to help. Without moving she must've stopped releasing her pheromones as slowly I began to notice a hideous transformation, not just in her but in the house too. The woman's legs faded away, her torso instead attached to a large bulbous abdomen. It was jet black and covered in fine hair and must've been at least five feet wide. Spreading out across the room from the gigantic abdomen were eight long spindly legs, each one ending in a singular claw and flat on the ground. The ceiling above us had changed too and I noticed that it was now covered in thick webbing, the same we had seen in the forest outside. With her true form now visible the Jorōgumo picked itself off the floor, her abdomen large enough that her human torso sat two meters above the ground making her tower over us. Again Takeyuki didn't appear bothered by the gigantic half spider half woman monstrosity next to him and Shiho appeared not to notice the difference, as if she had always seen her that way. I on the other hand completely panicked despite it asking me to stay calm.

Shiho was prepared for the Jorōgumo's transformation and immediately held up her lighter saying that she would burn the roof webbing unless the monster let the three of us go. That would bring down large molten globs of the stuff which would burn all of us. The Jorōgumo turned to her, looking confused by the threat, but stayed still and asked Shiho what she knew of her kind. The question took Shiho back a bit, probably because it's normally me asking these things not giant spider human hybrids, but she answered quickly enough. She said she had met two Jorōgumo before and that both had attacked her the second they saw her. The Jorōgumo nodded and then asked if either of them had ever spoken to her. Shiho replied in the negative and the Jorōgumo nodded before asking if she would judge her entire species on the actions of those two. She explained that it was the natural instinct of Jorōgumo to attack humans for food but she swore that she wasn't like that. She explained that she had been alive for four hundred years as a spider and then fifty as a Jorōgumo and that for the majority of that time she'd been alone. She admits that she's a monster and doesn't deserve pity but she says she was lonely until Takeyuki stumbled across her house. She claims that she too has fallen in love with him and that she means him no harm. She said that we were free to leave but asked Shiho if she thought that monsters like her didn't deserve some happiness in their lives. The question seemed to stump Shiho and she simply stared at the creature trying to process her story whilst Takeyuki declared his intention to stay yet again bringing a polite and grateful nod from the creature. Shiho didn't answer her question but posed one of her own, asking why the Jorōgumo was going against its base instinct and not attacking us. The Jorōgumo replied that after living so long it became clear to it that it wanted something else from life. It claims that it can still hunt in the dark forest next to the house for meat which suffices meaning it has little need to eat humans. It again admitted that it was a monster but said it couldn't change that and requested that even if we didn't understand we would leave them in peace as it meant no harm.

The way the Jorōgumo spoke puzzled Shiho, I could see that it went against everything she knew of their kind and as such she was keen to know more. Even so, Shiho is Shiho and first off she wanted to be completely certain that it wasn't a threat. She spent the next two hours quizzing the Jorōgumo, which went on to identify itself as Mika, in great depth whilst we stood in this odd face-off. Despite all her questions Mika maintained her story throughout and it did honestly seem as if she had developed feelings for Takeyuki and, despite the look of her I didn't think she was a threat to us. Eventually Shiho appeared to have the same realisation conceding that she'd never encountered a Jorōgumo as smart as Mika and that if she'd wanted to kill either us or Takeyuki she would've done so already. It had taken a long time for her to relax and agree that it was likely that Mika was telling the truth. She spoke again with Takeyuki afterwards, trying to check if he was serious about staying, but he confirmed that Mika had shown him her true form after the first three days and he had chosen to stay despite it. I can't imagine how he reacted nor can I say that either of us fully understood their circumstances but we did agree to pass on his message to his mother and he also promised that he would venture back down the mountain to visit her from time to time. They were clear though that Mika wouldn't be accompanying him on these visits and would instead forever stay on the mountain where no human would find her.

With that settled we prepared to take our leave although the afternoon had mostly passed and the light, although still abundant, would soon start to fade. Mika then offered us the chance to stay the night in her home. She said that it would be dangerous trying to descend in the dark and that the villagers wouldn't expect us back until tomorrow anyway. She also said that eating together would be a good way to cement our new found friendship. Shiho agreed, although I think this was more out of curiosity over Mika than any actual worry about the oncoming evening.

It was an odd evening, Mika pretty quickly reverted back to looking like a human, I think she simply prefers that as it doesn't mark her out as different, although at times it was difficult to remember that the great mass of her body and legs were actually still there and simply invisible to my eyes. I felt like I was about to trip over them at least a hundred times during the evening but never once did although I think that's due to her agility as she was often spinning around to get out of my way. I spent some time alone talking with her as we prepared our meal, an assortment of vegetables from their garden along with some unidentified meat that she'd caught in the forest earlier in the day. While speaking to her I found out many interesting things about Jorōgumo. She began life as a golden orb-weaver spider living in the very forest that the house backs onto. She says at that point the trees covered the entire slope and that their number have fallen year on year, a fact that upsets her greatly. She explained a great deal about her life as a spider yet it was bizarre to hear. Even the most mundane things like catching flies and spinning webs were fascinating to listen to although I credit Mika for her great passion for talking. She explained how at the age of four hundred she had transformed into a Jorōgumo and began her new life. It was during this time that she learnt how to excrete the perception altering pheromones and how to behave like a human, including her ability to speak. She explained in great detail how she had started off living in a cave behind the waterfall but had built her house after about a decade living as a Jorōgumo. On the previous two that Shiho has encountered Mika reckons they were young, most likely recently transformed. She says that Jorōgumo enjoy ensnaring their victims, seducing them and then devouring them. Mika herself freely admits to having eaten numerous humans in the past using this technique but claims that her tastes have since changed. The mountain path is rarely used, especially after the first few people went missing, meaning she was forced to hunt in the forest for smaller prey. She says that forty years of eating from the forest has meant she no longer has any desire for human meat but back when she was a young Jorōgumo she probably wouldn't have been able to help herself from attacking us. It's weird talking to such a creature, she's nothing like the other yōkai I've spoken too, I think she's the first which can actually hold intelligent conversation, way more than Hanako-san could. It's still weird though, on one hand she could easily kill me without any difficulty and is ultimately a terrifying yōkai yet when I speak to her she comes across as a friendly intelligent being that genuinely wants companionship.

The meal she laid out for us was delicious too and she and Shiho spoke long into the night. I can hear them downstairs even now, discussing names of various other yōkai which I do not recognise. It appears that even with all her knowledge Shiho occasionally has to bow to experience and after four hundred and fifty years I imagine Mika has seen more than her fair share of the strange on this mountain. Then again there's always the chance that she might eat us while we sleep. I'm sure Shiho will be watching out for that although truthfully I trust Mika.

I had an oddly terrifying experience this morning, I woke to find Shiho still asleep in our room, a strange occurrence as normally she wakes before me and it proved that she was no longer worried about Mika and was willing to sleep in her house without fear of being eaten. That, or she was exhausted having spent most of the night talking with our spidery host. Deciding to search for some breakfast I headed downstairs where I found our gracious host, hanging upside down from the ceiling and barely a foot away from my face as I entered the living room. I guess she must sleep in the webbing attached to the ceiling. I don't know if I woke her but she was staring straight at me and it was quite disconcerting to have a conversation with a gigantic half human half spider creature that was upside down yet had her face level with mine. She was, as always, in a talkative mood asking me how I'd slept and soon scuttled across the ceiling into the kitchen, returning through the door as a human with a plate of fruits for breakfast whilst we waited on the other two to rise. It gave me a chance to ask her why she bothered trying to hide what she was yesterday evening, we all knew about her so there was little point in the illusion and she explained that she did it for Takeyuki's sake. She believes that he prefers her looking that way so tries her best to project that image for him. I could tell that she was a little self-conscious about her spider like form regardless so I set about complimenting her on it despite my fear of spiders. She seemed delighted and dropped the illusion instantly, showing me all manner of things she can do with the webs she creates. Incredibly light yet stronger than I could imagine her webbing is truly a wondrous substance and I was fortunate enough that she offered to create a rope for me out of it, similar to that which operates the ferry outside. I have little need for rope but as a keepsake it is rather remarkable and might come in handy at one point. Mika was also very interested to learn more about Shiho. Clearly the two had spoken long into the night but Mika had found the same walls around Shiho that I'd spent months slowly breaking down. I guess it was only natural for her to want to know more about someone who knows her kind so well but I wasn't able to offer her much in the way of answers.

The other two joined us for a full breakfast and before long Shiho and I departed from Mika's house. It was definitely an odd experience for both of us but Mika told us that we'd be welcome back anytime and oddly I think I would take her up on that offer. I certainly hope that it isn't the last time we meet them. Shiho too admitted that she had grown to like them even in the short time we'd been there and wondered whether it was possible for other kinds of yōkai to have such varying personalities. On that matter I had no answer, but we both agreed that we wished them luck together and set off back down the mountain. On the way I asked Shiho what she thought about their future and she replied that it was unlikely Mika would eat him given that she'd already kept him alive for a couple of weeks. She said most likely they would remain together for his lifetime and then Mika would remain. Apparently Jorōgumo can live for centuries so she would definitely out live him but Shiho said there was no need to think they wouldn't have a number of good decades together first. After that Mika may find someone else in time, or even gain enough mastery of her pheromones to move into the village. I hope that's the case. I worry to think about Mika alone in that house for centuries so I hope she makes the most of her time with Takeyuki.

Back in the village we told Takeyuki's mother that he was still alive and had met a woman living in the mountains. We spared her a number of details about Mika's true form but she was glad that he was alive and immediately started fussing about when he would be visiting to which all we could tell her was that it would be soon. I'll admit it's nice to see a woman regain hope after worrying for so long, far nicer than confirming a loved one is gone.

Over all I think it was a successful job and one that certainly got Shiho thinking. After everything she must've seen doing this, I think it was surprising for her to find that even she believes that sometimes these yōkai are deserving of a little happiness too.

July 5th

Today I discovered something very interesting about Shiho whilst discussing the implications of Mika's existence. It's been playing on Shiho's mind for a few days especially as I kept saying how it was rare to find one as dangerous as Mika that turn their back on killing humans. That's when Shiho told me something unbelievable. It turns out she's not as alone in the world as she makes out. I was already aware that her parents had died when she was young, so too her mentor a few years back but today she told me about the only living relative she's got, if you can call her that.

She let slip about an apartment that she keeps in Tokyo, probably the one with her copy of the Gozu, but she told me it houses her 'sister'. It turns out that years ago, shortly after the death of her mentor, Shiho happened across a small girl who appeared to be homeless and alone wandering under the cherry blossom in Kyoto. It wasn't by chance that they'd met though, locals had asked Shiho to investigate the area after a series of deaths and her investigation led her to this homeless girl. Sakura, as she later became known, isn't an ordinary girl by any means. Shiho claims that she is in fact a spirit of an orphan who died yearning for a family. That desire brought her back to our world where she forever looks for a family to take her in becoming so possessive over people that eventually she kills them for fear that they might abandon her like her family in life. I guess in that sense she's similar to a Kuchisake-onna in the manner of her return to our world although I can't speak for her possessiveness. I am uncertain exactly how things went down that day but I do know that Shiho didn't banish the spirit and instead allowed it to form a bond with her. She claims this can be beneficial in that it can make other yōkai less inclined to seek her out although I wonder how she can trust something that can kill for want of having a family. Maybe it's just different for me, I have a family that's unlikely to try killing me, but I don't know how or why Shiho formed a bond with Sakura but she did. I guess something about Mika and her situation resonated with Shiho because she was surprisingly open about Sakura and what she truly is.

Life with Sakura seemingly wasn't easy. Cast in the role of an older sister to a psychotic spirit left Shiho forced to weigh up protecting Sakura from the yōkai she encounters against Sakura's unending need to be loved by family. It doesn't help that as a form of yōkai herself Sakura doesn't age, she is, and always will be, no more than a child yet somehow Shiho worked out a deal with her. She genuinely cares for Sakura and managed to convince her that she was protecting her by setting her up in Tokyo. Of course protecting her might not be necessary, the story of how she met Sakura included no fewer than five bodies suggesting the girl is more than capable of handling herself. Amazingly Sakura had agreed to Shiho's plan and the two remain in near daily contact. Shiho claims that Sakura is incredibly useful for information and that she is normally the one to pass leads onto Shiho. The colleague of hers that helped with information about the Teke Teke and the Aka Manto was in fact Sakura who seems to understand that world far better than Shiho ever could.

I asked why Sakura wasn't at school if she was just a girl but Shiho showed me a picture of her that she carries at all times. To say she wouldn't be accepted is an understatement. I have seen fewer things more demonic looking than Sakura who has two large horns on her head, large fangs and blood-red eyes. Certainly odd, Sakura is clearly a humanoid but unlike the Kuchisake-onna, Teke Teke or even beings like the Nure-onna or Mika who possess some human qualities, Sakura looks more like the traditional demons classical art depicts. Certainly a being that would cause concern in the local school.

Shiho told me that nobody else in the world knows about Sakura. Nobody goes into the house except her and when she's away deliveries of food are made and left at the door. On rare occasions Shiho even takes her out to wander the streets providing Sakura wears a hat, sunglasses and a face mask. Sakura seems pleased with this arrangement, or at least has never outwardly complained about it. I can tell that Shiho would prefer a world where she could go out without being in disguise though. I guess it's natural to want the best for those we love.

I never pictured Shiho as an older sister yet, despite the obvious nature of Sakura, it is clear to me that Shiho has grown to care deeply for her. It leaves me wondering what else she might be hiding.

I don't know if I'll ever meet Sakura, judging from her picture, I don't know if I want to. She's apparently less stable than Mika, more prone to showing her true nature, and Shiho is very protective of her. I'm glad she's told me about her though. It feels as if we're becoming closer as her trust in me deepens.

Death On Wheels

Honshu in the summer feels a world away from Kyushu in the spring and not just in terms of the temperature. The cities are vibrant and busy whilst the country is green and stunning. Travelling around in Shiho's car through long lazy days has truly been a surprising high point in the year. We've mostly headed North covering as many towns and villages as we can. I think Shiho's been to many of them before, possibly she does this every year in search of yōkai. On that front things have been quite quiet recently, almost as if the heat of the summer has driven them into hiding for we've not had a single useful lead for a week now. Still there is something that Shiho wants to check out.

Stories are circulating online and in the news about a possible serial killer operating in Sendai so that's where we've slowly been drifting towards although in no great rush. I remember first hearing about this case back towards the end of April when the news reported a grisly murder. I'd thought little of it at the time, preparing to visit my family and concentrating on my own articles, so my interest had been minimal. Anyway a man walking down the street in the early evening had been brutally decapitated. There were no witnesses to the event yet when the body was found blood was still pooling around his neck meaning the killer had to have been close by. The police couldn't find anything, no footage of anyone entering or exiting that area on the local CCTV and there were few leads. They did say that the cut to the neck was clean, a single blow dealt by a well-balanced katana according to their experts yet searching the local smiths brought no luck either. The case went cold and the press quickly forgot about it until around four weeks ago when a second body was found in the same street. The victim had also been decapitated and left at the side of the road but hadn't been found until the following morning. That sparked interest in the original case as it didn't take much to realise it was the same killer. Again there were no new leads and the police were forced to admit that they were stumped. About ten days ago a third body was found. Again it was on the same stretch of road as before and the poor soul had been decapitated. There seems little chance of the police being able to solve this one as their fresh investigations turned up nothing of note. Whoever, or whatever, is killing these people, they've vanished without a trace.

Mika had been following the story and pointed it out to Shiho who, immediately thinking that it might be something more than your average killer, suggested that we made our way to Sendai. She said that it was odd that a killer would be able to strike three times within a couple of hundred meters and not leave any clues whatsoever. Another troubling fact was that the attacks were seemingly becoming more frequent suggesting that something needed to be done before the bodies started to pile up. Sensing that something didn't add up we travelled to the local police station to offer our services.

Similar to the previous police stations I've visited with Shiho they had very little problem with accepting her credentials, especially after she said that she might be able to help them with the Sendai decapitator as the killer had become known in the press. Unfortunately there wasn't too much they could offer in terms of additional information. It was exactly as the press had reported, three murders, no witnesses and the only clue was that the murder weapon was a katana that couldn't be traced. There wasn't much to go on but determined to help investigate, we travelled out to the murder site to see if there was anything there that could point us in the right direction.

The murder site in itself was surprisingly pleasant but that was most likely due to the time of the year and the weather, a lovely summer breeze wafted down the street whilst the sun peeked out from behind a series of hazy clouds. It was perfect weather for a picnic and Shiho and I decided to have one in the small park at the end of the road. Evidently the fact that the beheaded bodies had been removed improved the ambiance too but the police had provided us horrific pictures of the incidents so that we could find the exact spots. The road was quite long starting with the parkland where we picnicked and running about a kilometre down to an old factory which had been gutted by a fire earlier in the year. The rest of the road was filled with residential blocks with the path set back and lined with trees all currently looking splendid in the summer sun. There appeared nothing particularly special about the actual murder sites either, they were all towards the middle of the road and all on the path. The victim files that we'd been given by the police suggested that all three victims lived in one of the various residential blocks that lined the street and that they had all been returning alone the evenings that they were murdered. The obvious suggestion was that the killer lurked in one of the blocks, probably towards the end and would pick their target and follow them although the police claimed to have searched the entire street and failed to link anybody to the murders or a katana. The whole affair seemed strange but it had driven people away. On a day like today the park should've been teeming with people but instead we were the only two enjoying it.

Walking up and down the street a few times with Shiho after our picnic turned up little in the way of clues but did give me a chance to discuss what she thought it might be. She replied that there was little to go on but few creatures behead someone and then simply abandon the bodies. Most yōkai that kill have some purpose to it whether it be for revenge or to sustain themselves, they kill for a reason. Whoever, or whatever, was killing the people on this street wasn't like that. The bodies were left unharmed, other than the missing head which was always found nearby. The killer had struck one powerful clean blow and then left which led her to believe that the killer was purely out for entertainment making it one of the worst kinds of monsters she could think of. I asked her what the creature was she had in mind but she wouldn't say instead saying that we needed to return that evening to put her theory to the test.

When the evening came we returned to the road and took another stroll along it in the setting sun. It was still pleasant but the wind had increased slightly bringing a slight chill if one was to stand still for too long. Together we walked up and down the street until it was properly dark and the path was only lit by the street lights. The whole time we didn't see another person nor a single vehicle on the road but that didn't deter Shiho. After the fourth round trip she told me that the killer prefers dealing with individuals not groups therefore our best chance of drawing them out would be to head down the street individually. Not particularly wanting to run into a crazy katana wielding maniac on my own I was quite relieved when Shiho volunteered herself for the task and I waited in the car as she set off into the night. Just under ten minutes later Shiho returned and silently slid into the car. Before I even had the chance to ask her whether she had seen anything she blurted out that she knew what the killer was and that it was a form of yōkai. I asked her what it was but she refused to say claiming that saying the creatures name will summon it and spell her doom. Unsure how that would work I instead asked her to write it down but before she did she made me swear not to read it out loud. I agreed and she carefully wrote out a single word on a scrap of paper, 'Tonkaraton'. I asked what one was and Shiho claimed the easiest way to explain would be for me to see the spirit myself. I firmly declared that I had no desire to meet such a creature but Shiho explained that an encounter with one could be easily survived if you knew what you were doing. She described the yōkai as a humanoid wrapped tightly in bandages on a bike that would ride up to individuals and announce its name. Shiho claims that if you respond by repeating its name it will simply continue riding whereas if you don't it will decapitate you. That was the only time it was safe to say its name, any other time and it would kill you. She then told me that now that I knew this trick I would be safe against it and insisted that I took a look at the creature so that I could truly know what we were dealing with.

Rueing not saying no, I soon found myself walking down the street alone just as Shiho had done. All the warmth of the day had long since passed and I was practically jumping at every shadow and each individual noise. Maybe about seven hundred meters down the street, well beyond what Shiho could see from the car I started to hear a strange noise in the distance. It took a while for me to recognise it but as it drew closer I realised that it was the sound of a man singing. The voice was hoarse though and cackled as it sang and then I started to work out the words to its song, 'ton ton ton'. That was when I first saw the yōkai. Coming towards me along the road was a rusted old bike, the last few remnants of red paint peeling off as it moved, movement that occurred despite the rusted chain that prevented the wheels from turning. Compared to its owner, the bike was in positively mint condition as the rider was almost fully bandaged head to toe in faded white bandages that had greyed to match the sallow skin that poked through from underneath where the cloth had loosened. The creature's eyes were strikingly blood red and its mouth hung open permanently showing rotted black teeth and a blackened burnt tongue creating a truly gruesome appearance. On its back hung a katana, the very weapon used in the three

124

murders which was in surprisingly good condition considering the rest of the being riding towards me. As it rode up to me it stopped and continued its rattling song without ever moving its mouth. It then turned its head towards me, very slowly as if the movement was difficult for it, until it was staring directly at me although it felt more like it was peering straight into my soul. That was when its song changed and it said 'Tonkaraton' to me slowly, again without ever moving its mouth. Fortunately, despite the terrifying appearance of the yōkai I managed to stutter out its name in response. The creature looked at me for what felt like an eternity weighing up my answer before I heard it repeat its original song of 'ton ton ton'. Its head then slowly twisted back to face forwards and then it rode off singing its song as it went. I waited a few minutes to recover my breath before I followed the Tonkaraton back towards the end of the street where Shiho waited for me in the car. When I finally got back to the car Shiho could tell that I must've seen the creature as she read my expression. She said that the positive was the bike hadn't passed her waiting at the entrance of the park meaning the Tonkaraton was only operating in that one street and wouldn't travel further. Once I'd manage to calm down after my encounter I asked how we were going to get rid of it as we clearly couldn't leave such a thing killing people randomly. Shiho's face scrunched up as she thought before she told me that they were a pain to get rid of but first she'd need to inform the police of what they were dealing with. That will be our first task come morning.

The first thing we did this morning was go back to the police station to inform them of what we'd encountered in the street last night. In order to protect them Shiho refused to tell them the name of the creature instead constantly referring to it as the Sendai decapitator or simply calling it a yōkai. I don't think they appreciated this and instead thought that we were crazy talking about a monster that we couldn't name. For whatever reason, probably a mixture of their failure to get anywhere on the case and their desire to get us out of their station they dispatched a junior officer, Kōichi to go with us back to the street as Shiho was determined to discover what had caused the spirit to appear.

During the journey Shiho told us that a Tonkaraton was formed when a man died in immense pain yet his body was left to rot. The spirit then returns, vengeful towards the living whom he sees as forgetting about him. She claims that repeating its name appeases the spirit as it shows the spirit that you know of it and haven't forgotten. Of course the fact that it repeats its name over and over as it rides means you don't have to know it but I'll admit a lot of these yōkai don't seem to be all there in the head department but maybe dying does that to you. I asked Shiho where the katana and the bike came into the story of the Tonkaraton and she said she didn't know. At first her community had thought that the vehicle was their preferred mode of transport in life having read early tales of them appearing on horseback yet nobody had ever recorded a Tonkaraton riding in a convertible which led them to believe that perhaps the tales were of a different sub-species of the yōkai. Either that or they were just very slow to adapt to new technology. Where they find the katana they carry is also a mystery, one I doubt will ever be solved as they don't appear to do much speaking. None of the local stores reported any stolen so somehow they just seem to materialise. Even Sakura, so often a font a knowledge on the strange, has little information on either of these questions leaving them a mystery. I asked Shiho how one manages to get rid of a Tonkaraton as, although they are easily appeased if one knows what to do, we couldn't leave it roaming the road for eternity. Shiho replied that the easiest way would be to find the remains of the person and bury them correctly although based on the time that the Tonkaraton had been operating that might not be enough. If that failed she planned on burning the remains and then burning the creature, a fact which she claimed would be easy since it was mostly made of bandages and dry skin. The only trouble with that method would be that we would have to actually find and then attack the spirit which didn't sound like the greatest idea. In the time I'd known her, not once had directly attacking a spirit worked in the way she'd hoped so I had little faith in it working this time.

Once we arrived at the road we began to pace ourselves knowing that it was highly unlikely the creature would show itself to three people in the middle of the day. Instead we were looking for anything that might fit the origins of such a creature. That was where Kōichi came in handy as he was quick to answer any questions Shiho had about the area. There had been no other unsolved murders in the street and no reported disappearances meaning that if someone had been killed in one the flat blocks it was probable that their body wouldn't have been treated correctly. The parkland at the end of the road would also be an ideal place to dump a body although Shiho pointed out that the Tonkaraton hadn't made it as far as the park last night and had disappeared further down the road. The only other alternative was the factory at the other end of the road which had been gutted by fire earlier in the year. That raised Shiho's suspicions and she asked Kōichi to tell her what had happened. He told us that back in March a fire had raged through the factory, all the evidence had pointed towards an electrical fault. Nobody was to blame but the fire had claimed the lives of five workers who had been trapped on the top floor at the time. He assured us that those bodies were properly laid to rest suggesting it couldn't be one of them. Even so Shiho pointed out that the police had already done a full sweep of the street inside all of the apartment blocks searching for the murder weapon and hadn't found anything to suggest that a body could be hidden amongst them. With the fire occurring only a month before the first attack she thought that it was best to start with the burnt out factory so we headed that way.

The factory was still empty, the cost of repairing it too great for the company so instead it sat as a scorched ruin at the end of the road, a plethora of signs outside warning people not to venture inside given the dangerous nature of the structure. Ignoring them entirely the three of us marched in surprised by just how damaged the interior was. The majority of the walls had been scorched black and in every room sat heaps of metal where once proud machines had stood only to be reduced to molten waste by the fire. Immediately Shiho asked to be shown where the bodies had been found and Kōichi led us up to the top floor, the stairs forever feeling as if they were about to give way under our weight as their supports had become charred husks. When we arrived the room was a mess, the door had been kicked in but everything else in there was entirely destroyed, just clumps of blacked ash that littered the floor. I asked what had happened and Kōichi, who'd been part of the team investigating the fire, told me that the door had jammed leaving the workers inside trapped. Unable to escape they had burnt to death. It was a grisly thought but there clearly wasn't any remains left in there. It was possible that a body could've entirely burnt away in the inferno but when I raised this theory Shiho informed me that wouldn't make a Tonkaraton and that the other five bodies had left remains. Clutching at straws she asked where else someone might have been that would've left them unable to escape the blaze. The obvious answer was anywhere that was far from the exits, the top floors or the basement area below. We searched the top floor in its entirety but couldn't find anything resembling bones so we moved onto the basement where we found a storage closet which had its door welded shut during the fire. Shiho asked what was in there and why it hadn't been opened but Kōichi replied that they had been told it was just a storage room and wasn't important. Even so Shiho insisted we open it and between the three of us we managed using a series of the burnt tools that had been left behind. There, in the back we saw the skeletal remains of one poor soul who'd tried to hide from the flames. The rest of the room was surprisingly clean suggesting his hiding place had been a good one but unfortunately with no way out he'd starved to death before he could be found. I asked Shiho if that could be the remains of the spirit and she nodded silently staring at the bones for a long time. Kōichi was in quite a state bemoaning that they hadn't helped him as the fire had only raged for a day before they'd brought it under control meaning the man could've easily been reached before he starved. Eventually Shiho shook us from our thoughts, telling us that we needed to bury the remains in order to drive away the Tonkaraton so carefully we extracted the bones from the room.

Once we'd collected the remains we drove to the nearest cemetery and convinced them to dig us a new grave. They had little complaints when they saw that we were with a police officer and were willing to pay twice the usual amount for a quick job. With no name to attach to our body we decided that the burial should be enough and investigations into the identity could be done afterwards by the police although given that nobody had reported them missing for six months, identifying them could be difficult. Our first priority had to be to get rid of the Tonkaraton. With that in mind we conducted a quick burial laying the bones to rest in the newly dug grave marked with an empty headstone.

As soon as it was done Kōichi asked if we had driven away the Tonkaraton but made the mistake of speaking its name. As soon as he did I saw Shiho's face turn to one of worry and her eyes darted around the graveyard in case the creature hadn't been banished. Then we heard it coming. The squeak of its bike and the 'ton ton ton' of its song as it approached. Kōichi looked terrified and pleaded with Shiho to save him but she backed away saying that she couldn't anymore. Then we saw it coming over the crest of the graveyard hill. The same creature which we'd met the previous night although this time it had its weapon drawn and was peddling as fast as it could. Kōichi screamed and began to run as I felt Shiho drag me behind a gravestone so that I was out of the way of the creature. Its song continued as it got closer and then we heard a swish of air as it brought its weapon down. A moment later the head of Kōichi was thrown down next to us and we both peeked round the gravestone. The Tonkaraton was staring at us, its cold dead eyes filled with rage. 'Do not say Tonkaraton without permission' it rasped, its mouth never moving before it rode off back the way it had come leaving us staring at Kōichi's dead eyes.

Unfortunately there was nothing we could do for him other than to report his death fighting the very creature he'd set out to help stop. The other officers clearly believed us because, instead of arresting us as I'd feared, they allowed us to continue our investigation with Shiho claiming that she was certain that it was the correct body that we'd found and that she would be able to get rid of the Tonkaraton now. Helping our case was the fact that the grave diggers had also reported seeing the Tonkaraton which confirmed that we weren't directly responsible for the death of Kōichi.

By the time the police had removed Kōichi's body and left us to our work the sun was already setting and, terrified by what they had seen earlier, the grave diggers had refused to return to the site leaving the two of us to exhume the body once more. The work was gruelling and we were constantly on the lookout should the creature return but fortunately it remained true to character and wouldn't show unless called for. That or it was busy elsewhere. Once we had exhumed the bones Shiho quickly piled them up and set fire to them, the flames taking on an ethereal green colour as they burnt away. It must've taken a good hour or so for the bones to reduce to ashes but as soon as they had Shiho swept them up and reburied them in an urn, saying an incantation as she did so. With that done I asked if the Tonkaraton would've been appeased and she shook her head telling me that the body was just its physical connection, to be rid of the yōkai we would need to burn that too.

With the darkness of the night fully engulfing the area Shiho suggested that we wait until tomorrow for that particular job. She wanted to set up some things in preparation and besides, the Tonkaraton prefers the early evening to hunt its victims.

I don't know why Shiho continually insists on using me as live bait when trying to stop these yōkai. I don't know why I allow her to do so. Today, not for the first time since knowing her, I found myself face to face with a demonic spirit that was inches away from killing me. One day she'll get it wrong and I'll be done for and when that happens I'll be sure to come back vengeful. I don't know why I put up with it. I know its good material for my articles and I enjoy my time with Shiho but I could definitely do without days like today.

It all started with her plan to burn the Tonkaraton. A foolish notion at the best of times yet I'm still not sure why I needed to be put in harm's way to achieve this goal. Her plan had been quite simple, knowing that Tonkaratons are hardly the brightest of creatures we were going to create a ring of fire on the road which the creature would have to pass through when summoned. One of us would then spray it with gasoline whilst the other threw a lit match on it. It was a simple idea yet should be effective. Having been told that the ring of fire would in all likelihood kill it anyway now that the body was burnt, I had been volunteered as the person who would call for the spirit, Shiho reasoning that she could act more freely without the attention of the Tonkaraton. As such as the day turned into evening I found myself on the pavement standing in the centre of a circle of oil which Shiho promptly lit lighting up the sky with the flames. At that point I called out for the Tonkaraton and sure enough a few seconds later we heard it cycling up the road making its 'ton ton ton' sound as it went.

By the time I saw it, it already had its weapon drawn and was closing in fast. The wall of flames was a good twenty feet before me so I thought I would be fine but when it reached the flames it seemed to part them with its katana, adding a burning layer of oil to the blade as it passed through. Instantly regretting my faith in Shiho I ducked away as the Tonkaraton approached with its now flaming sword only to have my faith repaid as Shiho flung herself at the creature, somehow knocking it off its bike and scrambling away so both her and I stood on one side of a burning ring whilst the Tonkaraton lay on the other. Once it got to its feet, a considerable effort as its legs were almost permanently stuck in one position as if its whole body had been burnt stiff by the fire, it appeared to scream at us annoyed by Shiho's intervention. Unfortunately it was staring straight at me and completely ignoring Shiho almost as if it could only attack the one who'd called it as opposed to one who'd attacked it. The Tonkaraton slowly stumbled towards me making an awful death rattle in its throat and holding out an arm ready to grab at me. Instinctively I backed away only to be reminded by the flames licking at my heels that I was trapped in a ring of fire. Unsure of what to do I looked at Shiho who abandoned trying to get the attention of the Tonkaraton and instead sprayed gasoline over it which didn't deter the spirit. Even at its slow pace it was still closing the distance between us and slowly cutting down my angles of where to go and I heard Shiho screaming about the match. Without taking my eyes of the creature I fumbled in my pocket for the matchbox and in my hurry dropped it. Panic ensued as I scooped down to gather the matches and

Shiho threw herself at the spirit careful to avoid the katana but was easily pushed away by the Tonkaraton which had its sights firmly on me. I managed to light a match but when I looked up the creature was only a few feet away. Still I threw the match at it and watched as it embedded itself in the folds of its bandages immediately taking hold as the Tonkaraton burst into the same peculiar green flames that we'd seen yesterday. Somehow it was still moving and I felt it grab my hair and pull me upright as I heard it growl 'do not say Tonkaraton without permission' at me raising its weapon. I thought about closing my eyes but something about the burning creature was mesmerising. The bandages that it had worn had completely burnt away showing its grey sunken flesh. There was a terrible burning smell too like overdone barbeque and from that distance I could tell that it wasn't breathing. Another odd thing was the fact that despite the whole Tonkaraton being on fire including the arm which propped me up, I felt no heat nor pain from the fire. As I looked at the creature, its red eyes burst into flames and the flesh on its head burnt away leaving a flaming skull which incredibly continued to snarl at me. Then I felt its grip loosening and realised that its arm had become no more than bone allowing me to pull myself away as the katana dropped to the ground, its other arm breaking off due to the weight. Terrified I scrambled away over to Shiho and together we watched as the Tonkaraton dropped to its knees and then eventually fell to the ground nothing more than a pile of burning bones.

It took another twenty minutes for the flames to die out and when they had I realised that the bones had been destroyed leaving absolutely nothing other than the katana. I asked Shiho why there were no ashes and even where those bones had come from since we'd burnt the bones of its actual body and she replied that those of the Tonkaraton were a construct only. The same as the flesh, they only existed as part of the creature and formed around the spirit. Once the spirit was removed they simply stopped existing. I asked why that hadn't happened to the katana and she told me to pick it up if I wanted to know. Curious I scooped down to pick it up but as soon as I touched the hilt the weapon crumbled into dust before being carried away by the wind leaving us no wiser as to where it had come from.

In order to be sure that it was dealt with Shiho called out 'Tonkaraton' at the top of her voice but nothing came leaving us thankful that there wasn't a second lurking in the city. The spirit had been dealt with and although four people had lost their lives Shiho was relatively pleased with the outcome. She tells me that Tonkaratons can often kill hundreds before anyone realises what they are. We told the police that we'd dealt with the Sendai decapitator and although they seemed happy with that outcome they offered no reward and asked us to leave. I think they blame us for the death of Kōichi.

Could we have saved him? Perhaps if we'd played it differently but it's difficult to second guess these kind of things. No doubt the police will claim that he was the one to catch the killer at the cost of his own life. He probably deserves the acclaim, I know that Shiho won't want it anyway. It makes a nice story for them too, hero cop gives his life to stop mass decapitator. Now there's a story I could sell to any news outlet.

With the case closed we immediately retreated to our hotel for the night. We'll have one night here and then in the morning we'll set out for Kyoto again. Shiho is leaving shortly to travel abroad and, unfortunately, due to the number of visas needed I cannot go with her. Her flight is in a few days but she wants to get back to Tokyo and Sakura before she leaves. It's certainly been an odd few months travelling with her and going back to Kyoto will be strange. She's promised to stay in touch though and I've made her swear to come pick me up again once she gets back to Japan. I'm not quite ready to give up this life just yet.

Today's the day Shiho left Japan to begin her foreign tour. As I write I believe she's about to touch down in Seoul. She appears to have a set schedule in place, no doubt jobs that have been posted to her throughout the year meaning she's on a strict timetable. I have no idea what she's likely to encounter over there. According to what little she would tell me, yōkai, like any other creature, have environments and countries that they are native to. Apparently those she's going to be looking into aren't the same as the ones you find in Japan. Even so, I have no doubt that she'll be able to survive whatever she encounters. I wonder if she'll meet other people like her whilst she's there.

Her absence will give me time to write up the last few adventures I've had with her as articles for there is only six weeks left until the next edition of the magazine and I'm yet to send anything to the editor. Still, I have a month to get things sorted before Shiho returns and plenty of encounters to write up.

Demons and Kittens

July 18th

I've done basic drafts of the adventures I've had with Shiho and truthfully I think the Tonkaraton will go down best with the editor. I'll change the name of course, I can't risk someone accidently saying the creature's name out loud and summoning one. Other than that I'm struggling with which one to submit. The Kunekune was simply too bizarre whilst the Nure-onna wasn't really their style. At least I've still time to think of which is better for submission.

In the meantime, the editor actually approached me with a bit of good news. Apparently one of the nationals really liked my articles and wants to reprint the three of them in their bi-annual review. Of course I said they could, it's more exposure for our magazine and more income for me. I can't wait to tell Shiho the good news. Six months ago I never would've expected this.

The editor loved the Tonkaraton story so that's definitely in the next edition. He did press me on a second article though and he didn't seem too convinced by the description I gave of the other two. Looks like I might need to find another if I'm to sneak in a second.

In other, somewhat related, news I heard from Shiho today. She's currently in Northern Vietnam having completed whatever she was doing in South Korea. She wouldn't tell me what she'd encountered there but said it was perfectly safe. She still has a few stops left on her tour so it seems like she's busy. She did however have a request for me although it sounded a little strange at first. She says that Sakura is acting a little odd, apparently she's quite distracted and bored whilst talking to her. Shiho asked if I could visit her to make sure she's alright. It's an odd request, nobody else knows about Sakura so I'm honoured that she's asked me but knowing Sakura's true nature leaves me worried. Anyway Shiho gave the address and asked if I could make my way over there at one point in the next few days to check up on her sister. Honestly I have no idea what to expect.

I always enjoy riding the train into Tokyo. It's not too far from Kyoto but it can feel a world away, the quiet calm atmosphere of Kyoto replaced with the bustling hub that is Tokyo. The perfect place to have a summer break although I didn't come here to have a break. I came here for a purpose.

Today was the day I finally met Sakura. Having seen a picture beforehand I knew what to expect but even so, after everything else I've seen, I still wasn't prepared for the demonic looking figure that lurked in the address Shiho had given me. She was small, similar in size to Hanako-san but very different in looks. Her face was an odd shade of pale with almost a purple hue and she had stark blood red eyes. On the top of her head were two sharp horns which slowly curved upwards and were maybe a foot long. I don't know if I'll ever get used to talking to these things but Sakura appeared capable of holding a conversation, intelligent well beyond her age although, as her body doesn't age, it's impossible to tell exactly how old she is. Shiho had once joked that we could count the rings on her horns but I don't think she works like a tree. Her voice is coarse and deep yet seems to contain great power. There's something about the way she speaks that I can't quite describe. Mika was intelligent, way more than I thought possible of a yōkai but Sakura seems to be something else entirely. She might be the most intelligent being I've ever encountered.

She appeared to have been expecting me, I don't think I would've made it through the door if she hadn't, but mostly kept herself in front of a bank of computer screens which I noticed included one permanently on Shiho's website and another which appeared to be a location tracker pinpointed on Shiho's position. The other monitors were open on a variety of news feeds, assorted videos and one which appeared to be an online game of chess. The rest of the apartment was quite dark, the curtains completely closed leaving the lights of the screens the only source of illumination whilst pop music blasted out of an old record player in the corner. Sakura didn't seem to mind, if anything she didn't seem to notice. She was very inquisitive to begin with, asking me plenty of questions mostly relating to my experiences and friendship with Shiho. It's clear that Sakura cares about her in her own way although at times it can border on the unhealthy with the precision of the questions she asks.

After a while I finally asked what was wrong with her and why she had worried Shiho so much. Sakura didn't realise that she'd been acting any differently around Shiho and appeared confused by my question. After a bit of coaxing I managed to get it out of her, she was simply bored and wanting an adventure. She'd heard the stories of our adventures from Shiho and wanted one for herself. She even had the perfect one lined up in her mind. A request had come in from a teenager living in Tokyo that Sakura wanted to investigate and saw no point in dragging Shiho back to look into it. Naturally I suggested that she wait for Shiho who knows what she's doing when it comes to this sort of thing but Sakura was insistent that she knew just as much as

Shiho and that we'd be looking into it tomorrow saying that she would do so with or without me. Knowing that Shiho would want to keep her safe I reluctantly agreed.

As I get ready to spend the night in Shiho's apartment, I wish I could say that I'm not afraid of Sakura. Speaking with her marks her as one of the most intelligent beings I've ever encountered and she did attempt to be friendly. Even so there's just something off about her. It's not like Mika who I trusted almost instantly. With Sakura I feel like I've walked into the lion's den. I can still hear her even now, typing away at her computer. She's not left it the entire time I've been here. I don't think she sleeps. She certainly eats a lot though, she went through a full uncooked chicken earlier this evening. Still Shiho trusts her, even loves her, so I have to believe that she wouldn't have sent me to my death. Hopefully the adverse effect it would have on their relationship is enough to keep Sakura from killing me.

I woke to a strange sight this morning. Sakura was perched on a stool at the foot of the bed watching me sleep. I have no idea how long she'd been there nor what she was doing but she didn't find it strange in any way. I asked her if she does that to Shiho but she was surprisingly coy with her answer. It's definitely true, the girl is weird. I'm pretty certain she read my diary too but I have no proof other than a few facts she scoffed at over breakfast that I'd apparently stated incorrectly.

With breakfast out of the way, Sakura was quick to state that she wanted to get going yet I was glad that she had remembered to put on her disguise of a large hat, sunglasses and a mask. I'm not entirely sure I would've been able to coax her into wearing it. The investigation she'd chosen had come from a teenager who believed that his girlfriend was a monster and trying to kill him. I don't know where these people find out about Shiho but as he was living in the city Sakura wanted to help him reasoning that if we left it he'd be dead by the time Shiho returned.

Finding the young man, a one Jin Hideaki, was quite simple, so desperate was he for protection that he pretty much found us. He didn't even appear bothered by the fact that I'd brought along a child although he only answered the questions I asked and ignored Sakura who just seemed happy to be out. His story was pretty simple, he'd met a girl that he'd liked and they'd started seeing one another. They had dated for about a month when he noticed that she was becoming more and more possessive, getting to the point where she would ask him not to see his other friends. He'd ignored this request and spent the night at the house of one his friends. He claims that during the night his friend had been killed by his girlfriend who had said it was because he wasn't spending the time with her. He'd told the police but they couldn't find this girl anywhere and he was worried that she was going to come after him. Sakura asked him few questions which I had to repeat before he answered yet they were odd, seemingly unrelated as if a curious child were asking them, constantly jumping back and forth before she became distracted by a bird. For starters we asked the name of his girlfriend to which he answered Fuku with no family name given. We also asked where this Fuku could be found but he replied he didn't know. If he wasn't even aware of where she lived then tracking her down wouldn't be easy. The final relevant question Sakura posed was how the two of them had met which he described as strange. Apparently she simply showed up at his house one day claiming to know him although he swore they'd never met. Quite why this hadn't appeared strange to him at the time seemed odd but Sakura didn't particularly find it strange.

We were both aware that finding this Fuku would be difficult as Hideaki had no real record of her. Asking around nobody appeared to know where she lived or even where she usually went. The only firm lead on her location was that she had shown up at Hideaki's home uninvited. Their other dates had been around the city but she'd always met him at the location or gone straight to his house. Never once had she mentioned where she lived and seemingly she had no phone. With little to go on, we

138

followed Hideaki to his home assuming that if Fuku really was trying to kill him then it would make sense for her to try and find him there.

Hideaki's house was in a rather affluent area and the building itself looked thoroughly modern. The small garden backed onto a local park but had tall enough walls to dissuade anybody from wandering in uninvited. A quick tour of the building easily told us that there hadn't been a break-in and Hideaki confirmed that Fuku wasn't currently there. The only thing Hideaki could offer us was a photo he had taken of the two of them giving us a first look at Fuku. She appeared to be on the smaller side with a cutesy look yet nothing about the girl in the image suggested that she was in any way a murderer.

Whilst I examined the picture Sakura had been busy strolling about the place sniffing the air randomly and running her hand across the walls. At first I ignored her but once Hideaki had left us to our work I had to ask her what she was doing. She told me that there was as strong scent of a yōkai in his home and that she might be able to pick up the trail. For the record, I couldn't smell anything and I have never heard Shiho talk about the smell of yōkai but I guess Sakura is better tuned for this kind of thing. Incredibly within a few minutes she had picked up the scent and started to lead us away from his house. Firmly on the trail of Fuku, I asked Sakura if she knew what we were walking into hoping that it wouldn't be too dangerous and she looked at me with utter derision. When it comes to explaining these creatures and what she's doing about them Shiho is difficult to get information from. Compared to Sakura she's practically a public speaker. The little demon would tell me nothing only that we were getting close. Eventually, after threatening to turn back she finally told me the name of the creature she was hunting, a Bakeneko.

Forced to trust that Sakura would know how to handle this Bakeneko given how nonplussed she seemed about it, I went with her and we soon came to a small park relatively near to Hideaki's house. Once there Sakura led us through a clump of trees until we came to a small stream. That was where she declared that the trail ended. There was no sign of Fuku, although I had the feeling that we were being watched. It's possible that if she really is a Bakeneko then she might be able to sense what Sakura is. If that's the case then she might have stayed away. I don't know how strong Sakura is. If she is anything like Hanako-san then if she thinks her family is in danger she might just be the strongest yōkai I've ever encountered. The other possibility is that she's simply incredibly confident.

Our search of the area threw up very little to begin with and after a while Sakura asked me to wade into the stream saying that was where the scent was strongest. I don't know why she couldn't have waded into the stream, maybe the water would've killed her, maybe she's just lazy, but for some reason I agreed. In the stream I finally found something that might be relevant to the case. There was a rice sack in the water, tied to a large rock preventing the current from taking it away. At the other end, the sack had been torn open by what appeared to be sharp claws. Sakura was delighted with the find and promptly told me that we'd need to talk to Hideaki again tomorrow but that she was done for the day. With that she simply turned tail and wandered off.

Unable to abandon her we went back to Shiho's apartment where Sakura finally told me more about Bakenekos.

The little that Sakura would say included a brief description of the yōkai, a cat like creature that is known to have shapeshifting abilities. She went on to say that there are many different sub-species of Bakeneko some way more violent than others meaning she couldn't be quite certain what type we were hunting. She did say that she didn't think it would be too aggressive as she confirmed that it had been watching us in the park from the trees and could've attacked if it wanted suggesting either it was quite docile, or it was afraid of us. On how they are created Sakura had many theories that mostly involved terms I do not understand but she suggested that the one we were dealing with had been drowned in the sack we found.

Who would do that to a cat I have no idea but Sakura said that would be the first thing we looked into come morning. It's odd, I know she's some demon and they're not related at all but at times it is difficult not to see bits of Shiho in her. They share traits for this sort of thing even if Sakura is slightly more detached.

Again I woke to the sight of Sakura watching me sleep. I got the impression she had done so for most of the night although what her purposes are for doing so I cannot say. Certainly if she wanted to attack me then she would've done so. Part of me wonders if she's acting as some sort of guard dog and trying to protect me as I sleep. Maybe I'm just thinking too much, or hoping for better intentions from her. Either way, she point blank refused to tell me.

Anyway, as promised, we set off for Hideaki's house shortly after breakfast. Sakura appeared to really enjoy being outside. I don't know how often she does go out but she takes an odd childish interest in the most mundane things, often stopping to simply watch people or stare at shop windows. Even so it was still morning by the time we reached Hideaki's house. Having been told what to say in advance by Sakura I informed him that Fuku was indeed a yōkai and was trying to kill him. After he'd calmed down a little I then told him that he needed to come with us so that we could deal with her together. I had no idea what we needed him for but I went along with what Sakura had suggested and quickly the three of us made our way back to the park and the stream that runs behind the clump of trees. It appeared to be a place that Hideaki was strangely familiar with.

He questioned why we had brought him there and Sakura showed him the sack we had found yesterday. He gasped at the sight and attempted to make a break for it only to stumble back towards the stream as Sakura revealed herself, terrifying him. I'll admit seeing her out in the open baring her fangs and her horns made for a terrifying sight and I certainly wasn't going to get between them. Despite her small frame she appeared to grow in that instant and all around us the skies turned darker. With her gaze firmly set on him Sakura asked him about the bag in what can only be described as a very threatening manner. Hideaki broke instantly and replied that he and a group of mates had found a stray cat in the park one day about a month ago. Horrifically, they thought it would be fun to trap it in a rice sack and drown it in the stream. As he explained I felt nothing but disgust toward him but oddly Sakura didn't seem affected only demanding further answers from him, her voice echoing through the park. He told us that was two days before he'd met Fuku and offered no excuses as to his behaviour that day.

Whilst Sakura was interrogating him I noticed that our strange party had been joined by a fourth person although this one, like Sakura, was no person at all. Emerging from the trees was Fuku, the same girl from his picture only she was half human looking, half cat. Her face and body appeared human but in place of hands and feet she had paws with sharp claws. She also had a set of razor sharp fangs almost rivalling Sakura's. Round her neck I noticed she still wore a collar suggesting she hadn't been a stray when Hideaki had found her. Hideaki noticed her coming too and trapped between two yōkai quickly lost his sanity and started wailing. Sakura didn't care and simply stepped out of the way letting Fuku deal with him. Her response was rapid and violent. In a flurry of swipes she tore at him with her claws asking him if she was good enough now until all that was left of Hideaki was a bloodied mess.

Sakura was delighted with the outcome wandering over to me as Fuku set about her work and whilst beaming declared that she'd loved the last couple of days. She thanked me for helping her and then said that she wanted to go home. Before we did I pointed toward Fuku who had finished and stood watching us. Sakura seemed shocked that I would still want something done with Fuku believing us to be done with the matter. I know Shiho has allowed yōkai to kill people before, normally it's required to banish them but I got the distinct impression Sakura couldn't care less about getting rid of Fuku, instead she was just happy that she'd had fun threatening a human.

That was when Fuku first spoke to us, or mostly to Sakura. Her speech was broken and a struggle to understand but she thanked us for bringing her justice, a thanks Sakura waved off. I asked her if she was going to kill again or if she was finished knowing that we couldn't just leave a killer yōkai to roam Tokyo. Fuku replied that she had no desire to kill anybody else although expressed regret that she couldn't return to her prior owner, whom she loved very much, and as such had no idea what to do with herself. Sakura was quick to point out that she could do whatever she wanted, Sakura didn't care. She then told me that she wanted to go home again and immediately set off. Knowing I had to keep her safe for Shiho I set off after her leaving Fuku to decide on her own future.

Working with Sakura is certainly different to working with Shiho, I'm pretty certain Shiho would've done something about Fuku but I'm not sure what. If only I knew then maybe I could help her. I even asked Sakura about it once I'd managed to get her home but she reiterated that she didn't care. Her job was finished and that was all that mattered. She even said that the last thing she needed was another yōkai moving in on her patch. I think that's something I was forgetting about Sakura, although she is this demonic being capable of incredible destruction, she's also a little girl and a surprisingly selfish one at that.

Today is the day I left Tokyo and Sakura. She was very polite when I left, thanking me for our time together although she let slip an interesting bit of information. It turns out that Shiho hadn't requested that I visit Sakura and that she had hacked into her phone to send the messages herself! Shiho is so protective of Sakura that if she finds out that I've been running around Tokyo with her then she'll kill me for sure! All Sakura would do about it was laugh and tell me how much she enjoyed it. I'm beginning to really dislike her.

Anyway the last couple of days I've been feeling bad for Fuku, the Bakeneko, after we left her in the park. I just know that it's not what Shiho would do so I went back to try and make things right. The area around the stream is still cordoned off whilst they deal with the police investigation into the recent unsolved murder but near the trees I called for Fuku and incredibly she emerged. Talking to her I asked if she'd decided what to do with her life but she replied in the negative saying that she wanted to be happy again like she was before. I don't think she's left since Hideaki died. That was when I had an idea. It might not have been what Shiho would've done and I'm not entirely certain how safe it was but I told her that I might be able to find a home for her if she was willing to trust me. Incredibly she was, although maybe that's due to a lack of options, and not an hour later we were on our way out of Tokyo.

The journey back to the Minami Alps was difficult and in the end I had to rent a car to avoid suspicion given how bizarre Fuku looks but as evening fell I found myself hiking up the mountain path with a new friend. As we came to the plateau under the waterfall I instantly felt comforted as I saw that house again and, after great difficulty getting Fuku to cross the stream, managed to knock on the door.

Mika was the one who answered and she was delighted to see me, embracing me instantly with her human arms, although Fuku was disturbed by her appearance. I think she sees Mika's true form. Mika explained that Takeyuki was currently visiting his mother but invited us in for the night. It took a while to convince Fuku that Mika wasn't going to hurt her and slowly she became more trusting. I explained Fuku's story to Mika, she, of course, knowing exactly what Fuku was, and she was quite moved, instantly offering her the chance to stay there. As I'd hoped Fuku eventually accepted. It's probably not exactly what she wanted but truth be told I think it's what both of them may need in time. Few others would be able to handle a cat like Fuku and here she would be safe.

Mika has offered me the chance to stay as long as I want and I'm inclined to stay a few days, at least until Takeyuki returns so that she doesn't get lonely and Fuku settles down. It's odd, here I am six months on from that Kuchisake-onna attack sleeping in a house with a Jorōgumo I consider a friend and a Bakeneko.

It's strange that I can find so much enjoyment amongst such otherworldly creatures yet I've found both Mika and Fuku to be exceptional company. They show a surprising amount of traits I thought unique to humans and it's really left me thinking that maybe we're not so different from yōkai.

Mika is certainly the friendlier of the two, Fuku still trying to really understand her circumstances. That is no clearer than in the way she speaks. Mika is fluent having perfected her human speech over decades of practise whilst it's all new and unfamiliar to Fuku. Her speech is basic and often broken but Mika encourages her to practise as much as possible, showing great compassion for her situation. She also assures me that Fuku needs time to get used to her environment and that she will eventually settle down. As such she offered to take me hunting with her. I can't say I was any help stumbling around the dark forest that backs onto her home but it was fascinating to see Mika in her element. She has incredible pace and dexterity which belies her size. She managed to ensnare a deer with her webbing but truth be told I think I was making too much noise for her to be truly effective. It's amazing how fast she moves given her size in addition to her ability to blend into the trees.

I think Fuku was glad to have the chance to explore the house by herself whilst we were hunting, she appeared more relaxed when we returned a couple of hours later. I'll stay a few more days and then head home.

It's been a good few days with Mika and Fuku. Fuku appears to be fully settled now and happy to be around Mika, as I'd hoped.

The stay has been enjoyable for me too. I've been able to sit and talk with Mika for hours on end. Her stories and views on the world are incredible to hear and she even permitted me to write them down for an article for the magazine. 'Tales of the Jorōgumo' I'm going to call it and focus more on her hunting humans in her earlier years as opposed to her life now. That would certainly be of more interest to my editor I think. It might be quite interesting to write one based on the monster's point of view for once too. I'll add the finishing touches myself and send it off to the editor before the week is out.

I've had a couple of calls from Sakura whilst I've been here. She wants to know why I haven't gone straight home. The demon must've put some tracking device on my phone whilst I was sleeping because she knows exactly where I am. I guess I should feel flattered that she's worried and based on her nature I'm not going to tell her to stop. Still, after the stunt she pulled to get me to Tokyo I'm glad to make her worry.

Takeyuki came back from visiting his mother today. He was happy to see me too, in his own way. Never as friendly as Mika I think he more tolerates my presence but Fuku took an instant interest in him. He seemed ok with the idea of having a pet cat, even one as bizarre as Fuku although truthfully Mika sort of steamrollered him into it. Either way Fuku is now officially part of their household and appears happy. It certainly has to be better than staying in that park in Tokyo. I noticed that she vanished into the forest herself earlier today, hunting no doubt. The fact that she chose to return later suggests that she's happy enough.

My work here is done. Not only have I managed to find a home for Fuku I've also been given a new article idea by Mika. It's certainly been a worthwhile visit but tomorrow I will return to Kyoto. It won't be long now until Shiho returns and I've got this article to finish before then. As much as I would love to stay here, life beyond the mountain continues and it's probably about time I return to it.

The national publication which carried my articles from earlier in the year was released today. It was interesting to see them in a different journal and one which has a much greater following. Again my social media has had a mini explosion of people wanting to ask questions. I try to respond where I can but it's slow progress. If only Shiho were here to answer all the questions readers posed.

I finished the article on everything that Mika had told me and sent it to the editor a couple of days back. I received the feedback today. He loved the idea of the role reversal and is happy to run with it for the September issue giving me my quota for the quarter. It's a shame he'll never get the chance to meet Mika personally. He had plenty of questions which I know she'd be very keen to answer in great detail. I'll have to be sure to send her an issue, no doubt she'll take great enjoyment from reading it.

I don't know the full details of what Shiho got up to during her time abroad, I don't even know exactly which countries she visited, but she returned to Kyoto today and turned up at my door unannounced. It was an odd way to find her, she was in a jovial mood and was happy to laze away the day recalling stories from her time away. Maybe the sun got to her or something because I don't think she's ever been this talkative.

She's done quite a bit too, her work out there had been lucrative yet busy and in the short period she'd been away she'd visited at least four countries, possibly more. She told me of work she'd taken in China, South Korea, Vietnam and Cambodia explaining the various creatures she encountered in each. I did wonder why Shiho, who by all accounts was an expert in Japanese yōkai, would be of use if she encountered a Korean version but she explained that most had similarities that she could exploit. She also explained that it was an ideal opportunity to learn about different species and that eventually she'd like to be able to take jobs all across Asia if not the world. She claimed that the trips helped her to build up a network of similar minded people across those countries that she would be able to call upon should she need them in the future.

Personally I don't know if she'll ever manage that but I will admit that hearing her tales left me wishing that I'd agreed to go with her instead of hanging about here. Even so, it was good to see her again.

She was aware of my trip to see Sakura but wasn't as mad as I thought she would've been. Instead she thanked me for putting up with Sakura's quirks and confirmed that the demon herself had admitted to tricking me into going thinking I was doing it for Shiho's sake. At least she had owned up to it instead of letting me take the fall I guess. Shiho seems surprised by the interest Sakura had shown in me but ultimately admitted it was always a possibility that Sakura would latch onto anybody she forms a connection to. In return for her understanding I offered her my account of the events which Sakura appeared to have been lapse about and although there were clearly points where Shiho disagreed with our choices she ultimately accepted that it wasn't the worst outcome. She didn't appear particularly pleased that I'd taken Fuku to Mika alone but, as nothing bad had happened to me, relented and admitted that Mika continues to surprise her by allowing a second yōkai into her home.

August 21st

Straight back to Japan and almost straight back to work for Shiho. Any hope she might have had of a lazy late summer has been dashed by a new request from the police that was passed to her by Sakura who seems to monitor her inbox. They want her to look into a series of deaths in a retirement home on the outskirts of Tokyo. At first they had thought little of it, deaths are hardly unusual in those places, but recently they've noticed that they have a significantly higher than average death rate compared with the rest of the country. They visited to investigate but couldn't find anything so have requested that Shiho looks into it. It doesn't sound like the sort of thing that Shiho usually deals with but the pay's good so we're going to head for Tokyo tonight and investigate the place tomorrow. It'll mean another night with Sakura but with Shiho there I don't think she'll be as creepy. With any luck she'll even let me sleep unobserved.

The retirement home is more of a complex than an individual building and it would be hours away from Shiho's place on public transport. We've been forced to get a hotel or we'd spend all day going back and forth. Fortunately there's a hotel on hand which relatives use to visit their family members. We've managed to get a room for the night so that we can continue our investigations in the morning.

We achieved quite a bit today and incredibly the police were right to call Shiho, this is something that they could never have dealt with.

When we arrived at the retirement complex we were met by a couple of staff members who showed us around. It's incredibly modern and the people living there all appear to be enjoying themselves. The way the staff gave their presentation as we walked through the halls showed little indication of the surprisingly high mortality rate that peaked our interest. It was only when we reached a locked door to the west building that the two staff members hushed up and we had to prize information out from them. After a little persuasion by Shiho, whereby she disclosed that the police had asked us to investigate, they told us that the building wasn't closed for refurbishment as they'd originally suggested but had been closed because the residents no longer wanted to live in that block. Sensing something was wrong we pushed them further and they told us a ghost story about a monster that supposedly walks the corridors of that building preying on anyone it finds. They said they didn't believe it but that some residents claim to have seen the monster in the middle of the night and that they spoke of nothing else. The number of deaths in that building only added to the tale and eventually management had sought to close it permanently after all the residents demanded to be moved. Asking about the monster, the staff were adamant that it was nothing more than a child's story but told us that if we were really that interested they could take us to a resident that claims to have seen it. As far as the management was concerned, there was no monster and the west block was simply closed for refurbishment indefinitely.

The resident they took us to was an elderly woman who'd been at the complex for many years and was so frail that she could barely walk. After the staff had introduced us and told her what we were there for she began to tell us what she had seen shortly before moving out of the west building. Her speech was slow and she was somewhat confused on the details but the general gist of it appeared to be that she'd seen a shadow bumping around in the night attempting to get into people's rooms. She'd hear it every night scratching on her door before moving onto the next and one day a friend of hers, who has since passed away, told her that she'd seen the monster in person from behind but described it as an old man pacing the halls. In truth it wasn't much to go on and I'm not entirely convinced that she wasn't just confused but afterwards Shiho asked the staff about the number of deaths and if there had been anything odd about them. They didn't answer her directly and appeared to be hiding something but we couldn't force it out of them. Instead they informed us that the west building was the oldest of the blocks in the complex and was where the oldest residents used to live so it wasn't that surprising that it had a higher mortality rate than elsewhere. Even so, Shiho wanted to check things out fully and we headed to the local morgue after ascertaining that was where all the bodies had passed through hoping to find autopsy reports or anything to suggest signs of a yōkai attack.

The local morgue was similar to the others I've visited, clean yet unwelcoming as places like that often are, yet when we arrived one of the workers was very keen to talk to us about the bodies from the retirement complex. He led us through to the freezers telling us on the way that he was glad someone was looking into the retirement complex. He'd held onto one of the bodies due to the strangeness of the injuries yet when he had tried to report it nobody had done anything and the police had ignored his claims. According to him most people were trying to cover up the events at the retirement home yet all the bodies he saw from there had the same inexplicable injuries. Despite remaining silent I could tell that Shiho was intrigued and she sprung to life as soon as we were shown the latest body.

It looked perfectly normal, an elderly lady who'd died of old age if not for the one noticeable injury. I don't even know if injury is the correct description of her affliction as her face had been entirely wiped clean. She had no eyes, nose or mouth and instead her skin stretched across her head uninterrupted until it reached her ears. It might have been an obvious question but I asked how she'd died and was told that her death showed all the signs of suffocation, hardly a surprise since she no longer possessed a mouth nor nose to breathe. There were no other injuries anywhere to be seen, and the worker was keen to inform us that there were no internal injuries either. Her death was quick almost as if someone had put a pillow over her head whilst she slept. Shiho examined the body closely, carefully running her hand across the eerily blank face almost as if she was trying to ascertain whether the features were simply invisible or had indeed vanished. It was clear however that they were not invisible as her search found nothing.

Ultimately I'm afraid to admit that the sight was quite disturbing and unsettling to behold so I left after less than five minutes with the dead woman unable to bare looking at her blank face. The morgue worker shared my queasiness and he too abandoned Shiho to her work happy for her to do as she pleased with the corpse. It was maybe ten minutes later when Shiho joined us in the waiting room, her hands noticeably wet as if she'd just washed them, and confirmed that she knew what had caused it. She wouldn't say in front of the morgue worker, waiting until we were outside but before leaving ordered them to burn the corpse alongside any similar corpses that might remain.

As always seems to be the way Shiho was aware of the yōkai that had caused such an infliction although she seemed shocked by the sheer number of deaths that have been reported. She claims that the creature is known as a Noppera-Bo, a faceless ghost that has the ability to both impersonate and, in this case, steal the faces of anybody they encounter. What confuses Shiho most is that she claims Noppera-Bo are generally annoying pranksters as opposed to cold blooded killers which makes the deaths all the more interesting to her. She's troubled by the fact that Noppera-Bo, due to their inherent ability, are shapeshifters capable of having any face. That means knowing whether you're dealing with one or one of the other apparent multitude of shapeshifters out there is a near impossibility. When I asked how she knows this was indeed a Noppera-Bo she explained that only a true Noppera-Bo would be able to completely wipe someone else's face leaving nothing but skin behind. She also confirmed that the dead woman's face had completely gone, a fact she had checked by cutting into the skin which I for one am glad I missed. Skipping that detail, I asked her the obvious question, what was a Noppera-Bo doing in the retirement home and why was it killing people if they normally don't. Shiho tried her best to come up with a reason but it was clear that she too was stumped. Her knowledge on Noppera-Bo is quite limited, due in part to her not generally considering them dangerous and therefore unlikely to be called upon to deal with them. She claims that there have been stories of them for centuries though. Apparently they used to sit by the side of roads at night to scare unsuspecting travellers for amusement although Shiho also stated that there were just as many stories to suggest that they helped lost travellers return to the path by scaring them and that many a lost traveller had later claimed their survival was due to the actions of the creature. She claims that as fewer people began to travel on foot at night they changed tactics and have since been known to frequent public places such as theatres or restrooms looking to scare people. Apparently this is only the second time Shiho has encountered one, and the first time it's still been living. The previous time one had taken up residence in the bathroom of a shopping centre only to be the unwitting victim of an Aka Manto that Shiho had been investigating. She had found the body sliced to pieces but it was only afterwards that she had realised what it was. As for what this particular one was doing in the retirement complex she had few ideas. Her best bet was that it had been attracted by an increasing number of residents although she admitted that was unlikely to be the true reason as there are far more populated areas of Tokyo. For the aggression this one demonstrated she had few answers so could only speculate based on other spirits. Following her thoughts, I asked if there might be something tying the Noppera-Bo to the retirement home or someone that it wanted vengeance on. Shiho told me that she doubted that would be the case. Unlike a lot of the previous spirits that we've encountered like the Kuchisake-onna or the Teke Teke who are created in their dying moments and then seek vengeance, a Noppera-Bo isn't formed in the same way. In fact, even Shiho is unsure how they come into existence. Without seeing their true face there's no way of knowing who they were in life. Indeed Shiho claims that they may never have experienced a life as we know it and might simply form as a Noppera-Bo. If her claims are correct then it'll be difficult to find a reason why it's hanging around the retirement complex or why it's started to kill people.

Still our journey to the morgue did at least give us the name of the creature we were hunting and we were soon back at the complex and keen to scout out the west building further. Unfortunately by the time we arrived it was quite late and the staff outright refused to allow us access tonight. Instead we made our way to the adjacent hotel where I currently sit writing this whilst Shiho stares out of the window towards the west building. Her eyesight must be better than mine for she claims to be able to see shapeless shadows stalking through the halls of that building. I can't see anything but now that night had fallen I do get the impression that there's something evil in that place. Something about it is just off-putting.

It feels like it's been another long day today although I know the worst of this one is still to come.

We began the day in decent spirits. I had slept well whereas Shiho barely slept at all instead choosing to spend her night watching the abandoned building forever searching for a sight of the Noppera-Bo. Whether the shapes she saw last night were actually it we'll never know but regrettably Sakura had little to offer about Noppera-Bo beyond what Shiho knew. She too has encountered one before although I got the distinct impression that she didn't enjoy its pranks and that it didn't survive the encounter with the demonic girl.

This morning, after last night's disappointment, the staff of the retirement complex handed us the key to the west building and allowed us free roam of the place so long as we agreed to remove the Noppera-Bo and allow them to reoccupy the rooms. They no longer bothered to deny the presence of something supernatural suggesting they had known about it much earlier and were simply trying to drive us off yesterday. Maybe it's Shiho's knowledge of yōkai that ultimately makes people relent and tell her stuff but I've noticed she appears able to draw information from people even if they don't want to give it at first. The west building wasn't that different to any of the other buildings in the complex save for being a few decades older. It had been well looked after though so despite a few tired areas it maintained a modern feel. As we walked the long corridors, stopping to peer into each and every room it became clear that the evacuation from the building hadn't been particularly rushed. Although all the furniture remained in place any personal belongings and official records had been removed leaving rooms of empty beds and wardrobes. It was surprisingly clean, as if they had a deep clean after moving the residents giving everything the feel of a hotel room waiting for guests to check in. At times Shiho stopped to inspect something that she thought was out of place but each time she simply shook her head and continued to wander the halls. What exactly we were looking for she never told me but an odd assortment of generic items were inspected and then discarded without reason. I had thought we were on the lookout for the Noppera-Bo itself although Shiho rejected that idea. She stated that the creature hadn't been seen other than at night, a common trait amongst its kind, and although it had broken other rules of its kind by killing people Shiho doubted it would break that one.

The hours ticked by slowly as we examined every room of the three storey building and there was still no sign of the Noppera-Bo nor whatever Shiho was looking for. With a preliminary search turning up nothing we returned to the main building and questioned the staff on the location of the rooms where people had either died or seen the yōkai. Although they refused to come with us they did give us a list of rooms which Shiho thought might be useful in trying to track down the movements of the creature. Returning to the building we headed straight to the rooms they'd listed. Shiho spent a long time in each room, desperately searching for anything she could link to the Noppera-Bo. Unfortunately the rooms were spotless, the only thing she found was a slight scratching on a couple of the doors, too high to be from an animal yet she assured me that Noppera-Bo don't have claws making the scratches an enigma.

We came out of the last room ready to give up for the night having spent hours searching when we finally saw it. The Noppera-Bo, an exact replica of a human except without any facial features was standing outside the room waiting for us. Despite its unsettling look, it didn't appear particularly dangerous nor did it try to attack us. It simply stood there facing us, it's hands down by its sides. Shiho marched straight up to it as if unafraid, that or had some method for dealing with it in mind. She immediately demanded to know why it had been killing people. As expected the Noppera-Bo was silent. Shiho had previously mentioned that they can speak when they want to by putting on a face but this one was choosing to remain faceless. Instead it simply raised an arm and pointed down the corridor. At first Shiho laughed, unwilling to fall for the oldest trick in the book but I turned to look knowing that she had my back covered. Terrifyingly at the other end of the corridor stood another creature. At six and a half feet the humanoid creature was taller than the Noppera-Bo and slightly similar looking although unlike the Noppera-Bo it wore no clothes and had long clawed hands. Again, this creature had a bald head and was missing eyes and a nose although this one had a mouth. It was large and filled with rows of razor sharp teeth while an impossibly long tongue licked the air in front of it putting me in mind of a snake. I tapped Shiho to get her attention and she turned to see it letting out a slight gasp. Slowly the creature lifted one of its arms and held its hand up to us as if motioning for us to stop. To my horror I then noticed something on its palm, it was an eye which blinked open and stared at us. Behind us I heard the Noppera-Bo shuffle away but didn't turn as the other creature began to shuffle forward slowly churning its long spindly legs into a run as it kept its palm eye fixed on us. I heard Shiho scream for us to run and we both turned and fled eager to get away from this new threat.

Our escape wasn't dignified, we charged through the rooms with little knowledge of where we were going with the creature thudding along behind us. We could hear the smacking of its lips as it chased us and knew that it was closing fast. We managed to get to the ground floor before the creature caught us but knowing that we wouldn't reach the front door we went out of a window, landing in the small courtyard and breaking into a run despite suffering several cuts. We charged forward but fortunately the creature stopped, standing in the window and staring at us with eyes in both palms. We took one final look at the monster and ran back to our hotel lucky to have escaped with our lives.

Once we had reached the safety of our room I demanded to know from Shiho what that thing was along with why she wasn't prepared for it. Previously she's always had something in mind for the yōkai we encounter but this time she was just as shocked as me by its appearance. She was annoyed at herself for not noticing any signs of it earlier but replied that it was no Noppera-Bo instead she named the creature as a Tenome. Apparently they're vicious yōkai who feed off the bones of the living. Shiho explained that they're usually created when a blind person dies but maintains a desire to see. They are then born again as a Tenome with the ability to see through their hands, similar to how they 'saw' in life, yet they are apparently blinded by hatred and rage. Shiho says they are monstrous killers and she expressed amazement that more people hadn't been killed by it especially if it had been there a while. Despite having limited vision, especially during the day, they can use their long tongue to sense prey from a great distance and have extraordinary tracking abilities often stalking their prey for hundreds of kilometres. The big question I had was if the Tenome would usually eat people's bones, how come all of the deaths had been from having their face wiped by the Noppera-Bo not having their bones eaten. It appeared to me that although the Tenome was a far more gruesome looking creature, the Noppera-Bo was the one causing actual harm. Shiho agreed that did appear to be the case but stated that something was wrong about it all. The Noppera-Bo we met didn't try to attack us even when our backs were turned as we focused on the Tenome. It also didn't attempt to speak with us which surprised Shiho as normally they like to pull pranks on people by having their face disappear midsentence. Starting with that point we considered why it wouldn't speak to us and swiftly came up with our answer, because of the Tenome. Shiho theorised that a Tenome could easily overpower a Noppera-Bo if it wanted but as a fellow yōkai it probably wouldn't bother as it can't eat it, it has no bones after all. However, if the Noppera-Bo was wearing a face then the Tenome could mistake it for a human and attack it. Shiho reckoned that the Noppera-Bo is afraid of the Tenome and was protecting itself by not creating a face. That brought us to our next question, why hadn't it attacked us. Shiho replied that given normal Noppera-Bo behaviour it wouldn't. She reminded me that they scare humans but have been known to help them escape danger. As she reminded me of this her face changed as if she was having an epiphany. She repeated that they have been known to help people escape danger and then questioned if that's what it has been doing. Her thoughts were that if the Noppera-Bo was aware of the Tenome and its nature, a fact we know to be true, then it must've worked out that it won't attack a faceless person hence keeping the Noppera-Bo alive as it never shows a face to the Tenome. Shiho suggested that what if, to try and help the residents, who had no chance of outrunning the Tenome given their ages, the Noppera-Bo had wiped their faces. This would've stopped the Tenome from targeting them as it would believe they weren't human but would also kill them. Shiho suggests that maybe the Noppera-Bo wasn't aware that it would kill them or that it was so desperate to help that it figured it could save them from an even worse death at the hands of the Tenome. If that was the case then the Noppera-Bo is only killing out of mercy in which case Shiho thinks the deaths will stop if we can get rid of the Tenome. Even if that isn't the case the Tenome is too dangerous to be left to its own devices and needs to be stopped before we can deal with the Noppera-Bo.

We'd just reached that conclusion when we heard a scratching coming from the door to our room. As the closest to the door I softly crept over and looked through the peep hole. On the other side, staring back at me was the palm of the Tenome, its black eye widening as it saw my shadow approaching. Instantly the scratching started to intensify, as if it was trying to break through the door and reach us. I didn't even need to tell Shiho what was happening, she already knew and sprang into action. She leapt towards the bed and started to make a rope out of the various sheets calmly stating that the door wouldn't keep the Tenome at bay for very long and she didn't think she could fight it. From the tearing sounds that started to come from the door I figured that she was right yet wondered what she was planning to do. Before I could ask she was finished and not a moment too soon as the Tenome burst through the door, its long tongue licking the air and dropping foul looking black saliva to the floor. Fortunately Shiho had been quick with her knotting and threw her makeshift rope out of the window having tied one end to the bedpost. She ordered me to climb down and swiftly followed as the Tenome bundled across the room. We got to about the height of the first floor before the Tenome worked out a way to stop us. Horrifyingly it began to drag the rope back into the room barely having to work against the weight of the two of us. Desperate, we simply let go and crashed to the ground grateful for a flower bed that we landed in. Instantly the Tenome vanished from the window and Shiho pulled me to my feet saying that it wouldn't take long to get downstairs. Together we ran to the parking lot and into our car, Shiho in the driving seat. She struggled with the ignition and we saw the Tenome emerge from the hotel and charge directly at us. I was convinced that we were about to die but fortunately Shiho got the car moving just in time, although the claws of the Tenome did take some of the paintwork off the passenger side door as we sped away.

We've been driving endlessly since. Shiho says that this way the Tenome won't be able to track us too quickly. She says that it will do eventually but for tonight it will probably return to the abandoned west building of the complex. Despite everything I think Shiho plans to return tomorrow but I wonder what she can do against such a creature.

When I woke this morning Shiho was still driving and she'd managed to put at least fifty kilometres between us and the retirement complex on the edge of Tokyo. She'd taken a meandering route throughout the night but assured me that it was the best way to throw the Tenome off our scent. Even so, her effort seemed pointless as by the time I awoke she was already heading back determined to get rid of the creature.

I asked how she was planning to banish a yōkai which so far we had only managed to escape by fleeing. She explained that it was difficult to get rid of a Tenome, the easiest way is to blind them hence robbing them of the one thing they desired in life. Of course doing so provides its own set of challenges. Tenome are, by nature, incredibly fast and vicious. Even with their eyes in the palm of their hands it's nigh on impossible to stab at them such is their speed and the sharpness of their clawed hands. Shiho's plan is to use acid to blind the creature although that too requires her to be close to the Tenome in order to ensure enough of the liquid coats its hands. She claims that her best bet is to creep up on the creature but for that she'll need a distraction as the natural hunting abilities of a Tenome make them almost impossible to sneak up on. I didn't even need to offer to be the bait, Shiho just told me that I would be. It seems as if that's become my position in our little team, permanent bait. I really will have to raise my objections next time because it's beginning to happen too often for my liking. Apparently now that the Tenome has seen us it will pursue us when it gets the chance and as such would presumably drop anything else it was doing to try and catch us. I told Shiho that I didn't like the sound of being the bait for such a creature but she assured me that I wouldn't need to outrun it for long. When I asked why we couldn't switch roles she simply replied that I couldn't be trusted with the acid and that she needed to prepare something else whilst I distracted the Tenome although she wouldn't tell me what.

We stopped off at a supermarket as we made our way back and bought a selection of their finest bleaches which Shiho mixed into a foul smelling cocktail in a bucket in the car park of the retirement complex. I can't say how many different liquids she added but it was clear that getting any of it on one's eyes would blind them. Honestly, I think getting any on one's skin would cause significant damage such was the toxic fumes that rose from the bucket. With that done she carefully poured her mixture into a number of jars and handed me a few just in case I needed them before explaining to me where she'd be waiting inside the abandoned building. With very little fanfare she then bid me good luck and pushed me inside, straight into the lair of the Tenome.

The building was dark despite it being the middle of the day and I remembered Shiho telling me that Tenome see better in the dark so it was likely that it would've used the night to draw the all the curtains to replicate the darkness. Quite why it hadn't done this before I don't know, perhaps it knew we would come back or maybe we'd disturbed it yesterday. Without Shiho beside me, and now knowing exactly what lived there, the empty rooms and long corridors felt far more threatening than they had yesterday and I could hear each of my footsteps echoing off the carpeted floor even above the noise of my beating heart. Each shadow set me on edge as I slowly crept forward towards the staircase. Shiho had told me that the best place to start looking for the creature would be where we first saw it last night but she reassuringly confirmed that there was no need to worry about finding it. So long as I walked around long enough the Tenome would find me, I just needed to be prepared for it.

Without really knowing where I was headed, I wandered through the hallways never looking into any of the rooms for fear of seeing the Tenome until I heard the sound of its long tongue licking its lips. I turned in time to see it sneaking up from behind me, barely fifteen meters away. It had one of its horrendous eyes looking right at me as it grinned wildly. Terrified I used the only thing Shiho had given me and hurled my bottle of bleach mixture at it before running. Unfortunately my aim wasn't that great and the glass smashed into the wall next to the Tenome which I hoped would at least daze the creature. I don't know if it helped at all but it gave chase almost instantly as I fled from it for the third time.

I had a vague idea of where Shiho had suggested she would wait and knew that it was near the entrance giving me a chance of escape providing I could outrun it. As it was, the Tenome was incredibly fast and as I ran I could feel the air move behind my head as it swiped a clawed hand at me. Fortunately the staircase was bathed in sunlight from an uncovered window and I was able to gain a little bit of time as it slowed, dismayed by the light. Once we'd reached the ground floor it was back at full speed again and I quickly realised that I wouldn't be able to reach the entrance. That was when I heard Shiho's voice. She shouted out to us, or more likely just at the Tenome, from down a perpendicular corridor as we ran past. Whatever she had said it caught the attention of the Tenome and immediately it changed its target and ran towards her. Pausing to catch my breath I turned to watch as the Tenome advanced on Shiho who just stood at the end of the corridor waiting for it to come at her.

I could see from my position that Shiho wasn't holding any of the bleach bottles that she'd prepared and didn't seem to have any way of defending herself especially as she was backed into a dead end. The Tenome reached her quickly and paused right in front of her raising one of its clawed hands ready to strike. That was when the oddest thing happened. Shiho calmly lifted her hand to her face and wiped it clean, removing her eyes, nose and mouth to leave a flat surface. The Tenome halted, its hand still raised as it blinked at the sight before it and I realised it must be the Noppera-Bo. From the nearest room, the real Shiho emerged holding the bucket filled with the bleach mix. She asked if the Tenome was surprised which gained its attention, both of its hands spinning to face her so it could look upon her with both eyes. As soon as it had done that Shiho hurled the liquid all over it. From a range of just a couple of meters the Tenome was drenched in the stuff, its hands completely covered. I noticed that its eyes instantly turned red as the bleach rapidly blinded the creature. It threw its hands in the air as if it was in pain and an odd gurgling sound

158

came from its mouth, the only real sound I ever heard it make, before it simply faded away, vanishing into nothing.

Incredibly it was gone although I was now left with two identical versions of Shiho as the Noppera-Bo had reapplied her face. When it spoke it even used her voice making the two all but indistinguishable. The only difference was their memory which allowed me to find the real Shiho easily. I don't know how she managed to get the Noppera-Bo to help her, perhaps it was fear of the Tenome that caused it to act or maybe it was simply the fact that it could play a prank on it. Either way it appeared delighted at the result and took great pride in telling us about its part in the proceedings despite us having witnessed it first-hand. It was difficult to remind myself that the blabbering version of Shiho before us, it refused to change its face to anyone else even after she'd asked, was the same creature that had killed so many people yet it confirmed that it had only done this to spare them the wrath of the Tenome. With the Tenome gone the Noppera-Bo promised Shiho that it wouldn't kill again. In exchange she agreed to allow it to continue to use her face whenever it wanted and it confirmed that it would still play pranks on the residents. Personally I don't think allowing a spirit to play pranks on elderly people, especially pranks likely to cause heart attacks, is a good result but Shiho was at least satisfied that the deaths would stop. Quite what the Noppera-Bo will do with Shiho's face is another matter but Shiho didn't appear too bothered. Maybe it was aware that she hunted its kind. I'm sure that if it ever does cause problems for her Sakura will eat it or something.

As we left we informed the staff that their problem was solved, the building was safe and that they could, and should, start using it again. They were thankful and promised that they would move residents in starting with the next arrivals.

It's been a long few days and I'm left wondering how long it's going to be before I can sleep without picturing the awful sight of the Tenome. Perhaps it's for the best tonight. Maybe if I can't sleep I can catch Sakura in her act of watching me sleep and finally get her to tell me why she does it.

I've spent the last few days in Tokyo with Shiho and Sakura. You would've thought being one the biggest cities on the planet it would be crawling with work for Shiho but she claims it's usually surprisingly quiet around the summer. Maybe the heat drives them away although Shiho theorises that it's to do with the longer days with most yōkai preferring being out at night. With little in the way of jobs, Shiho's been happy to spend a few days with Sakura. Truthfully I don't know how often they actually get to see one another, I know that from mid-April through to mid-July they didn't but Shiho did spend a few days here before she went abroad. Even taking that into account this might be only the second or third time she's seen Sakura in person this year. Guess it depends if she was exclusively in Kyoto at the start of the year or kept traveling between.

To her credit Sakura appears much friendlier towards me when Shiho is about. It's almost like she's actually making an effort on Shiho's behalf. She's a little less sharp with her words and has given up watching me sleep. She still hasn't told me why she did it nor why she stopped but honestly I'm relieved about it, hers isn't a face you want to wake up to in the middle of the night staring at you.

Unfortunately for the two of them Shiho's work means that she's often not here and when she is it's over far too soon, especially in Sakura's mind. That was the case today as Shiho announced plans to complete a route of Northern Honshu which she expects to last around a month. As much as she'd like to Sakura can't go but Shiho was keen to invite me to travel with her again which I accepted without hesitation.

The Midnight Feast

September 4th

Our journey around Honshu has so far been very lacklustre with nothing sparking an interest in Shiho. The closest we came to anything was last night when we were driving along the road and I noticed a woman waiting on the curb hitchhiking. I told Shiho that we ought to stop since there was nobody else around and it was raining but Shiho refused telling me to look closely at the woman in the mirror after we'd passed. When I did I noticed that she was actually levitating slightly and that her eyes had been stabbed out. She was clearly a yōkai yet Shiho showed no interest in stopping to deal with her. When I asked why that was she replied that the spirit wasn't harming anybody currently and that she knew what it was and that it was nearly impossible to get rid of. Instead she simply suggested leaving it be and we continued driving. I don't know what would've happened if we had stopped but Shiho was pretty relaxed about the whole affair. Maybe sometimes I'm better off just not knowing.

In other news, the publication of the next magazine edition is tomorrow. I'll have to pick up a copy next time I'm in Kyoto and remember to send one to Mika. Come to think of it I'll need a couple more articles for the December edition. Maybe I could fashion something out of the Tenome, that's the sort of thing my editor likes.

As we were driving around eastern Tohoku today the worst happened. We ran out of fuel. I felt like such a fool as I had been driving at the time and I know that Shiho judged me for it. The only thing that I can console myself with is the fact that there hadn't been a petrol station for kilometres so it's not like I deliberately let it run out. Of course, she had reminded me that it needed filling before we set off for the day so blamed me for my incompetence as she put it. I guess worse things happen but if anything it was the disappointment in her face that bothered me the most.

Anyway, it was early evening when the car stopped and we were slowly winding our way up a gentle wooded slope maybe a kilometre or two from the top. In that moment we had to make a choice, whether to spend the night in the car or get out and search for a source of fuel, or lodging. In the end it wasn't surprising that our desire not to sleep in the car won out and we were swiftly on our way on foot making for the summit of the hill in the hope that would show us a town where we might find some fuel.

The trek up the hill wasn't that bad, it was a warm evening and there was enough light left in the setting sun for us to see by. The slope was relatively gentle too, hardly the same gradient as the hike to Mika's home. Anyway at the top of the hill we came across an old temple. It wasn't much to behold but what there was had been well kept. Shiho suggested that we ask there for fuel, although there was no vehicle present, or for lodgings for the night. The door was answered by an elderly priest who didn't look pleased by our arrival. He attempted to keep the door mostly closed but I managed to spot two other priests behind him tending to a large offering of food spread out across the temple. To her credit Shiho put on her best damsel in distress impression informing the priest of our predicament and asking for help. To our amazement he simply replied no and slammed the door in our faces. I've seen a lot with Shiho this year but I don't recall seeing her ever this taken aback, the priest's actions were so rude and uncharacteristic of his profession. Not to be deterred Shiho tried again and this time one of the other priests answered. Slightly shorter than the first, he appeared no less annoyed by our intrusion. Despite this he was more helpful than the first and informed us that although they couldn't help, there was a small village at the foot of the hill where we might be able to find some assistance.

Looking down from next to the temple we could see lights coming from a small row of houses that lined the bottom of the hill suggesting the priest hadn't lied. Unlike the way up, which was a winding route, the way down this side of the hill was an overgrown path that appeared rarely used yet led almost directly to the houses. We struggled down the bank, Shiho's mood seemingly falling with the sinking sun clearly still upset at my carelessness in letting the tank run dry.

By the time we reached the houses, only six of them standing in a line, the sun had completely set. It was clearly a small farming community and although there was no petrol station in the village we were encouraged that a few of the houses had cars parked outside. All of the houses were dark other than the central one where lights were blazing from every window. With our options limited we headed for that house where we were greeted by a middle-aged man who, although surprised to see two strangers on his doorstep, was kind enough to invite us in. He told us his name was Kazuaki and as Shiho explained our situation he listened intently and nodded. When she was done, he explained that although they had no fuel that they could spare he would be happy to take us to a larger town nearby where we would be able to procure some. He explained that he couldn't do that today though and it would have to be in the morning. He did however offer us the use of his spare room for the night which we gratefully accepted.

Kazuaki led us through his house to his spare room on the second floor overlooking the road. The house was filled with people, presumably the residents of the other houses and to our embarrassment we realised that they were holding a wake. As soon as we realised we offered to leave but Kazuaki insisted that we stay and eventually we relented promising to remain in our designated room whilst they conducted their mourning.
Confined to our small yet comfortable room Shiho once again criticized me for allowing the fuel to run out although part of me wonders if that was simply to cover her embarrassment at crashing a wake. Either way, she ranted for a while and then fell silent staring out the window up towards the hill and the temple that sat upon its crest. After about an hour our host returned to our room bringing us a small selection of food from their spread. We were grateful for it and he sat with us for a while whilst we ate. He explained that the deceased was his father and, as a small community, everyone in the village was in attendance downstairs. Again he brushed aside our apologies for intruding and reaffirmed that he would take us to the local town in the morning. We were grateful for his assistance and after about half an hour he bade us a good night and returned to his guests downstairs.

That must've been a couple of hours ago and since then we've sat pretty silently in this room waiting for sleep to overcome us. Shiho made a phone call at one point, I think it was to Sakura from the way she was talking, whilst I've taken the opportunity to sit at the small desk by the window and write this. Shiho's been sleeping for a while now and I'll try and get some soon although as I write something strange seems to be happening outside. The wake must be over because people are leaving but the manner of their departure is odd. It appears that they are all leaving at once filing out in a single line. They all appear to be wearing the same dark hooded cloaks whilst those at the front and back are carrying lanterns to light their party. I swear that amongst them is Kazuaki too, I recognised him as the final member of their party. As I watch they're slowly making their way down the road, not towards the other houses but away from the village entirely. The noise downstairs has halted too suggesting we've been left alone. This is odd, why would anyone leave their house in the middle of the night with two strangers lodging there? I'm going to wake Shiho and see what she thinks.

163

I woke Shiho, much to her distaste, and dragged her to the window to see the last traces of the strange procession vanishing into the night leaving only two lanterns bobbing in the darkness slowly moving further away. She was groggy but not particularly alarmed and immediately declared that she would go downstairs to check with our host making up some flimsy excuse of wanting to help him tidy up after the wake.

She was gone for only two minutes before she returned to our room, fully alert now and looking concerned. She confirmed that we had been left alone, there was no sign of our host and the outer door was locked trapping us inside. The only thing that she did note was that the corpse of Kazuaki's father was still downstairs, as was the food which had been set up for mourners. I was now becoming freaked out and asked why everyone would leave especially after locking us in the house. Shiho clearly had a few theories as to why, none of which I wanted to hear but suggested that she had plenty of experience dealing with weird death cults, experiences she'd obviously survived. Again she returned to the window and stared out into the darkness hoping to see anything but even the lanterns of the strange party of mourners had now vanished into the night. I suggested that we make a break for it, back up the hill to the safety of our car, escape from the house unlikely to cause us that many issues. Shiho, however, disagreed, pointing out that in the darkness we'd struggle to find the route back and even then, there was enough worrying Shiho about the party's behaviour for her to wonder what else might be lurking out there. She also pointed out that the car had no fuel and was nowhere near as defendable as a house should the need arise.

Her earlier anger at me seems to have vanished given the odd situation we find ourselves in and when Shiho suggested that we try to wait out the night in our room she even offered to take the first watch. She's taken up a position by the window and sits staring out as I write. I'll stop now and get some sleep. I hope that nothing happens to us during the night.

After a few hours' sleep I was woken by Shiho for a change in our watch. Nothing had occurred whilst I slept and as such she settled in whilst I took up position looking out over the darkened valley. There was still no signs of life in the small village but the moonlight bathed the road and the adjacent fields in an eerie whitish glow that seemed to stretch on throughout the valley.

I must've stayed on watch for a few hours before I heard a faint noise. At first I was unsure what could be making such a noise, an odd mix of cracking and slurping. It sounded nearby yet I still couldn't see anything outside nor had I seen anything approach the house. Concerned I went to wake Shiho although to my surprise she was already awake and listening to the noises. I guess she chose not to sleep, it's possible that she never does in these situations and I just never noticed before but she signalled to me that the noises were definitely coming from inside the house. Cautiously we crept out of our room onto the landing and slowly made our way to the top of the stairs. The room underneath, where the wake had been held the evening before was lit by the moonlight flooding through the front windows and allowed us to see the remains of the food and the coffin which sat open against the back wall as it had been when we passed through earlier. The only difference to the sight that had greeted us previously was that the mourners were no longer present, instead they had been replaced by three monstrous creatures that squatted on their hind legs close to the floor. They each were an ashen grey colour with sallow yellow eyes and sharp fangs in their blood encrusted mouths. At the end of each hand they had sharp claws and from their heads ran long wispy white strands of hair. Two of them were hunched over the food which had been left out, untouched by the mourners, and were tearing into it with their clawed hands, devouring everything they could reach in a ravenous frenzy. Worse was the third, the largest of the creatures, slightly taller than a human, which was standing over the coffin. Its long blood-soaked claws were wrapped around the head of the corpse which it had split open whilst it feasted on the poor dead man's brains. To my horror, I realised this was the slurping sound I had heard and despite the demented way the three creatures went about their business they made very little other noise. Alarmed by what I was seeing I wished to return to our room and escape via the window however Shiho seemed intrigued by the creatures and held a finger to her lips to silence me before she crept forward to take a better look.

We'll never be sure whether those creatures would have left us alone had we retreated to the bedroom as I had hoped, for as Shiho crept forward the floorboards creaked which caught their attention. The three creatures looked up immediately, dropping their food and snarling, a horribly deep sound that clearly wasn't of this world, as they realised the potential for fresh meat. Before they could move, I felt Shiho's hand wrap around mine as she yanked me away from the staircase back towards our room. I saw one of them lunge at the staircase using all four limbs to scale it faster than any human could but fortunately the bedroom was on hand and Shiho slammed the door shut before they could reach us. Without wasting a second I re-enforced the door with all the furniture in the room whilst Shiho tried to keep the creatures at bay. It was during this panic-stricken moment that I was finally able to ask Shiho what they were. To my disgust she told me that they were Jikininki, corpse eaters and that we shouldn't have disturbed them. Still, as a clawed hand ripped through one of the panels in the door and slashed at the air, I hoped that Shiho had a plan for how to deal with them since she had at least heard of such creatures. My faith was poorly rewarded as she informed me that we would need to survive until daylight. Apparently Jikininki only maintain this horrendous form during the night or when called upon and will shy away from the sunlight. A quick glance at my watch told me that it was coming towards half four, still a number of hours before sunrise and with the Jikininki rapidly breaking through the door, the chance of us seeing daylight was looking thin. Fortunately, even in dire situations, Shiho is not without some fight and quickly drew her knife slashing at the clawed hands now appearing through the door and forcing them back as she stung their palms. Unable to help, I went to the window to see if there might be any hope of outside assistance but to my horror saw one of the creatures crouched in the road looking up at me. I watched as it bounded forward, taking a leap beyond anything I could imagine to reach the second floor window and haul itself through into the bedroom with us.

With one of the Jikininki now in the bedroom we had nowhere left to hide and immediately Shiho went after it with her blade. As I had been the one visible through the window, the creature focussed on me allowing Shiho the opportunity to get a good slash to it with her blade. Her knife cut right across the creature's face leaving a long scar that drew no blood. The Jikininki didn't seem bothered by the wound, barely reacting to the strike and instead attempted to claw at my face. Its arm caught Shiho, more by accident, and sent her to the floor, landing near the door where the claws of the other two grabbed for her. The one in the room took another leap towards me, the foul stench of its last meal still fresh on its breath. Before it could reach me, Shiho was back on her feet, barging into the side of the creature and knocking it to the floor although it quickly recovered, snarling at her like an injured dog. At the same time we heard the snapping of wood as the door finally gave way and the other two Jikininki burst into the room leaving us surrounded. Before I could do anything I felt myself being dragged backwards by Shiho towards the window. The three Jikininki advanced but before they could attack Shiho pushed me out of the window, jumping out seconds later.

I hit the ground heavily, fortunate that there was a relatively soft landing in the small garden and saw Shiho land perfectly, rolling forward before coming up into a run. Without stopping to see if I was ok from the fall she yelled at me to run and somehow I was able to pick myself up and spur my legs into motion whilst the calmness of the night was shattered with the howls of the Jikininki. We ran for a couple of kilometres before Shiho finally stopped coming to rest beneath some trees. I was concerned about stopping whilst the houses could still be seen bathed in moonlight behind us but Shiho assured me that we were safe, if the Jikininki had pursued us they would have easily caught us so it was more likely that they had returned to the food already available to them inside the house. I was convinced and glad for the break as my legs were in agony from the fall. Unfortunately with several hours until daylight and no easy way to find the car in the darkness we were forced to halt and wait for morning.

Since it was clear neither of us were going to sleep again, the remainder of the night gave me plenty of opportunity to quiz Shiho on the Jikininki and what they were doing. She explained that they're not too different from some of the other yōkai we've encountered. Neither spirit nor living but stuck in some in-between state, Jikininki are born from a strong greed manifested into an insatiable hunger. They will feast on anything although human remains are their favourite cuisine and they are drawn to them when near. I asked if she knew how to get rid of them and she was surprisingly vague, saying only that normal techniques wouldn't work but she did know of one fail safe way to destroy them. Now with a slightly greater understanding of our foe I asked about the people of the village. The way they had acted the previous evening, leaving in such a bizarre fashion, not to mention the fact that they hadn't touched the food and had left the corpse suggested to me that they had done so in the knowledge that the Jikininki would come. Shiho agreed, saying that it was known that some people actively offer tribute to Jikininki for fear of the creatures. When I asked if that's what we were meant to be she shook her head saying it was doubtful. Jikininki tend not to take live prey preferring the dead and only really go for the living when they are disturbed whilst feasting. The fact that everybody left suggested that they knew of the creatures and expected them to come hence the food left out and their departure. Shiho was also certain that there would be no benefit to the people living there to feed the creatures live prey. She claims that Jikininki are dumb, single-minded creatures incapable of doing anything other than trying to satisfy their appetite and that there has never been a recorded incident of one actively helping humans nor one of them even providing a benefit to their presence. As such Shiho is convinced that the residents did not mean for us to be prey as it would serve them no benefit. Either way come the morning they had plenty of questions to answer after all, what sort of man invites people to stay at his house when he knows it's going to be invaded by yōkai?

At the first rays of sunlight we were met with the sight of the villagers returning in a similar manner to their departure. Again they came in single file wearing their hooded cloaks only this time in the light of day we could clearly recognise Kazuaki at the back of the party. They shuffled past the tree we were under without casting a glance towards us although the general tone of the party appeared to be in good spirits. Not missing our chance we gave chase and quickly caught up to the back of the line. Kazuaki was shocked to see us out wandering a couple of kilometres from his home but didn't appear to expect us to be dead. If anything he appeared to expect us to be asleep in his home. He was very cordial though and reiterated his promise to take us to the local town to collect fuel. He made no mention of the Jikininki and when pressed replied that their reason for leaving last night was a village tradition whereby they would spend the night passing on the news of the death to the other local villages. Neither I nor Shiho bought his tale and a quick flash of her blade informed him that we wanted real answers and that we were prepared to do anything to get them.

The threat of being stabbed was enough to make him talk and he immediately admitted that he knew about the Jikininki although he stressed that he thought we would be safe so long as we remained in our room and left them to their feast. He then told us that he would explain all once we got back to his house and he was away from the other villagers who were beginning to pull ahead.

Taking him at face value we continued the walk back to the village in silence and entered his house stealing him away from the rest of the residents via the use of Shiho's knife. The house was surprisingly clean considering what had happened the night before. There was no sign of the Jikininki nor of their feast. The food that had been placed around the room had vanished, the plates licked clean, whilst the coffin was now empty, no traces of the corpse remaining. It appears as if the appetite of Jikininki includes human bones too. The only sign of the night before was the broken door to our room which had been thoroughly torn apart much to Kazuaki's surprise. Getting back to questioning Kazuaki, he claimed that the whole village knows of the Jikininki but have no way of dealing with them. The first time they had come for a corpse, the family of the deceased had tried to fight back. It had resulted in a massacre. Since then nobody has tried fighting back and have instead left plenty of food for them in case they aren't satisfied with the body and still want meat. They believe that this offering prevents the Jikininki from coming after them and devouring them in their sleep. Their beliefs about the Jikininki were enough to make Shiho roll her eyes clearly dismayed about their lack of knowledge of the yōkai. I think she pitied them though. It was clear they were living in fear of the creatures yet had no way of fighting back against them although that didn't excuse leaving us trapped in the house with them. Focussing on their history, Shiho asked how long this had been going on and Kazuaki replied that it had been that way for decades, most people living there had no memory of a time when they didn't have to deal with the corpse-eaters. Her next question surprised me, she asked why they hadn't sought help from any of the nearby temples. Kazuaki replied there wasn't one nearby willing to come at such short notice of a death and when Shiho mentioned the one on the hill he looked confused. He replied that there had been a temple on the hill years before but it no longer stands. This statement intrigued both of us. We had definitely come across a temple last night on the very hill he was talking about. Pressed further he told us that the temple on the hill had been used by the locals but the priests running it were unreliable. He had been told stories that they would charge excessive prices for everything and even then people received less than they paid for or nothing at all. They had kept asking for more and more from the local villagers and eventually, unable to pay, the locals had abandoned the temple. That had been nearly fifty years ago though so he was unsure why Shiho was asking about it. Shiho listened to his tale carefully but silently until he had finished at which point she muttered something about insatiable greed and a hunger for money before she stood up, thanked Kazuaki for the information and said that we'd help them with their Jikininki problem. I still wanted to see some payback for abandoning us but Shiho appeared satisfied with merely scaring him with her knife and was, if anything, more keen to prevent it from happening to someone else than annoyed at him.

As soon as we had left his house I questioned Shiho on her thinking and she explained that she now knew how to get rid of the creatures. It obviously had something to do with that temple which Shiho confirmed telling me that the greed of the priests in their life had brought them back as Jikininki. Now that she knew where they were bound she could remove them. When I asked how she replied that she knew of an ancient ritual that would cure their hunger and banish them from this world. The only issue she had was that beginning the ritual would draw the ire of the Jikininki and they would inevitably attack us. The ritual in question is a Segaki, a presentation of rice and water which when done with a certain incantation can act as an eternal source of food for the creatures. Of course this can only happen if we can prevent the Jikininki from eating the rice whilst the ritual is performed. Not an easy task considering their insatiable hunger.

With the required items collected from the village, our host Kazuaki had been more than willing to help by providing the rice, we set off for the temple atop the hill once more. The day was turning into another pleasant one, masking the horrors of the night before, and despite the hot sun and the steeper incline on this side of the hill we made good time and were quickly back at the temple.

I had expected Shiho to simply start there and then with her ritual but instead she calmly knocked on the door which was answered by the same priest as yesterday, the first one who had been incredibly rude to us. Today his mood was much improved and he apologised to us, noticeably not for his behaviour yesterday evening but for 'showing us his true form'. Bizarrely Shiho took this in her stride and informed him that she was there to make their hunger stop. The priest looked as amazed as I was. From my experience rarely do you inform such a creature that you're planning to banish them but the priest appeared delighted with her statement. He begged Shiho to follow through on her offer and moved aside to invite us in. Crossing the threshold of the temple created a strange effect. It was almost as if there was some illusion on the place as the second we entered we saw that the temple, which had looked rather well cared for from the outside with golden statues and awash with food offerings inside, was actually in a rundown state. Timbers from the roof hung down rotting away, plant life crept through the floor and ensnared any columns whilst the food that we had seen turned out to be naught but ash. In the temple were two other priests, the other Jikininki, and both were just as apologetic as the first. I couldn't help but notice that one, the second to have answered the door yesterday, now carried a faint scar across his face, presumably from Shiho's blade.

The first priest informed the others of what Shiho was there to do and they were equally desperate for her to succeed although when she explained her plan to them they all warned her that they would not be able to control themselves at the sight of food and would eagerly wolf it down. Shiho acknowledged that this would be an issue and that she was aware of their nature. As such her plan was for me to hold them off whilst she conducted the ritual. I did ask if we could switch roles, not fancying my chances against the three creatures we'd faced the night before, but as Shiho so graciously pointed out to me, my knowledge of incantations isn't great and I wouldn't know what to say. Again, trying to think of a way whereby I wouldn't have to face them, I asked if the priests could simply leave whilst we did the ritual only to be informed that wasn't possible. If they left the temple they would transform and instantly return for the food Shiho was preparing. Sensing my distress one of the priests, the one we hadn't yet spoken with, offered me a walking stick as a crude weapon. It wasn't much but at least it would give me something to beat the creatures away with.

With the plan set, Shiho prepared herself in one corner whilst the priests huddled together in the opposite one with me in-between the two parties not feeling particularly confident. They had promised to try and prevent transforming for as long as possible but everyone there knew that their nature would quickly overcome them. Even so Shiho laid out three bowls, filled them with rice and began her incantation.

The second she revealed the rice I saw a change in the priests, their eyes went wide and I could see them sniffing the air. Saliva began to run from the corner of their mouths as they instantly became very fidgety. I told them to stay in their corner but they were clearly struggling to maintain control and within seconds the first of them transformed. Gone was the priest who had offered me my weapon, replaced by one of the terrifying Jikininki who immediately focussed on the rice bowls. Fortunately before it could move the first priest we had encountered threw his arms around its waist preventing it from leaping forward. The Jikininki, deprived of its food, turned on him and quickly wrestled him to the floor. I couldn't watch to see which of them won out any longer as the third priest, the friendlier one from yesterday, transformed, also immediately focussing on Shiho. It leapt towards her, taking just two great bounds to cross the temple floor and, without thinking, I brought the walking stick down with a crack on its head. The Jikininki collapsed to the floor, spinning around to face me and snarling, baring its blood encrusted fangs. I then heard the same snarling coming from the corner and realised that the final Jikininki had transformed leaving me facing the three of them. Behind me I could still hear Shiho going about her work so, unsure of how to hold them off, I started slicing the walking stick through the air in front of me in the hope of frightening the creatures. It was a plan that didn't work. The one I'd struck on the head leapt at me and again I tried to strike it but it managed to catch the end of the walking stick in its mouth as it jumped. It then crashed into me knocking me to the ground where it landed on top of me digging both of its clawed hands into my shoulders. Fighting for my life I still held the walking stick in front of my face which kept its head at bay as it tried to snap at me. I was unsure where the other two Jikininki were, my only thoughts were on my own survival although I'm certain that they would've gone for Shiho and her rice bowls. The breath of the Jikininki was atrocious, a vile mixture of rotting meat and blood and I could feel it slowly inching its way closer to me, the claws in my shoulders digging in fast as it attempted to lick my face. The pain was unbearable and I felt like I was going to pass out when suddenly I heard Shiho stop.

To my amazement, the Jikininki that was on top of me simply faded away leaving nothing but ten bloodied wounds to my shoulders where its claws had been. Shiho came straight over to check if I was alright, puling me up where I could see that the same had happened to the other two Jikininki leaving us alone in the abandoned temple. The only other thing there were the three rice bowls, each now noticeably only half full despite Shiho filling them to the brim. She explained that by providing them food she could banish their hunger meaning they were no longer cursed to an unending existence. As such they simply melted away. Before we did anything else she checked my shoulders and assured me that there was nothing serious about the injuries I'd received and that they'd heal quickly now that the Jikininki were no more.

Leaving the temple we noticed something that we hadn't before. I'm not even sure if they had been there until that moment but outside the entrance to the abandoned temple now stood three gravestones next to one another. Shiho paused before them and bowed her head. They belonged to the three priests that had maintained the temple over fifty years ago. Their greed in life had turned into an insatiable hunger in death but now, thanks to Shiho, they could truly rest. As too could the villagers in the valley. We returned to the village and informed Kazuaki of our victory which delighted him. Whilst we had been away he had fetched some fuel for our car which we thanked him for although he declared it was the least he could do. That's certainly true given how they left us for dead but Shiho wouldn't let me shout at him. How long it will take for them to believe that the Jikininki have actually gone is another thing entirely. Presumably the next time there's a death they will continue their strange practice only to find that the body is still there the next morning. That will come as quite a shock to them I'd imagine.

We returned to our car by the same route we'd taken the previous day but I noticed that as we reached the summit of the hill Shiho refused to look towards the temple yet when I did I couldn't see the building anymore, only the three gravestones standing watch over the valley. It's odd, the Jikininki were the first yōkai I've encountered that genuinely didn't want to exist. It's almost like they themselves were victims too. I wonder where the first Jikininki came from. It appears to be a form of punishment yet who's doing the punishing? Where did the first yōkai come from and why? There's probably answers in Shiho's copy of the Gozu yet somehow I don't think she's going to tell me.

With the car refuelled we were back under way and incredibly I received a form of apology from Shiho. She apologised for not listening to me and leaving the Jikininki to their feast the night before saying that they would've left us alone and I wouldn't have ended up injured. She did however point out that we wouldn't have been there at all if I hadn't let the fuel run out. I guess it's the best apology I'm going to get out of her.

This has definitely been the shortest of the road trips I've taken with Shiho but unfortunately it has been cut short. It's my birthday coming up and my family have decided to visit me in Kyoto to celebrate. That means I have to return there and leave Shiho to continue her work. I did invite her to come back to Kyoto with me but she's become intrigued by a woman who claims to have entered a game of hide and seek with a spirit. I can't say that there's much to it but Shiho seems to think that the spirit is dangerous and the woman requires expert help. I wish I could be there to help out, or at least document it but as it is we must go our separate ways for now.

Shiho's destination is Aomori meaning we're heading in opposite directions so she couldn't even drive me back. Instead I had to leave her at the station and take the train back to Kyoto. Much like during the summer it feels oddly quiet around here without her.

Today was the day my parents and sister arrived in Kyoto to celebrate my birthday. It was great seeing them again. I guess it was April when I last saw them. It also gave me a chance to properly talk to my sister about Hanako-san and whether there have been any additional incidents at her school. She told me that there had been no further deaths, although those that had occurred officially remain unsolved. Despite not killing anybody, Hanako-san has been busy. According to my sister a number of the school bullies have found themselves traumatised after visiting her bathroom and Hanako-san has told her that she had attacked them. I'm still not certain about her having contact with such a spirit but it's true that she hasn't yet been harmed. I guess I'm in no place to talk either what with the yōkai I've seen since.

Shiho also called today for my birthday. It was a surprise as she doesn't normally go in for birthdays or anything like that. Her investigation into the spirit haunting the woman appears to be over although she said little about it. Sakura sent me a message and a gift too. That one was a surprise. It was clear she didn't really know what she was doing and was very awkward but it's the thought that counts. She even gave me a new diary in preparation for next year. I really can't figure her out at all. I guess I've got to learn when their birthdays are now although I don't know if Sakura even has one nor what she could possibly want.

My family's stay in Kyoto was short but pleasant and I will admit feeling disappointed as they left this morning. Without Shiho being here and them leaving I certainly feel quite empty.

Still, the alone time has given me a chance to jot down a basic draft for articles on the Tenome and the Jikininki. The editor tends to prefer the ghost based tales but he liked the one on Mika so it's possible that these two will suit his tastes. I hope so, even if one is accepted then I'll only need one further article in the next six weeks.

Again I've heard from Shiho, she's returned to Tokyo after her last case but assures me that she'll be active again soon. I hope that when she does take jobs again, she'll get in touch.

Footprints in the Snow

October 4th

Shiho turned up at my doorstep today unannounced and in great spirits. It appears that she has been approached with a new job that she's quite excited by. From what I can tell she's not due to start for at least another month but wants to get going to see if she can pick up any work beforehand. She also says that the chance to get away can be considered a late birthday present and that we were going to the snowy land of Hokkaido. I must admit, it's an area of Japan which I've never visited but Shiho assures me that it's a stunning part of the country filled with fascinating types of yōkai for me to meet. I can't say whether they will be fascinating, knowing Shiho that actually means dangerous but I was excited to be back on the road with her. There can be no doubt that my life is far more exciting when I'm with her.

With a plan set, I quickly packed and together we began the long drive north. As usual Shiho travelled light but was happy for me to load multiple bags into the car which she drove. Unusually for Shiho, she's taking the fastest route this time and it shouldn't take long before we make the crossing onto Hokkaido.

Having arrived in Hokkaido we've journeyed further north than I expected. I thought we would've stopped at Sapporo to see if we could find anything there given its status as the largest city on Hokkaido but instead Shiho kept pushing onwards until the world became white as snow piled up all around. We travelled towards Wakkanai but stopped this evening at a small village on the way, hoping to gain some rest. I don't know why we didn't stop at Sapporo, this far north there aren't that many people and it seems less likely that anybody would report a yōkai. It does appear that Shiho knows the roads around here. I think she must know every town in Japan by now and I'm sure she knows what she's looking for.

The village itself is very picturesque especially with the constant snowfall making it appear like a winter wonderland, and I considered the place to be quite quaint. There are few amenities, it only has one inn so we booked a room and before we settled down for the night Shiho insisted on visiting the local temple and other places of interest. We set out on foot, slowly trudging through the fresh snow. I wasn't surprised that Shiho wanted to visit the temple, she often did claiming that it was an ideal place to find out more about the spirits that inhabited the local area. This one was quite similar to many that we'd been to before with one key difference that Shiho noted. In a small box outside stood four ornate statues, similar to the jizo statues that you see in most temples but these were clearly something else. They were deliberately kept away from the temple and unlike many others had been left to the elements leaving them heavily worn. One of the statues was cracked too giving all four a rundown appearance. I asked Shiho if she knew anything about them but she shrugged saying it was probably something unique to the village but she was surprised that they had been left outside and untendered. The priests inside couldn't give us any useful leads so instead we returned to the inn for a traditional meal and a good night's sleep.

We woke to the sound of screaming this morning. If I'm honest I think the whole village did. A woman was running through the streets wailing for her child who had vanished overnight. There were others in the village that tried to calm her saying that her son had simply wandered off and would be found before the day was out. In these conditions he'd be lucky to see out the day being only ten years old and the snow falling heavily. Desperate to help find him we joined the search party of around fifty locals hoping to offer assistance but there was no trace of him. Fresh snowfall had masked any tracks that we could follow and nobody seemed to have any clue why he would wander off in the middle of the night. It was clear that he had left of his own accord, there were no signs of a break-in at his house. The search lasted all day and as a thanks for our help the inn offered us a free night's board and lodging so we could continue the hunt tomorrow. It was nice of them considering we didn't find anything that could help. Shiho and I are the only people from out of town too and therefore easy to blame but nobody was suspicious of us.

I'll admit I'm running out of hope that we aren't searching for a corpse. I don't see how anyone can survive outside in this temperature for this long but we'll try again tomorrow.

After yesterday's fruitless search, today Shiho took the lead based on her investigative expertise, and instead of scouring the wilderness outside the village she decided to interview the family and the boy's friends hoping that they might be able to shed some light on why he had suddenly disappeared. The rest of the village would continue the search of the surrounding countryside.

To begin with we tried to get information from the family but it was as you'd expect. They all said that he was a good boy who'd never run away of his own accord. When asked if they thought anyone in the village could've kidnapped him they were shocked by the very suggestion. The idea that someone in the village could've been responsible was alien to them and they were swift to tell us that it wasn't that sort of village. Nobody living there would want to harm him and they get so few visitors that it seemed unlikely any strangers would've whisked him away. They also referred to the fact that there were no signs of a struggle but didn't appreciate it when Shiho theorized that he could've opened the door for his possible kidnapper replying that he knew better than to talk to strangers in the middle of the night.

When we left the boy's family I could see Shiho was puzzled. She told me that she was troubled by the idea that the boy had simply vanished without a trace. Sure people wander off and go missing from time to time but she didn't believe the boy would've been able to get far from the village and should've been found by yesterday's search. It did seem unlikely that he hadn't been found considering the size of the village and the near constant snowfall which would sap a young boy's strength very quickly. I asked if she suspected something out of the norm and although she didn't answer, the glint in her eye told me that she did. I guess it's only natural that even out here in the back of beyond Shiho would stumble across a supernatural occurrence.

With the boy's family offering little we moved on to his friends starting with his best friend who lived further down the street. His mother invited us in and told us that her husband was still out searching along with most of the village. Their son, Kiyonori, meanwhile was allowed to play in their garden. The mother had seen and heard nothing the night the boy vanished and agreed with the general consensus that nobody in the village could be responsible but even so allowed Shiho to question her son to try and find out more about the missing boy. She showed us to the garden where he played, slowly building a snowman in the fresh snow.

As always Shiho was the first to question him but acted surprisingly gentle, not wanting to suggest that she thought his friend had been murdered by a ghost, or something worse. She can be friendly when she wants to be although I still find it odd seeing her like that. It seems to be only for her interactions with children, I guess the softer touch with them is probably more constructive. Again he added to the picture of the boy being well liked and couldn't say anything of any use. That was until we began to leave when he remembered that the boy had mentioned talking to some woman that he'd never seen, or heard of, before, an unlikely occurrence in such a small village. Shiho immediately asked for a description of the woman but there was little that Kiyonori could tell us. All he could give us was the fact that the boy had told him she was tall. It wasn't much to go on but Shiho set about asking anyone she met about this woman. Nobody had an answer as to who she was nor where she'd come from. In fact nobody in the village had seen this woman making me wonder if the boy had been mistaken given that the missing boy's mother proclaimed it to be impossible that he'd talk to a strange woman.

We waited for the search parties to return to ask them but they too hadn't seen this illusive woman leaving us stumped. The search parties still hadn't found any trace and after two whole days of searching few still had hope of finding the boy alive.

It is exactly as Shiho thought and I feared. The disappearance of that boy was due to a yōkai and as I write Kiyonori's life hangs in the balance.

It all started this morning when desperate to find out more about this mystery woman, Shiho had abandoned using her description and was instead asking about any strange woman seen in the village figuring that was the best way to gain information. Again there was no knowledge of any new people in the village, except us, which led us back to Kiyonori as we looked to confirm our facts.

We found the boy in his back garden again admiring and improving his snowman despite the newly laid layer of fresh snow that coated his garden. Again Shiho asked him about this woman and he repeated everything he had told us the day before, that in the days leading up to his disappearance the missing boy had mentioned talking to a tall woman. I looked at Shiho and we both agreed that there was no way a stranger could hide herself in the village for a number of days without anyone other than the missing boy noticing her. We asked Kiyonori for a better description but he had gone pale and was staring at the gate which led from their garden to the street. He pointed towards it and we both looked but there was nothing there so we turned back to him, again asking for a description. This time he gave a full one. Without ever moving his eyes from the garden gate he described an impossibly large woman, at least eight feet by his reckoning with long black hair who wore a white summer dress and matching wide brimmed hat with no shoes despite the cold. Her face was friendly enough but something about it seemed scary to him, off-putting as if she was somehow evil. Asking how he'd suddenly been able to provide this description he again pointed to the gate and whispered "because she's there". We both spun round but again there was nothing there so we put it down to the child's imagination. He then told us that she was making an awful noise which he said sounded like she was saying "po" over and over in rapid succession almost as if she wasn't speaking but making the sound involuntarily. There was nothing at the gate but he grabbed hold of my arm and attempted to hide behind me when he screamed and shouted that she was coming for him.

Again we turned to face the gate and although it had opened we put that down to the slight breeze. It was a rather flimsy gate and it wouldn't have taken much of a breeze to open it. I looked at Shiho quizzically who was also looking puzzled by Kiyonori's fear. That's when we saw something I thought impossible. In the snow, just inside the garden we saw a fresh human footprint, then a second one appeared quite a way in front as if something was taking giant strides towards us. I heard Shiho whisper "it's invisible" to nobody in particular and I felt Kiyonori's grip on my arm tighten as he panicked. I asked Shiho what it was but she didn't answer instead she took a number of steps towards the oncoming footprints and stopped around five meters ahead of us, halting the creature noticeable only by the two footprints that appeared directly before her. It was clear that, like me, Shiho also couldn't see this thing but she spoke to it calmly and firmly as if she was trying to convince it that she could. She told it to leave, informing it that we didn't mean any harm to it but that she couldn't let it reach Kiyonori. She offered to let the thing leave peacefully the way it had come but all the time there was no answer from whatever stood before her although I have no idea if it could speak. Growing impatient Shiho asked if it accepted her terms and this time she received a response. We watched horrified as Shiho was thrown backwards as if struck heavily, she spun through the air and landed a good ten meters away. It was the sort of force that no human would've been able to produce yet the thing in the garden hadn't moved. It's feet had remained perfectly still proving that whatever it was, it wasn't human and despite being invisible, it was capable of interacting with physical things. The sudden pain in my arm as Kiyonori gripped onto me even tighter pulled me back to worrying about what it would do but even so I stepped forward eager not to let it harm the child. I watched the snow carefully as I saw one footprint appear four meters away, then another three meters away. Another couple appeared and then I knew that I was less than a meter in front of the thing. Breathing heavily I looked straight ahead of me, seeing nothing but the open gate beyond, and asked what it wanted. Not too surprisingly I didn't receive an answer but I felt a slight rush of wind as whatever it was must've raised its arm ready to strike me the same way it had Shiho. I took a deep breath to brace for the impact but heard a whistling sound before a snowball exploded just in front of me, the snow sticking to the air and floating impossibly. I saw Shiho to the side of me looking on amazed and preparing a second snowball and then I realized what she'd hit. Six feet into the air just before me, her snowball had hit the creature's shoulder and as the snow trickled down the outline of an armpit and dress strap became apparent. This thing, which clearly Kiyonori could see, stopped, presumably checking to confirm that we could see it and a second snowball struck its back revealing little new information other than confirming it was definitely humanoid. I heard Shiho shout that we needed to see it so without thinking I kicked out showering the legs of the creature with snow as Shiho threw another snowball. The snow I kicked up revealed the shins and knees of what looked like a woman although she was clearly tall whilst Shiho's throw was higher and caught what appeared to be the rim of a hat that stretched well out to be level with her shoulder. I continued to kick snow at the creature but suddenly the snow fell to the ground as if it had shaken it off leaving us able to see it once more. I heard Shiho shout to ask where it had gone as she ran over but there were no new footprints and as she reached to grab at the space where the creature had stood her hands passed through the air uninterrupted. She asked again where it was desperately scanning the garden until her eyes fell on Kiyonori still clutching onto me and asked him if he could still see it. He replied that he couldn't and Shiho relaxed slightly telling him to inform her when he next saw the tall woman before leading him back to the house where his mother had heard the shouting and was coming to check on him. Shiho explained briefly what had happened and that she could help but asked Kiyonori to draw what he had seen reasoning that she needed to know what it was she was facing.

Kiyonori's picture was crude but was much as he'd described previously, a tall woman, long black hair, white summer dress and hat but he'd included a manic smile that gave the whole image a demonic look. When he'd finished he showed us the drawing and Shiho sighed and whispered that it was going to be a long night. I asked her if she knew what it was and she replied that she had a suspicion but couldn't be certain as she'd never encountered one before. She thought it was a Hachishakusama. I asked what that was and her reply wasn't entirely clear as she wasn't sure herself. She'd heard tales of them but had never seen one but then again few people had. The tales suggest that only the victims of a Hachishakusama can see them and that their victims are exclusively children. As such little is known about them, nobody has ever successfully conversed with one and beyond the kidnap of their victims it's not known what else they do. It's not even clear why they want to kidnap children or indeed if they kill them although Shiho is pretty certain that they do. Her theories ranged from them being a type of onryō that longed for its own missing child to something else entirely that feeds off the unspent years of the child it takes, sustaining itself for another lifetime which would make them incredibly old. What was clear was that they have an impressive array of skills. As pointed out by Shiho, the Hachishakusama is a physical being, it can be struck with snowballs yet it remains invisible to any adults and despite having the ability to kill Shiho had chosen not to yet hadn't held back when striking her suggesting it wasn't afraid of encountering adults yet had little desire to kill them. It also clearly has the ability to vanish at will having disappeared once covered in snow. Shiho claimed to know of two other skills listed under the Hachishakusama in her Gozu book, the first was an impossible speed and the second was the ability to mimic voices of humans which it uses to lure children by pretending to be their parents. Adding it all together it makes this thing an apex predator for children and I had no idea how Shiho planned to stop it since she couldn't even see it and I doubted the yōkai would be dumb enough to fall for the same snow trick twice. Kiyonori's mother followed this up with the obvious assumption that the creature would be back. Shiho nodded grimly. She said that Hachishakusama never give up on prey unless they have a strong reason to. She reckoned that the woman would return that evening to try to steal Kiyonori away given that he now was the only person capable of seeing the yōkai. His mother was rightly terrified and asked if there was anything we could do since we'd somehow managed to drive the Hachishakusama away in the garden. Shiho agreed that we would stay and help but said she needed to gather some things first but we'd be back before night fell doubting that the spirit would return during the day.

As soon as we left I asked Shiho what she was expecting that evening when the Hachishakusama returned and what she could possibly do to get rid of it. She replied by telling me the only method mentioned in her book of yōkai. According to Shiho the Hachishakusama will return overnight when her prey is sleepy in the hope that it will be able to entice them to go with her. She said that the only method she knew to prevent this was to lock Kiyonori in a room that night and wait for the creature to appear. It would then try to entice him to allow her in so that she could steal him away. It was crucial that he didn't respond to her. I asked what we were trying to find since that only involved Kiyonori not opening the door. She replied that in her experience scared children didn't think straight and couldn't be trusted not to let the creature in. It was therefore imperative that she took measures in case that happened. I asked what her plan was and she replied that she needed rice and a statue of the Buddha. I must've looked confused because she replied that those were the items mentioned in her book. Desperate for further knowledge we called Sakura for her input but even she admitted to not knowing anything about Hachishakusama although she was keen to know if they would see her as a potential victim. Quite why Sakura would want one of these things after her is beyond me, but so are many things about her although Shiho suggested quite earnestly that she might fancy eating one. What was clear was that we were going to have to use Shiho's limited knowledge on this one.

Finding the items Shiho needed was fairly simple, large bags of rice could be found in the local store and the family themselves had a Buddha statue. Even so Shiho insisted on taking the rice to the local temple to get it blessed. Apparently the Hachishakusama is entirely adverse to religion, presumably something about them being demonic creatures not mixing too well with religion in general. When we reached the temple Shiho immediately told them what the blessing was for and although they were scared they gave her what she wanted. They also handed her the cracked statue that we'd noticed the other day saying that she could trap it in there. Shiho accepted it although neither she nor they could explain how she was meant to do that but they were aware of an old legend of a child killer, the spirit of which was originally trapped within. Quite whether that's true I don't know, Shiho appeared unimpressed and they admitted it was only a local tale.

With that task done we returned to Kiyonori's house and waited for night to come. Shiho had chosen a fairly large room for her task which we duly emptied leaving only a single bed inside. She placed a bowl of rice in each corner and the statue at the foot of the bed. Confused about how we would be able to help out if needed Shiho said that we'd be staying just outside the room all night so that if Kiyonori did open the door we'd be on hand to act before the Hachishakusama could carry out its vile work.

When night came we locked Kiyonori in the room and Shiho and I took up our positions outside the door. I offered to take turns keeping watch with Shiho but she refused saying that she would stay awake all night if she had to, the Hachishakusama was too dangerous to lose time waking her. Not wanting her to suffer alone I agreed that I would do the same and together we waited.

That's the situation we're currently in. I'm sat on the floor writing this whilst Shiho sits opposite me, the door to the bedroom in between us. Occasionally I ask for reminders about information she's dropped throughout the day and she's happy to repeat things to me. I don't think she fully understands my desire to document everything as it occurs but at least she doesn't complain. It distracts her from the cracked statue which she stares at endlessly trying to work out what secrets it holds.

I'll admit I'm feeling tired now. I might take a quick nap so long as Shiho is fine with it and hope that the Hachishakusama doesn't pay us a visit while I sleep.

I was woken by a noise tapping on the door to the bedroom and immediately sprung up worried that the Hachishakusama might be standing before me. In the darkness my eyes met Shiho's and she assured me that the noises were Kiyonori tapping on the door trying to speak to us. Apparently he'd been doing it a lot, complaining about the Hachishakusama calling "po" through the window and tapping on the glass whilst looking at him. It had now vanished and he was wanting to get out. I asked Shiho why she didn't respond and she replied that she couldn't. Speaking to him would mean that she'd have to do this again tomorrow night. When I pointed out that he claimed the creature had gone she simply replied that it hadn't. It was instead forming a new plan and would still be hanging around, eager to strike before the night was out. That's the trouble with something you can't see, it could be anywhere. It was presumably in the house somewhere just biding its time watching us, waiting for the perfect opportunity to strike.

Another hour or so passed with relative silence until we heard Kiyonori speaking again. This time he was far calmer and sounded quite relieved about something. We didn't know why but then we heard what he was saying, "I'm coming mother" and I saw Shiho's face drop. She'd told us how Hachishakusama could mimic voices and it slowly dawned on me that Kiyonori was having a conversation not with his mother but with the invisible woman instead. I saw Shiho clench the statue tightly, its purpose still unknown, and climb to her feet as we saw the door handle slowly turn before the door opened a crack. As soon as it opened Kiyonori started to scream and I realised that the Hachishakusama must've been standing directly between myself and Shiho without us realising. I guess the only reason it didn't attack us was that its sole focus was on Kiyonori and nothing else. Before I could do anything I heard Shiho yell at Kiyonori to get back before she leapt at the doorway. Incredibly she hit something which must've been the Hachishakusama as she tumbled through into the room beyond struggling against an unseen foe. I burst into the room seconds later desperate to help any way I could and saw Shiho struggling on the floor, lying on her back with her legs wrapped round something that couldn't be seen whilst Kiyonori had scurried away into the far corner. I heard Shiho grunting before I realised she was asking me to help pin the creature down. I yelled at Kiyonori to go find his mother and then charged at whatever Shiho was struggling with, trying to avoid the invisible limbs that had dealt such a fierce blow to Shiho in the garden. The task wasn't easy, and being unable to see the Hachishakusama, I wasn't sure whether it or Shiho had the advantage. Instead I just aimed for where Shiho was, throwing myself at her and hoping to hit the creature. To my horror I felt an arm connect with me as I got close and I spun across the room into the corner spilling one of Shiho's rice bowls which scattered across the floor. I heard Shiho moan that it too was on its back and I'd just wasted any chance of subduing it although quite how it was my fault I wasn't sure. Before I could climb to my feet I saw that Shiho was right as the Hachishakusama clearly found its feet and staggered upright carrying Shiho on its back. She desperately clung on trying to choke the creature but it slammed her back into the wall and she was forced to release her grip dropping to the floor. With nobody attached to the creature we had no idea where it was but I heard Shiho mutter "black rice" and looked at the floor towards the rice I'd inadvertently spilt. Incredibly the grains closest to the door were turning jet black and I figured that they must be closest to the creature. Not thinking about the consequences I hurled myself at the area where the rice was turning colour and to my amazement hit something solid which must've been the midriff of the Hachishakusama as we both fell to the floor. Unlike Shiho I hadn't maintained my grip on the creature and I quickly felt a pair of strong hands around my neck attempting to squeeze the life out of me. Fortunately Shiho was on hand to deliver a firm kick at the creature forcing it to roll away into a corner, the entire rice bowl turning black as it landed next to it. I clambered to my feet and joined Shiho in front of the door blocking any escape for the creature which we'd trapped in the corner. I whispered to Shiho to ask how we were going to get it into the statue to which she replied she was still working on it. Then we heard a scream from upstairs. Confused Shiho kicked some of the spilt rice towards the corner and it remained white. She swore at her stupidity, forgetting that the creature could vanish entirely before she scooped up a bowl of rice and ran out of the room. I did the same and followed her upstairs towards the screaming.

We didn't even reach the top of the stairs when we saw the odd site of Kiyonori being carried through the air as if the Hachishakusama had simply hoisted him over her shoulder. His mother was following screaming but was unable to catch up as the creature was surprisingly fast. Shiho was quick to react and placed herself in the middle of the staircase blocking the creature's way. Like before the creature moved to push her aside but with Kiyonori on its shoulder Shiho could guess where the blow was coming from and ducked out of the way catching some part of the creature, I'm guessing it was her arm from the way her shoulder jerked dropping Kiyonori to the floor. As she caught the creature's arm Shiho pushed away from the wall with her foot and caused both her and the Hachishakusama to crash over the banister and down onto the floor below. It wasn't a long drop but it would've been enough that she'd have definitely felt it. The only hope was that the Hachishakusama would've felt the impact too.

Not sure how best to help I threw my rice bowl over the two of them and it immediately turned black as it struck the Hachishakusama giving us the vague outline of the gigantic woman as the grains covered her. She squirmed violently as if the rice was burning her and temporarily forgot about Shiho who was able to roll away and observe. I screamed at Shiho asking how we were going to kill it but she just stared at the creature watching as it dissolved into thin air.

Carefully we all huddled round Kiyonori making sure that the creature wasn't there by spreading a ring of rice around us. We waited out the rest of the night like that and by the time morning came the Hachishakusama hadn't returned despite the fact that it could have easily fought its way through us. Kiyonori's mother asked if that was that and whether the creature had gone but Shiho shook her head saying it would be back to continue the hunt and that all we'd succeeded in doing was anger it. Both Kiyonori and his mother were scared, rightly so considering the creature was hunting the boy and refused to be separated from Shiho until the Hachishakusama was stopped. Agreeing that this was probably for the best Shiho allowed them to come with us as we went back to the temple to ask about the statue, carrying the spare rice just in case.

There had been another snowfall over night so we were able to easily check that the Hachishakusama wasn't sneaking up on us as we made our way to the temple. Fortunately there were no unexplained footprints although at one point Kiyonori did claim that he could hear it calling to him on the wind. This seemed to spur Shiho on and she forced us to go even faster for fear of being ambushed by the ghostly woman. The temple priests weren't that surprised to see us again but were concerned when Shiho told them that the Hachishakusama wouldn't be far behind. Unsurprisingly they asked why she had led it there and she replied that she needed the other three statues from the case outside. They fetched them immediately and Shiho explained that she thought the broken one had previously been used to house the Hachishakusama as a form of prison but now that it was broken the creature was free. Quite how it had ended up in there she didn't know but her plan was to trap it in one of the other three that were still whole. When she had worked out that it was a prison I have no idea. Maybe she'd always thought that after the story we were told yesterday. The others agreed but when I took Shiho aside I saw that there was doubt etched across her face. Her mind seemed even more clouded when I pointed out that if the broken statue housed the Hachishakusama then whatever was trapped in the other three might be even worse. She acknowledged that it was a good point but admitted that she'd never heard of a different yōkai that could be kept imprisoned in a statue. She said it was more likely that whoever originally trapped it did so via a ritual and will have used four statues just to increase the chance of it being dragged into one. Even if there was something else trapped in the statues she saw no other way of saving the boy so I agreed that it was worth the risk.

We allowed Shiho to set up her trap, first creating a ring of rice around the centre of the room and placing the three unbroken statues equidistant round the circle. She then told Kiyonori to remain in the exact centre of the circle and not to move whilst the rest of us took up positions around the circle. She claimed that the prayers of the temple priests along with the rice would be enough to drive the creature into a statue so they would pray whilst me, Shiho and Kiyonori's mother would throw rice at the creature. I'll admit I thought it sounded like a long shot but with nothing else I was willing to help out however I could.

It wasn't long before the Hachishakusama arrived, Kiyonori informing us he could hear it calling "po" through the open temple door. The priests looked worried but Shiho told them to keep calm and that their prayers would keep them safe. As instructed they began repeating the same short prayer over and over at first quietly

188

but growing louder as the rice closest to the door in Shiho's circle turned black as the Hachishakusama crossed over it. It was clear that Kiyonori was frightened and he closed his eyes tightly refusing to even look at the creature which stalked him. Watching him carefully Shiho judged when the creature was getting close to him and threw some rice grains watching as they bounced off the invisible woman and turned black as they fell to the floor. Seeing that was enough to increase the volume of the prayer as the temple priests realised that Shiho had been telling the truth. With the location of the Hachishakusama discovered by Shiho's rice throwing both myself and Kiyonori's mother got involved throwing our rice at the creature until it was under constant bombardment by the three of us. I don't know if the Hachishakusama is allergic or something but it began to writhe about in pain as the rice struck it, the colour changing rice on the floor testimony to its wild movements. When she believed that the creature had fallen to the floor, Shiho ran over and dumped the remaining rice out of her sack onto it. That seemed to cause it to snap as part of its illusion fell away and suddenly we could all hear it. It wasn't like I expected at all. Like Kiyonori had said it was constantly repeating the word "po" although it was rapid yet softly spoken and despite this, the noise reverberated around the room causing an increase in the volume of the prayers to counter. Following Shiho's lead I too unloaded the remainder of my rice on the creature which continued to writhe on the floor as the rice blackened. The prayers reached a cacophony as the shape of the woman became visible under the rice and then it scuttled away almost as if it was being vacuumed up as it slid towards one of the statues, darkening the rice around it before everything became perfectly still. For a moment there was complete silence as we wondered whether it would reappear then Shiho asked Kiyonori if he could still see it. When he replied no Shiho took the statue to him and asked if he could hear the Hachishakusama inside. He nodded saying it was still making its "po" sound but was clearly inside. I don't know if it was the rice, the prayer or a mixture of both but somehow Shiho's plan had worked and the Hachishakusama had been trapped within the statue.

Kiyonori's mother thanked us profusely for saving her son although there was going to be no such joy for the missing boy's family, he was forever lost, a victim of the Hachishakusama like so many before. The temple priests thanked us too although they refused to keep the statue with them saying that it was not safe there as it had already escaped once and that should it ever break free it would target Kiyonori yet again. Shiho agreed and reluctantly accepted their advice that it would be better for her to take it with her. I suggested that we drive to the ocean and toss it in there but Shiho seemed less than impressed with the idea saying the water could break the statue so now we have an odd passenger in the back seat of our car as we drive. I have no idea what Shiho plans to do with it, if she wants to keep it that's on her but I wouldn't fancy living with an angry invisible woman who could break free at any moment. Maybe Sakura can find a way of dealing with it permanently but I don't know if Shiho will ever allow her try. I guess the only positive is that we can no longer hear it but the thing gives me the creeps. I still wonder what else might have already been in that statue but if something did escape, it hasn't made itself known. I also wonder who, or what, it was that first trapped the Hachishakusama and how it managed to escape.

After agreeing to take the statue with us the villagers were keen for us to be off, fearing the creature would return, so we weren't able to rest there another night. Instead we continued to push north towards Wakkanai. Hopefully things will be more peaceful there.

October 17th

We've spent the past few days in Wakkanai without looking for yōkai, at least Shiho doesn't appear to have been actively searching them out and has declared this a mini-holiday, the late birthday present I was promised. I'll admit that I like it here although it is very cold.

The break has given me a chance to get some feedback from my editor. He likes the two articles I sent him but is unsure whether they fit the kind of thing they normally go for. The Hachishakusama will definitely be up his street so I'll use the break we're having here to write up an article on it.

Speaking of the Hachishakusama, the statue that houses it still creeps me out although we can't hear it making its awful noise and it doesn't do anything. It isn't helped by the fact that Shiho doesn't trust anyone else with it. She refuses to have it posted back to Tokyo for fear of it breaking and dislikes leaving it in the car overnight. Instead she brings it into the hotel and leaves it in our room. I'm thankful that we can't hear it anymore or it would be unbearable. Even so I still dislike it watching over us as we sleep given that I can still feel those cold hands wrapped around my neck.

Shiho declared an end to our mini-vacation by suggesting that she wants to visit Sapporo. She wouldn't say why but she said she was in no great rush to get there. I guess it has something to do with the job she's slowly gearing up for. Either way I'm happy to visit and see what we can find there.

I've used the time to finish up my article on the Hachishakusama and send it across. Hopefully that one will be accepted quickly. The creature, unfortunately, remains with us although I'm thinking Shiho might be coming round to my idea of simply tossing it into the ocean, even she's admitted that it freaks her out a bit having it so close all the time.

Of Monsters and Men

November 3rd

Our reason for coming to Hokkaido was made clear to me today. It hasn't solely been to get away from the city at all but because Shiho has been invited to take part in a hunt for a legendary creature that supposedly lives in the Kitami Mountains. She says she was approached by a small band of five hunters when I was back in Kyoto who are attempting to capture a yōkai called a Yuki-onna. Shiho says that she's never encountered one such is their rarity yet for a long time she'd heard of one that lives in that mountain range. She's even visited the area a couple for times before but never seen the creature making her doubt its existence.

Apparently a Yuki-onna is a spirit that has perfectly adapted to the snowy conditions found in Hokkaido and very little else is known about them. Shiho is excited about possibly finding one though saying that she couldn't pass up such an opportunity to join other hunters. She says that we're going to meet the group in Asahikawa in a couple of days and that they'll be able to explain more.

That's why we've been in Sapporo, Shiho's been purchasing supplies for the hunt.

We met the rest of the hunting party today in Asahikawa. They had been here for a couple of days already preparing. There were five of them, all male with a clear leader, Takaaki, who was the oldest. The other four were a ragtag group of followers who each filled a particular role within the team. There was a navigator, Hideo, whose job was to successfully steer us through the mountains, a marksman, Atsuhiko, in case we came across any animal predators, a local expert, Kazunari, who had conducted many searches for the Yuki-onna and a camera man, Hirohide, who was going to film the entire adventure. With Shiho acting as the expert on spirits we had a full team ready for anything. Apparently I get in on account of Shiho although I was surprised by the group. They didn't appear to be the sort of people that Shiho would normally spend time with and I'm not convinced they're hunters in the same manner as Shiho.

As evening fell, Kazunari told us what he knew of the Yuki-onna and what we could expect. He claimed that the Yuki-onna was a snow woman who never left any signs of her presence but had been known to freeze people to death on sight. He said that she lived somewhere in the mountains and that she was to blame for the surprising number of hikers that vanish in the area and he recounted a tale of one of his previous adventures when he'd been the only member to survive. He claims that tales of the Yuki-onna living in the area have been around for decades, possibly centuries but that nobody had ever secured credible evidence of its existence. He claims that people have seen it but to get the proof others would want you'd need to get close to the spirit and that it would kill any that did. The rest of the team were hooked on his every word especially Takaaki but Shiho appeared sceptical. After he'd finished she pulled him aside to ask if he'd ever actually encountered the Yuki-onna in person. It didn't take long for him to admit that he hadn't but said he liked to tell the tale to keep hiking parties visiting the area. I asked Shiho if she thought the whole thing was a hoax but she admitted that the tales of a Yuki-onna in these parts far outlived the guide's stories. That alone was enough for her to be convinced that something was out there in the mountains but she couldn't be sure what. We agreed not to rat out Kazunari but were both now aware that he had little to offer the team.

Tomorrow we set out towards the mountains. There's a village near the foot that Kazunari knows takes lodgers who are hunting the creature. Right now I'm not sure that there's anything out there but the rest of the party, including Shiho, appear convinced.

The journey to the village at the foot of the mountain was long and uneventful. There were no signs of the Yuki-onna, although nobody expected there to be until we reached the mountain itself. Instead the journey gave us time to get to know the rest of our travelling companions better. Takaaki, the leader of the group spent most of the day chatting with Shiho, picking her brains about the Yuki-onna and everything that it might be able to do. For Shiho's part, she was mostly quiet about it preferring to admit that she hadn't encountered one but that they should be ready for anything. She had chosen not to expose Kazunari's story as a lie though, protecting him for some reason I wasn't aware of. From what I can gather she was also able to ask him about his own experiences. I spent the day chatting to the rest of the party. The marksman, Atsuhiko, was very quiet preferring his own company to the rest of the group and I don't think I managed more than a couple of lines of conversation with him throughout the day. When he did speak it was with purpose and he seemed under no illusion about the potential dangers. Hideo and Hirohide knew each other well and had worked with Takaaki several times before. Hirohide was slightly younger than the other two and way more enthusiastic, telling me about the other adventures he and his cronies had taken to find similar creatures. They conducted searches all across Japan looking for a multitude of beings, some of which I've had the unfortunate pleasure of meeting in real life, yet it didn't take much questioning to realise that they'd never actually encountered anything supernatural. He spoke of filming odd tracks in the sand of river banks, of footprints appearing in snow and of hunting odd spectral beings that were forever just out of their reach yet he'd never actually seen one of the creatures. He was desperate to catch a glimpse of one though and didn't think there was any need to be scared, perhaps the clearest sign of all that he hadn't encountered anything. As the day wore on, it became more and more apparent to me that if we were to actually encounter something in the mountains then Shiho and I were by far the most experienced of the party, the others would be of little help.

The village that we're stopping at this evening is so small I'm surprised it passes as a village, just a few buildings scattered about a small inlet at the foot of the mountains. There was a single lodging house, the closest building to the mountain and when we entered we were met by a stunning looking woman behind the counter who claimed to be the owner. She appeared interested as Takaaki told her of our plans but no doubt she'd heard them all many times before as she seemed to know Kazunari. She did allow us to use the reception area to plan for tomorrow which we were grateful for, I don't think I would've enjoyed squeezing into one of the rooms with six others. The plan tomorrow is simple, there's a set of cabins a decent way up the mountain which we'll head towards for tomorrow night. On the way there's a known bear habitat where a number of bear carcasses have recently been found, something our leader has decried must be the work of the creature we're hunting, so we'll swing by there first. With the arrangements made we spent the rest of the evening in the reception area chatting before bidding our host goodnight, who remained behind the counter awaiting any other guests who didn't show, and retired to our rooms.

I'm sharing a room with Shiho tonight. She didn't seem surprised when I told her that the others hadn't ever found anything, she'd worked out as much from chatting to Takaaki. When I asked if that worried her she said no claiming that we weren't likely to run into anything out here and as such it was easy money as they were paying her a lot to go with them. She assured me that if there was anything on the mountains then we'd be perfectly safe but most likely we we're just going to spend the next few days on a long snowy hike.

Our hunt continued much in the same vein today as it did yesterday. We set off early this morning on the hiking route out of the small village heading towards the bear habitat along our way up the mountain yet found little evidence of a Yuki-onna. We did find the remains of a bear, killed not too long since meaning we could conduct an autopsy on it. There were no obvious external injuries, it hadn't been shot but its neck was clearly broken and Shiho found a couple of puncture wounds in the skin. When the group asked her if it could've been the work of the Yuki-onna Shiho agreed that it was possible although she also listed another five creatures, none supernatural, which could also achieve the same effect. Ultimately it was impossible to know for certain what had caused it. With fresh snow falling daily it was also impossible to see any tracks in the area which we could follow so instead we pressed on towards our overnight stop. I later asked Shiho about the bear and whether a Yuki-onna would kill one and she repeated that it was possible. So little was known of them that she couldn't say whether that was regular behaviour for one.

I was fortunate today, in that I had Shiho to speak to. Hideo and Kazunari led our way towards the overnight stop whilst Hirohide was constantly filming, mostly just Takaaki babbling on about the creatures you could find out here including bizarre tales of the Yuki-onna which he appeared to be making up on the spot. It was interesting to listen to if only to see Shiho's reaction to him, she found very amusing yet uninformed. Again Atsuhiko kept to himself.

The overnight resting spot is very picturesque indeed, a series of three log cabins built next to a frozen river which is overhanging with trees, their long branches forming a constant row of icicles. Again, with three cabins, I've been able to snag one for Shiho and me so we're all set. We have three nights at these cabins so it's from here that we're going to strike out into the mountains on a daily basis in the hope of finding the Yuki-onna. I'm still not convinced that there's anything out here but I can see that Shiho is concerned by the bear we found even if she refuses to admit it was killed by a Yuki-onna. It's probably nothing too but I can't help feeling there's someone, or something, watching us.

Our expedition has taken a turn for the worst. Shiho's been injured, badly. I'm worried about her stuck out here with little chance of getting help. I don't know what I'm going to do if she doesn't pull through. She has to pull through. After everything we've done together she can't die like this.

It all started this morning when we set off from the camp into the wilderness in search of the Yuki-onna. Takaaki was desperate to get the search started early so we'd set off despite heavy snowfall and the threat of further flurries. We'd travelled about an hour into the snowy mountains when we were set upon by a bear. I have no idea where it came from but I can only presume that it had been following us for quite some time. As it was, I was at the back of the group when it happened meaning I was closest to the bear so I was the one the animal went for. I saw it quite late and barely had time to turn before the creature struck me to the ground but before it could maul me Shiho quickly jumped in between us to protect me. The bear continued its assault regardless and brought down a paw across her back, its claws cutting deep into her. That was when Atsuhiko finally reacted and shot at it. His bullet hit the creature but didn't kill it however it was enough to drive it away. As soon as we saw Shiho's back I was worried about her, blood was seeping all over and she was already going white from blood loss. With nowhere else to turn I bandaged her up the best I could and as a group we carried her back to the cabins.

By the time we'd managed to get back, Shiho was almost frozen so I built a large fire in our cabin and moved her bed next to it in the hope of keeping her warm. I don't know if it's working, she's barely conscious but her body feels warmer so that's a good thing. The rest of our party were all concerned too, although to varying levels. Kazunari declared that he was going to go down from the mountains to seek proper aid although who knows how long that might take. Atsuhiko and Takaaki both decided that the best thing to do was to seek vengeance on the local bear population and immediately set off in pursuit of the one which attacked us. I'm not entirely sure what the other two did, I didn't see them after we got back to the cabins so it's possible that they went hunting too, I didn't really care. All that I focussed on was trying to help Shiho pull though.

I don't know how long it will take for proper medical assistance to reach us. My heart says it won't be too long but my head says it might be too late. There's a swirling blizzard outside at the moment so that'll no doubt slow everyone down too. Shiho is currently out so I'm going to try to get some sleep too. Hopefully the morning will bring better news. It just can't be possible that after all the deadly yōkai she's faced and beaten that she could be undone by a bear. I'll never forgive myself if she doesn't pull through. I don't think Sakura will either. If we can get through the night, she just has to do that. Survive the night and things will be better in the morning.

My night took an unexpected twist during the early hours. I was woken by a sudden freezing sensation gripping my entire body and I struggled to move, suffering with what I presumed to be minor sleep paralysis. I did notice that the door to our cabin was somehow open and the wind howled as it brought through the snow of the blizzard covering the floor nearest the door. The large fire that I had built last night for Shiho was also out, it's remains blanketed with snow.

Knowing that the cold could be detrimental to Shiho's state, I tried to stir myself into action but in doing so noticed that we weren't alone in the cabin. Standing over Shiho's bed was a spectral woman. She was dressed in a thin white dress and had an unearthly beauty to her which combined to raise my suspicions of her nature. Her skin was a pale icy blue yet appeared to be made of porcelain and her hair was well kept. At first I thought she was unaware of my presence but as I tried to rise she told me not to be scared and withdrew to the other side of the bed so that I could approach to check on Shiho. As she moved I noticed that she had no feet and instead glided, the bottom of her dress a couple of inches off the floor. That was when I realised that the woman in front of me must be the fabled Yuki-onna of the Kitami Mountains. She didn't appear to be an immediate threat, although truthfully I had no idea what she could've been capable of, so I proceeded to check on Shiho whilst remaining aware of the Yuki-onna. She was pale white and absolutely freezing, hardly surprising considering the situation. Even so, I immediately attempted to shut the door and restart the fire only to be stopped by the Yuki-onna who politely requested that I refrain from doing so. Now I've encountered numerous spirits and creatures this past year, most of them loathsome beings that exist purely to torment humans but some, like Mika and Sakura, have been kinder. I don't know about the general Yuki-onna populous but the one in our cabin seemed very polite and sincere in its request. Of course it wouldn't be the first spirit to use a display of kindness as a method of putting its prey at ease. Even so I obliged seeing as most I've spoken with in the past haven't attacked me and it could've easily killed me in my sleep. Confused I asked what it had been doing. The Yuki-onna replied that Shiho was in a bad state, something I could already tell, and that medical assistance was too far away to help, something I didn't want to hear. It then told me that it had placed Shiho into a hibernation like state that would keep her alive longer to allow her a chance of survival. When I asked how that was possible the Yuki-onna didn't explain but instead stated that it could spare Shiho's life and heal her. Experience told me that this wasn't something it would do for free and that indeed proved to be the case as the Yuki-onna explained that even with her current actions Shiho wouldn't survive for too much longer and that to save her I needed to help the spirit. That's how I ended up working on behalf of a yōkai that, as far as I know, could be planning to kill me and Shiho regardless of what I do. Knowing that working with it may well be the only chance I had to save Shiho I asked what it needed and the Yuki-onna explained a little of its life. It told me that unlike some of its sisters it had decided not to hunt humans, a terrifying prospect considering I only had its word for that. Instead it claimed to have weaned itself onto bear blood, the carcass we had found the other day was indeed its work. The issue the Yuki-onna had was that our own hunting party was now focussed on the bears and if they killed too many the food supply would dwindle or additional protection measures would be put in place making hunting harder. To help Shiho, it wanted me to drive the hunters away so that it didn't have to revert to feeding on humans. I pointed out that it was in a far better position to do this than I as the very sight of such a being would likely be enough to drive off the others but it declined saying that it had been in the area for a long time and had rarely allowed a human to see it. The spirit claimed that if it were to show itself then others would return and disturb the hunting grounds. It was a fair point and, perhaps against my better judgement, I found myself trusting the Yuki-onna and agreed to help. The crazy thing is even without the perilous position Shiho was in I think I would've helped anyway, maybe it's an unseen side effect of the spirit. The Yuki-onna told me not to tell anyone that it had spoken to me or that I'd even seen it and then placed a hand on Shiho's forehead for one last time before gliding softly out of the door and vanishing into the blizzard. As soon as it left, I quickly closed the door to stop the icy chill and restarted the fire hoping to get some heat back into Shiho but despite everything I tried she remained almost frozen in the hibernation state that the Yuki-onna had placed upon her.

By the time night gave way to the morning's sun the blizzard was still raging and I had completely failed to warm Shiho. Instead I was faced with the fact that I needed to drive off the rest of our hunting group to have any chance of saving her. Not long after the sun rose Takaaki did come to visit to check up on Shiho's condition. I don't know if he genuinely cared about her health but he appeared slightly concerned by her freezing temperature. He informed me that they had yet to hear from Kazunari and therefore they planned to set off into the blizzard to hunt the Yuki-onna but would kill any bears they encountered as revenge for Shiho's injuries. It seemed a pointless endeavour but did confirm what the spirit had told me overnight. He said that I was free to stay with Shiho or go with them but either way they'd be back by nightfall. I pleaded with him to return with me and Shiho down the mountain so that we could look for medical assistance but he disagreed saying that the only hope Shiho had was for assistance to come to us. It was clearly an excuse so that he could continue his hunt and I could see that all he truly cared about was the fame of finding the fabled Yuki-onna.

The four of them set off not much later and, despite an innate desire to stay and protect Shiho, I followed shortly after knowing that in the blizzard I might be able to scare them into leaving. It was gut-wrenching having to leave Shiho behind but I built the fire as high as I could and swore to her that I'd be back as quickly as possible. Of course she couldn't hear me but it calmed me to talk to her.

It was only as I followed the rest of the group up the mountain path keeping my distance that I realised I had no clue how to scare someone, it had been many years since I'd last jumped out of a cupboard to scare my sister and I didn't think that would be appropriate, especially as within their ranks was a supposed expert marksman who would shoot on sight. His presence, and that of a permanently rolling camera, meant that I needed to avoid detection and preferably not get shot. The walk was long and I spent all the time trying to think of ways to scare them. Eventually I decided that the best way would be to use my knowledge of the type of creature they were hunting in the hope that if they thought they were being stalked by something unnatural they would flee. It seemed worth a shot and I quickly came up with a few ideas from the yōkai I've encountered recently. My first thought had been to simply unleash the Hachishakusama that Shiho carried around in a statue but I'd left that in the cabin with her and truthfully I had little idea if that would go after them. They weren't really it's sort of prey and there was a good chance that it was still angry with us for trapping it. I certainly had no way of negotiating with such a being. If I had more time, I could've turned to Sakura or Mika for help as they would terrify them but it would take too long for them to get here. Instead I quickly realised that I was going to have to be their monster.

I waited until the party stopped for a bite to eat and built a small fire and then sprung my master plan. With the blizzard still swirling I slipped off my shoes and ran about jumping into the snow to leave deep footprints, ones which wouldn't be covered instantly by the snowfall. As I did, I built up a small arsenal of snow balls and scattered them about the area before finally I started to softly whisper 'teke teke' slowly increasing the volume until it could be heard drifting through the wind towards them. Quite what a Teke Teke would be doing up a snowy mountain is beyond me but I was relying on them not knowing their regular habitat yet having heard of the creature. It was on my sixth call that they finally reacted, Takaaki saying something to Atsuhiko who scanned the area. I called again, this time louder and all four heard me, glancing up and questioning one another about the sound. I continued and finally got what I wanted, Atsuhiko and Hideo both got up and headed towards me, following the sound of my voice. I immediately became quiet knowing that they were heading towards the deep footprints I'd left and crept around them in a wide circle until I came to the first of my snowball piles. I heard them discover the tracks and stop to inspect them, Hideo asking what could've left them and Atsuhiko responding that they were fresh. Whilst they discussed that, I hurled my snowballs at the others, pelting them with snow as I moved around them towards my next pile. The duo stumbled to their feet and searched for me but fortunately the blizzard was thick and I was nearly impossible to see. To them it would've seemed like they were being attacked by a ghost. At least that was the effect I was going for. Their shouts quickly brought back the two who'd gone looking for the sound and the four briefly discussed their findings. I continued to work my way around forever throwing snowballs and shouting 'teke teke' and I could hear their responses. One of them suggested that I might be the Yuki-onna that they had been looking for whilst Takaaki spoke only of a Teke Teke. His words were meant to reassure his team but they came across as hollow and frightened. From what I could tell, he had clearly heard of a

Teke Teke although never encountered one. Atsuhiko then reminded them that the footprints were similar to the others they had seen on one of their previous adventures and that appeared to scare them. I have no idea what they encountered previously but it was a stroke of luck that they drew a comparison. I could see them wavering so I continued to throw snowballs at them and then they broke, fleeing blindly towards where I was hiding. This was when I played my trump card, I dropped the snowball I was holding and ran straight at them almost being barrelled over by Takaaki as he came the other way. They stopped as they met me and panting I explained to them that weird things had been happening at the camp. I told them that things were moving around on their own, strange noises could be heard in the blizzard and that tracks of creatures unlike any I'd seen before had appeared in the snow next to the cabins. I then told them that I'd seen half the body of a woman as I'd made my way up the mountain to find them, her entrails scattered in the snow. I saw Takaaki go completely white and then the group fled in a blind panic, fleeing back down the mountain despite the blizzard raging around them. At one point I told them that we were in the place I'd seen the body, of course there was nothing there but when I suggested that it must've moved they started to shriek making me wonder what they would've done if they'd actually encountered the Yuki-onna themselves.

As we neared the camp I veered to check on Shiho but the other four completely abandoned her unwilling to go back into the cabins, insisting on not spending one further night in the mountain range. They called me mad for wanting to help her and swiftly left me behind to deal with Shiho on my own.

With them gone I went back to the cabin, happy to see that the fire had survived yet there was no change in Shiho's condition. Knowing that I wouldn't be able to get Shiho down the mountain on my own I've bunkered down for the night. As the darkness takes over the mountain and I hear the blizzard howling outside I'm left wondering if I've just scared away the only assistance I might have if the Yuki-onna turns out not to be trustworthy. Either way, we're now entirely at its mercy.

The Yuki-onna didn't visit us overnight. I had hoped that it would so that it could cure Shiho but the fire burnt all night and the door held firm against the raging blizzard. By dawn the spirit hadn't returned and I'd lost hope. That was when the oddest thing happened, Shiho sat up complaining that she felt stiff. Amazed I ran over to check up on her and incredibly she was warm again and the wound on her back from the bear was hardly visible. She asked what had happened and I told her about the bear attack but when she asked how she'd recovered without assistance I told her she had done so naturally and failed to mention the Yuki-onna. I couldn't be certain that the spirit had done anything but it seemed to me that it must've played some part in Shiho's recovery. Shiho asked about the rest of the party as she slid out of bed and I lied, telling her that they'd abandoned the hunt after her injury giving up any chance they had of seeing the elusive creature that haunts the mountain range. She didn't seem hurt by them abandoning her, I think she's become used to that kind of thing but she admitted that it was a shame that we hadn't been able to prove the existence of such a creature. Even she had been looking forward to seeing such a rare form of yōkai.

I thought we might have to spend the day in the cabin yet as the morning wore on the blizzard died down and Shiho incredibly appeared to have the strength to make her way back down the mountain with limited assistance. We did so at a slow pace, aware that she was still recovering and it was dark by the time we reached the small village at the foot of the mountains. We took refuge in the same lodging house that we'd departed from just a few days earlier and were greeted by the same stunning woman as before. She informed us that the rest of our party had rushed through the village the night before without stopping and she was wondering if she ought to organise a rescue party for us. She also took pity on Shiho whom she said looked tired and weak and needed to rest. As such she offered us a free room for the night which Shiho immediately went to. I wasn't as tired and stayed in the reception reading through some of the local books they had on the area giving Shiho some time to sleep in private. After a while our host offered me a drink which I accepted gratefully.

It was only when she delivered my drink and turned to return to her counter that I noticed something odd about her. Her dress ended a couple of inches above the floor and underneath she had no feet, she was simply gliding through the air. The sight shocked me so much that I fell off the chair and by the time I'd recovered she was behind the counter again. Plucking up courage I approached her somewhat cautiously and she appeared to know what was coming. Before I could say anything her face flashed into the same pale icy blue colour and she simply thanked me for my help and glided away through a side door before disappearing.

I have no idea what a Yuki-onna is doing owning a lodging house. I doubt I ever will. The only thing I can say about the one I met was it appeared to be friendly and most certainly is the cause of Shiho's miraculous recovery. Whether all of them are like that, I highly doubt. I think instead I met the anomaly but ultimately I'm glad that I did.

I returned to our room and found Shiho spark out. The Yuki-onna may've used some trick to help her heal but I still think it'll take some time for her to fully recover. I guess tomorrow I'll head out for Sapporo again and get her checked out at the hospital just in case, I somehow doubt she'll enjoy that.

We left the lodging house early today, our spectral host was waiting for us behind her counter as usual although appeared human again. I don't know if Shiho was aware of her true nature, if she was she didn't show it and I didn't want to point it out especially after the Yuki-onna had asked me not to mention her to anyone so we simply bade each other farewell and hit the road again. I guess she'll wait for the next group of hunters to come to her lodging but it still seems strange that she's an active part of their community and not hiding out up the mountain.

With the hunting trip wrapped up, rather unsuccessfully, Shiho's purpose being on Hokkaido is over. I can't say that I'll miss the cold but I have enjoyed some of what we've done here. It'll still be a couple of days until we leave, Shiho has, under great protest, checked into the hospital for tests. They appear to suggest that she'll be fine but it'll be a few days before she's discharged and we can get back to Honshu.

Shiho was discharged from the hospital today. They couldn't find anything wrong with her other than the faint mark of the bear's claws across her back which have healed remarkably well. They have suggested rest and relaxation for a couple of weeks. At first I offered my place as a good spot for her to recover however she has shot that down saying we ought to head to Tokyo instead as she'd rather see Sakura. She was quick to point out that she'd like me to stay with her whilst she recovers. That way she can keep her eye on both of us as she puts it.

I'm not going to begrudge staying there for a couple of weeks. It'll give me the opportunity to write up an article on the Yuki-onna, my editor is really pushing for another story before next month, and it's a good chance to learn more from Sakura about some of the yōkai we've encountered.

We've been in Tokyo a week now and I've had the chance to write up an article on the Yuki-onna and the haunted mountains. It's a bit different to the others but I was able to contact the rest of the hunting party for quotes to make it more believable. I don't know if anyone will actually think the area to be haunted but perhaps it'll drum up more business for the Yuki-onna's lodging house. Hopefully that's what she wants and I haven't just made her life much harder. I must've done something right with it as the editor accepted it straight away. Along with the article on the Hachishakusama it'll be published in the December edition.

Speaking of the Hachishakusama, it was handed to Sakura on our arrival here. She seemed thrilled to receive such a gift although Shiho was very firm that she should never release it from its prison. Sakura appears to have understood. At least she hasn't released it yet. Instead she placed it on her desk and I can hear her talking to the creature at night. I asked her one morning about it and Sakura replied that the Hachishakusama was strong, strong enough to worry Sakura, and that it was angry. She says it talks to her, mimicking voices, specifically Shiho's and mine to try and convince Sakura to release it. At least that's what it started doing. After Sakura didn't fall for the trick it started wailing. Eventually when Sakura informed it of her own nature the yōkai appeared to have a change of heart and started conversing normally with her. I don't trust it at all. I still don't get how Sakura can hear it and we can't. Shiho shares the same apprehension although Sakura appears to delight in having it trapped. From what Sakura says, the Hachishakusama is surprisingly intelligent and practically ancient. Truthfully I think she's a little too attached to her new 'friend' and Shiho has already registered her concern that Sakura might start to trust it.

Speaking of Shiho, her recovery is coming along quite nicely. She moans about wanting to get back out there but fortunately Sakura is playing the role of strict nurse and forcing her to stay in. It means she spends a lot of the time watching the website for any leads. So far there's been little although I've noticed that she has taken a few calls from acquaintances in foreign languages suggesting that she was able to make some connections whilst abroad.

We've still got at least a week left here before she's able to go out again and truthfully even then I don't know if Sakura will allow her to.

Shiho is now fully recovered and even more anxious to get out again. Today we allowed her to do that much. A visit to Tokyo Tower may not have been what she had in mind but out is out. Sakura joined us too, it was the only way that she'd allow Shiho leave and truthfully I think she enjoyed the experience. It's the first time she's been to Tokyo Tower despite living in the city. There was one scary moment when she dropped her sunglasses and a young boy saw her eyes but fortunately his parents wouldn't believe him. That particular episode appeared to amuse Sakura the most.

Despite the enjoyment of today Shiho is keen to be away. I don't think she likes staying in the same place for too long, that and her fear of Sakura becoming too attached again. A fear which she only recently told me and could make sense although from what I've seen Sakura would easily be able to handle herself against anything that we come up against, if not help. Despite that Shiho has declared her intentions for the two of us to return to Kyoto next week. I don't think Sakura is too thrilled by that plan.

The Impossible Girl

December 4th

Back home for me and straight back to work for Shiho. No sooner had we got through the front door we were heading back out again. The police had contacted Shiho whilst we were travelling explaining that whilst we'd been in Tokyo they'd been dealing with a serial killer that they couldn't find any leads on. It had piqued our interest and immediately we set out for the station in question to try and uncover the details of the killings.

As is their way with her, the police spared Shiho no details as they recounted the events. It had begun ten days prior when three separate bodies had been found one morning. Each victim had been a school girl and all had been stabbed multiple times. There had been no witnesses to the crimes and nothing had shown up on any security cameras, the victims either being home alone or in isolated areas at the time of death. Examination of the wounds suggested that all three had died within half an hour of one another, ruling out the possibility of the attacks being committed by the same person as even with sirens on it had taken the police forty minutes to travel between the first and last murder sites without stopping at the second. Intriguingly the blade used in each murder, most likely a kitchen or butcher's knife, was the same size suggesting that it might have been the same weapon, or a version of the same weapon. This had stumped police as the timings didn't add up. The three victims had known one another, they attended the same school and from interviews with parents, teachers and other students it was apparent the three were close friends. Searches of their houses and possessions threw up nothing to suggest that they were involved in something untoward and the police had struggled to find anyone with a clear motive for the killings. At first I wondered if there might be another Kuchisake-onna at work in the city but the images they showed us ruled that out. The victim's faces were mostly left untouched but across their torsos and necks were a multitude of deep cuts. It was apparent that their deaths would have been quick and painful.

With their investigation into the three murders throwing up little in the way of solid evidence, the police were dealt a blow when another body was discovered the following morning. Again there were no witnesses to the crime and the technique was the same, multiple stab wounds to the neck and torso. Oddly the report reckoned that the killing occurred exactly twenty-four hours after the killings the night before. This time the victim wasn't a school girl but a middle-aged man however the link to the prior victims remained, he was a teacher at their school. A second round of interviews at the school had informed the police that he wasn't well liked amongst the faculty or the student body yet there was no clear motive for killing him. Again the police had an issue placing anybody at the scene of the crime. He'd been killed in his own home with no sign of a break-in and all the doors and windows locked. It was almost as if the killer had simply vanished into thin air after completing their gory task.

The third morning of the police investigation brought further bad news. A fifth body was found. Another girl from the same school, a couple of years older than the first victims with no other links to them. Again she had been killed in her own home, stabbed multiple times with no witnesses to the event. Normally suspicion would've fallen on the parents, who were out at the time, but the evidence from the body suggested that it was the same blade used on the other four victims. Again the time of death was recorded at an exact twenty-four hours after the previous one. With five deaths in three days the police were now getting worried about a serial killer and drafted in more men to help the investigation. Again their efforts threw up nothing in the way of solid evidence. Despite the suspicion on the school where all the victims had attended mounting, they couldn't secure a motive.

Things got worse the following day when a sixth body was discovered. The situation deteriorated even further on the fifth day when another was found and became steadily worse each day as more and more bodies were discovered. This being the tenth day since the first bodies were discovered, there have so far been eleven bodies found. By the time we arrived at the station last night's victim had not been discovered. Each victim has suffered the same impossible fate, stabbed multiple times by an unseen assailant who has somehow slipped away through locked doors or windows leaving no trace. There is little for the police to go on, they're convinced that the weapon, and therefore culprit, are the same for each case, except the first night when timings ruled that out, and have linked most victims to the same school although not all. Of the eleven victims, six have been students at the school, the four mentioned earlier plus a couple of males the same age as the first victims. There have been two teachers killed, the mathematics teacher who was disliked plus the gym teacher. The other three are all adults and have little connection to the school if any. The adults, one of which lives near the school, had a range of jobs; a vet, convenience store owner and a dentist. If not for the same method used the police wouldn't have linked them with the school cases.

With their investigation going nowhere and fearful of more bodies over the coming days they had turned to Shiho hoping that she might be able to help as they suspected that there might be something more to the case than they could handle. Shiho agreed with them but had been mostly quiet as they had told their story. She did ask a few questions but far fewer than usual and at the end paused to think for a good few minutes before saying anything. When she did speak her concern was for today's body which hadn't shown up. She asked what time the bodies were usually reported and quickly ascertained that this would be the latest by a number of hours. This seemed to puzzle her greatly as it appeared unlikely that the killer would simply stop or switch their modus operandi. After she had confirmed that the last death had been the dentist she focussed back on the school demanding to know if there was a way to check on everybody who should be attending so that we could locate today's victim. The police set about her request immediately and before too long they came back with a report on the school attendance. There were thirty-seven students absent, all of which they had confirmed with their parents were planned absences or merely ill and not dead. There were two members of staff missing, a history teacher and the janitor who had reportedly been taken to hospital the night before. As soon as she was told Shiho's eyes lit up. There was a chance that this janitor may have been the latest victim and had survived the affair. Wasting little time Shiho told the police she'd look into it and we headed straight for the hospital.

On the way I asked Shiho what she thought might be behind the attacks and she was vague in her answer. She told me that there were many things capable of killing humans, most of which wouldn't leave much trace but it was clear that whatever was killing them was vicious and unrelenting. She did though suggest that at this point even she couldn't be certain that we weren't looking for a deranged human. If it were from another world then it didn't fit with most of the spirits I've encountered, of those that stab their victims Aka Manto is the only one which would do so multiple times. The others such as the Kuchisake-onna or Teke Teke tended to deliver one quick yet fatal blow, the exceptions being those with claws yet a blade had clearly been used. I asked Shiho if it could be a version of an Aka Manto we were looking for but she shook her head reminding me that they wouldn't roam so far for their victims and would simply wait in their bathroom for people to come to them. Although one victim was found in their own bathroom, it ruled out the possibility of an Aka Manto attack.

Once we arrived at the hospital we were led straight to the janitor who had his own room and was still in shock from the night before when he had apparently been the victim of an unprovoked attack. Instantly it was clear that this wasn't the same as the killings. The man's torso was completely untouched, in fact his entire body was perfectly healthy other than around his eyes. Both of the man's eyes were missing having been plucked out. All around his eye sockets were stab marks as if someone had driven their blade behind his eyes and then popped them out. It was horrific to see but I noticed Shiho glance through a clipboard detailing his wounds. The information confirmed that the blade used matched the dimensions of the one used in the killings. The man was fairly spaced out, probably pumped full of drugs to ward off the pain but Shiho was cleared to ask him a few questions. She started with the obvious one, could he tell us who, or what, had attacked him. His words were slurred and broken, due to the drugs, but he did manage to give us a vague description of his attacker. He'd been attacked from behind in his own home, his assailant using strength to turn him around before setting at his eyes with their knife. He said that it was a woman although details were thin, he claimed that she had blood red hair that matched her blood stained dress and that he could remember her cackling with delight as she attacked him. He apologised for not being able to give us more information but the attack had been rapid and he'd been unable to fight back. Shiho was noticeably quiet, her face one of deep concern, so I took up the questioning. Unsurprisingly he hadn't seen this redheaded woman before neither could he think of someone who would have wanted to harm him. He claimed that, before he lost consciousness yet after the attack, the sound of the woman's laughter vanished and he never heard her footsteps as she left. The entrance to his house had been locked and it was only when he regained consciousness this morning that he'd been able to call for help. By that time his attacker had disappeared. Wanting to reconfirm I asked him to give us the description again to check that he wasn't mistaken but he repeated his story word for word. Once he was done a second time Shiho simply stood up and walked out. Confused by her behaviour I thanked the man for his information, wished him a speedy recovery, although I doubt there is anything that can be done to return his sight, and bade him farewell.

I caught up with Shiho in the car, she was in the driver's seat, hands on top of the wheel with a face of pure dread. Taking my position in the passenger seat I asked her if this was bad and she simply nodded. It was clear that she had an inkling of what we were chasing so I asked her to confirm. She was silent a long time before answering. She said that she wasn't certain but she thought this was something beyond anything we'd encountered together before, something which even she thought was only a myth. She told me that she had little doubt that this redheaded woman that the janitor had seen was responsible for all the deaths yet she was unsure how it was possible. When I pushed her further she explained that the yōkai I've encountered can be easily categorised, for example the Kuchisake-onna and Teke Teke are both subspecies of onryō. There may not be many of them at a time but there will always be a few and more can be created. Shiho believes that this is something different, the rarest type possible, an individual yōkai that cannot be replicated. I asked if that was even possible and she replied that she hadn't thought so. She said she'd heard stories but never believed them. Nobody she'd spoken to had confirmed the existence of these legendary yōkai so she'd assumed they were simply stories, imagination combined with a more common yōkai to create a myth. It was only after seeing the Kunekune that Shiho had taken a passing interest in the stories but still found them too unlikely. Apparently this case is similar to one of these stories. When I asked Shiho told me about one of these yōkai, she named it Hocho-san.

Reluctantly she told me what she'd heard. Anybody could summon Hocho-san provided they knew how. Although the exact details weren't documented, one would simply need to call on her, offer her a weapon, usually a knife, and a target alongside what you wished her to take from them. Provided that you summoned her at the correct time, in the correct manner, and that she chose to answer, she would take the weapon and be relentless in hunting the target. The story goes that Hocho-san enjoys her work, a little too much, but doesn't do it for free. Summoning her forms a contract between oneself and the yōkai. After she's completed her end of the bargain she comes to collect. According to Shiho the story goes that if you know what you're doing you can dismiss her although it's not entirely clear how. More often than not she is said to kill the one who summoned her and then torture their soul in the next life. According to Shiho there is no recorded information, nor stories, on the original life of Hocho-san nor how she became what she is now but it's clear that whatever she might be, she possesses immense power. After hearing the story I had only one question for Shiho, why would anybody possibly make a deal with such a creature? Shiho's answer was simple, desperation. She knew of no way to stop Hocho-san, in the stories she'd heard no target had ever escaped her wrath and as we sat together in the car Shiho made it clear to me that she couldn't fight such a yōkai. She couldn't even be sure that such a thing truly existed. To my surprise she then offered me the chance to walk away from this one saying that Hocho-san, if that is truly what is targeting members of that school, was more dangerous than anything we'd ever come across and that she couldn't protect me from her. She declared that she was going to continue the investigation and try to stop the killings but she had no hope of actually destroying the spirit. Without hesitation I informed her that I wouldn't be going anywhere and that I would see it through with her. She seemed pleased but it was clear that the events of the morning had shaken her. Seeing the Kunekune all those months ago had shaken her but this was like that to the extreme. Truthfully, for the first time, I felt as if even Shiho had no real answers.

Now that we had a name for the killer Shiho explained that our only hope of stopping the deaths was to pinpoint who had made a deal with Hocho-san. If we could do that then we would know who the future targets are and would be able to convince the one behind it all to stop feeding the spirit names. Of course the number of deaths so far suggested that the person we were looking for either had a lot of stored rage against the world or was plainly psychotic and had no plan to stop. Either way our only hope was to find them.

With that in mind we ventured to the school that connected most of the victims to have a look around. Unsurprisingly there was a lot going on. The recent deaths and police presence had caused quite a stir yet the student body mostly appeared scared more than anything. There certainly wasn't any obvious suspects for the one who had a made a deal with Hocho-san. The faculty provided more options, they ranged from terrified to completely uninterested in the deaths yet there was no clear motive for any of them. Brief interviews with teachers threw up a few bits of information about some of the deceased. It seemed that the original three were known to bully some of the younger students and that the dead teachers were known for being quite strict with their students. Even so, it wasn't much to go on and as the school day ended we retreated to my apartment to search through the records given to us by the police and the school.

It was clear that the most likely suspect was somebody at the school, the sheer quantity of deaths directly related to the place was too high to be a coincidence. What we were missing, but Shiho thought crucial to our case, was the link between the three external deaths and the school. She was determined that if this truly was the work of Hocho-san then someone at the school must've had a motive. If we could find links between them and anyone related to the school then we might be able to find the one responsible. It was an arduous task but we did what we could. The convenience store owner lived near the school. It was therefore possible that he would've come into contact with all manner of people at the school. The vet and dentist leads were slim too. We had managed to get a list of all their clients in the last six months but cross-referencing them against people at the school threw up a large number of students as well as three members of staff. Working long into the night we were able to cross reference the lists to come up with suspects that we knew had links to both the vet and the dentist. In total there were twelve students who'd seen both in the past six months and one member of staff. It was a decent start and I was confident that we'd be able to talk to them all tomorrow yet Shiho wasn't as impressed. As I spoke to her the truth dawned on me, another night was passing and with it Hocho-san would likely strike again.

It was a tense atmosphere this morning when I woke. Shiho was already up and had been in contact with the police hoping to find out where, not if, Hocho-san had struck. Crushingly they confirmed that there had been another attack last night and a senior from the school had been taken to hospital after being set upon by an unseen assailant. Wasting no time we were immediately on the way hoping to question her for information before interviewing our list of suspects.

Shiho hadn't been told the extent of the girl's injuries over the phone but when we arrived it was clear what had happened to her. Both of her legs were missing, sliced off slightly above the knees in a scene which reminded me slightly of the Teke Teke. This had been no clean cut though, instead the work of furious slashing with a blade that matched our suspect weapon yet again. The girl was unconscious and truthfully there was nothing her parents could say that helped us. They confirmed that she'd been in her room when they heard her screams and by the time they arrived the attacker, along with the girl's legs, were gone. They were worried about how she would take the news when she woke as she had apparently been accepted into college on a sports scholarship as the star athlete in her school. Now with one swift attack her dreams had been taken from her yet it was clear that with no deaths in two days whoever was controlling Hocho-san had now decided not to have her kill. That was something picked up by Shiho too.

I questioned her on it as we travelled back to the school but she was unsure why that was the case. She stated that she was surprised by it as usually one would expect someone who's ordered a killing to continue killing but the last two attacks hadn't resulted in death. She theorised that whoever was behind the attacks may have begun to target people that they didn't want to hurt as much, or more likely in her opinion that the guilt of having people killed was eating them up, at least that's what she hoped. Her third theory hinged on the notion that as the last victim was a star athlete maybe they were now targeting something personal to each victim which could damage them even more than a quick death.

It was an interestingly horrific notion and something I pondered as we arrived at the school. The latest attack victim being a student there had sparked another frenzy and unfortunately didn't help narrow our list of suspects drawn up last night. They all could have had links to the girl simply by attending school and although one was in her class and another in the same athletics club neither contained the other victims from the school suggesting the link wouldn't be that simple.

The interviews we conducted with our suspects turned up very little too. They all confirmed that they knew the victims, hardly a surprise as we'd done the research and few offered anything solid to go on. The majority of the students interviewed shared no liking for the original victims nor the teachers but none seemed like a cold-blooded killer. By the end of our interviews we'd manage to narrow it down to five possibilities based on the others either having little more than a regular check-up with the dentist or having no issues with the vet. Shiho reasoned that they wouldn't have been targeted unless they had done something bad to the person and by all accounts the vet had helped save the pets of the eight we excluded from our list of suspects.

We were about to give up for the day, Shiho reasoning that we ought to check out the homes of our five remaining suspects when there was a knock on the door and a young girl walked in calling herself Hoshiko. She was in quite a state and claimed to be in the same class as the girl attacked last night. She was also part of the athletics club and was utterly terrified that she was going to be targeted next. I could see straight away that Shiho didn't believe her, from what I had been told of Hocho-san there was no chance of knowing who the next victim would be yet she was adamant that it would be her. Willing to hear her out, we asked why she thought that and she explained that she was best friends with the girl attacked last night. She also claimed that she thought she knew who was behind the attacks but declared that she wouldn't tell us unless we could protect her tonight. The girl was in quite a state though and whether from pity or a lack of anything better to follow, Shiho agreed to her terms and we found ourselves acting as bodyguards to a teenager.

Hoshiko's house wasn't too far from the school and she was grateful for our being there. Her parents are currently out of town so she's on her own and terrified. Once we'd managed to get her settled and fed she began to open up a bit telling us more about the students. She says that rumours abound that the attacks are supernatural and that it's the will of demon worshipers within the student body. She says there are rumours that certain students have sold their souls for the power to take revenge and that's what she's scared about. Asked why she believes she'll be the next to be attacked she recounted a story from two weeks earlier. She and her best friend had witnessed a group of three students from the year below bullying a girl a year younger after school. She could see that the bullying was really getting to the young girl but as they had seen the janitor was nearby they had decided not to intervene and instead ran home reasoning that he would sort out the matter. The three girls bullying the younger had died that first night and the attacks of the last two days had targeted the other two people who had been present. She says that during recess today she had seen the bullied girl watching her carefully with a dead expression and it had terrified her. Hearing the rumours going around the school she's started to believe that this young girl has summoned a demon to seek her revenge. Telling anybody else in the world would've resulted in her being laughed at but Shiho and I sat there stone faced as she told us. Eventually Shiho asked if she could tell us the name of the young girl she had witnessed being bullied. Ban Miwako was the name she gave us, a name which we had seen before. It was one of the names on our list of suspects. Immediately I locked eyes with Shiho and knew what she was thinking.

Hoshiko became even more scared by our response but before we could say anything of comfort we heard the sound of glass breaking as if someone was smashing through the window of the other room despite us being on the eighth floor. Shiho offered to check telling Hoshiko to stay in the corner where she could see the whole room. A minute later Shiho returned and shook her head, there was no broken window anywhere and no sign of break-in yet as she finished talking the lights flickered and went out. Instantly I rushed for the light switch but before I could reach it we heard Hoshiko scream. I flicked on the lights and turned to see Hoshiko unconscious on the floor, her legs severed in the same place as her best friend's. Above her stood a woman grinning at us. She had long blood red hair and wore a matching red dress and was deathly pale. In her hands she carried a large kitchen knife and small scrap of paper. She stared at me and Shiho for what felt like an eternity and I could feel myself withering under her gaze. I even noticed that Shiho backed away. Undoubtedly there is a dark aura around Hocho-san that I've never felt before. She simply emits evil and as she stared at us it felt like all hope was lost. She could've killed us quite easily I imagine, I certainly could not have put up a fight and Shiho appeared to shy away, yet all she did was stare at us and then laugh. A cackle of pure joy that hurt my ears to hear before she simply faded away into nothing taking Hoshiko's legs with her.

We rushed Hoshiko to hospital but it was clear that nothing could be done for her. She would live, much like her friend, but she would never walk again. I think Shiho took it quite hard, she stayed quiet almost unable to comprehend what had happened. I think she felt like she'd failed Hoshiko. The girl had come to us for help and we'd let her down. I pressed Shiho on it after we'd made sure Hoshiko was treated but all she focussed on was the fact that she had given us a name. With Hoshiko being Hocho-san's victim this evening the clock had reset and we had twenty four hours until the next attack. We retreated to my apartment knowing that tomorrow we had to deal with this Ban Miwako.

The very existence of Hocho-san has rattled Shiho to her core. She placed a call to Sakura this evening to find out if she could dig anything up. The answer was nothing at all. Even Sakura didn't believe she existed and sneered at the thought. Whatever this thing is, it's beyond our comprehension.

It was a bitterly cold morning and when I rose I could see that our failure last night still weighed heavily on Shiho's mind. It was only over breakfast that she finally spoke. She told me that she was amazed that Hocho-san existed. It was something she had never considered but opened the door for other myths to actually be real, a thought which terrified Shiho. I have no idea what these other beings are, she wouldn't tell me, but I know that if Shiho is this scared of them then they're things I do not want to meet. It was clear though that if Hocho-san existed then Shiho thought she might be the least of our worries and that there might be other unimaginable yōkai out there waiting to strike. Creatures which didn't show up in her Gozu book.

Bringing the attention back to Miwako, I asked what we needed to find out from the girl and whether we were actually targeting her. Shiho replied that killing her could potentially stop Hocho-san but she wasn't certain that wouldn't just turn the spirit on us. The fact that killing a school girl in cold blood even crossed her mind showed just how afraid Shiho was of this yōkai. Not wanting to turn Hocho-san on us, Shiho suggested that we had to force the girl to end her agreement with the sprit. She was also intrigued to know quite how such an innocuous school girl had managed to stumble across such a being in the first place. Finding that out might be key to stopping Hocho-san from ever returning. Truthfully that appeared to the best thing we could hope for as killing it was out of the question.

Our first task was quite easy, as soon school started, using the authority the police had given us, we pulled Miwako out of the class so we could talk to her. Having spoken to her yesterday in a similar manner she wasn't too concerned at first but that quickly changed. A small girl, probably the youngest in her class, Miwako was pale and slightly sickly looking and the bruises on her arms suggested that the bullying she'd received had gone far beyond name calling. Still, I imagine none of it came close to what Shiho did to her. Initially she denied any knowledge of Hocho-san, acting as if we were simply making up a ghost story for her benefit. We weren't buying her act though and Shiho quickly pinned her to a wall and held a knife under her chin. It wasn't the nicest thing in the world to see her do that to a school girl and I'm not entirely sure that Shiho was proud of this turn of events but it worked. Almost immediately the young girl broke down and admitted that she knew about the spirit. I guess, in the end, she was just a school girl and threatening to slit her throat was an obvious way to frighten her. As soon as she admitted that Shiho released her and we were able to have a normal conversation.

It was a bizarre encounter, I had thought that we were going to see Hocho-san again or that she would come to protect Miwako but the spirit never appeared. Instead we were able to talk feely with her. She admitted that she had been the one to summon the spirit and had been giving Hocho-san targets every night but as she spoke it became clear to us that the girl was absolutely terrified. She explained how she had first come to hear about Hocho-san, a fact that interested Shiho no end. She said that she'd been on the internet doing some homework when she'd seen an advert pop up suggesting ways to prevent bullying. It was through this advert that she'd heard the story of Hocho-san and learnt how to summon her. Interestingly when we searched for this website, we could find no trace of its existence. Shiho suspects that it may well have been Hocho-san herself that targeted the girl with that advert, a worrying development if true. Anyway Miwako informed us that she'd found the story amusing and had tried it as a laugh. Following the instructions on the website she had taken a knife from her kitchen and placed it next to a piece of paper with the names of those who had bullied her the most on it. She had then repeated the summons written on the website and gone about the rest of her evening as normal. It was only a few hours later when she noticed the knife and paper missing that she suspected there might be more to the story than she first thought.

The following day she noticed that the three girls whose names she'd written on that missing bit of paper weren't at school. By lunchtime the whole school had heard that they'd been found murdered and Miwako began to get scared. That night brought even more horrors as exactly twenty-four hours after writing out the names Hocho-san herself appeared before Miwako in her room. According to Miwako the spirit bore down upon her, cackling away in glee and stating that as it had fulfilled its side of their agreement it demanded payment. Miwako told us that she was terrified that Hocho-san was going to kill her, a theory supported by Shiho which did little to calm the girl. Desperate to escape the spirit she declared that her side was not fulfilled and quickly scribbled another name on a piece of paper. She claims that once she did that Hocho-san stopped cackling and stared at her for a moment before snatching the paper from her. Miwako stated that the spirit told her she would be back for payment once she'd finished her side of the agreement. She then vanished before Miwako's eyes taking the paper with her.

Of course, as we know, Hocho-san carried out her new mission and returned to Miwako yet again although she had now worked out how to stall the spirit. By providing a new name each night on a new bit of paper she could, in theory, postpone her own payment as Hocho-san would never be finished. Miwako told us that she didn't want to kill anybody but fear for her own life meant she continued to provide names to Hocho-san. She said that after the first few days the guilt was eating away at her but she realised that there was a way not to have Hocho-san kill her victims, she merely needed to take something from them. Focussing on others who had turned a blind eye or ran from her bullying issues she began to have Hocho-san punish them. She said that she was trapped, forever feeling increasingly guilty about condemning others yet feeling more scared by the spirit that stalked her every night. She says we're the first people she's spoken to about Hocho-san and begged Shiho to help her after we explained that we deal with these sort of beings on a regular basis. Shiho agreed to help and told her not to prepare any names for Hocho-san as that evening we were going end their agreement.

Miwako spent the rest of the school day a nervous wreck whilst Shiho and I prepared for the evening. We knew what time Hocho-san would show, the same as every evening, so we had plenty of time. I asked Shiho what the plan was and she wouldn't explain it to me, she simply told me to go with her on this and not to interfere. She was also very clear on two things, never mention our names to Miwako or Hocho-san and in no circumstances was I to converse with the spirit for fear that it might latch itself onto me. I also took the opportunity to question why Hocho-san was so easily tricked into thinking she hadn't finished her side of their bargain. Shiho gave a haunting answer. She doesn't believe Hocho-san was tricked in the slightest, instead she believes that Hocho-san sees it as an additional victim and a way to prolong her enjoyment. So long as Miwako provides names, Hocho-san will be happy to keep her alive but Shiho was clear that the young girl hadn't tricked the spirit in any way.

After school we went home with Miwako and waited for Hocho-san to come. The girl was petrified but Shiho spent the time coaching her in what to say when the spirit arrived. She was very clear that she needed to break off the agreement with Hocho-san or else the spirit would forever torment her. Despite how harsh Shiho was at times in her instruction it seemed to work and Miwako began to hope that she might gain her freedom from Hocho-san.

When the time came the room became very cold and Hocho-san appeared. She was exactly as she had been the previous night, long red hair dressed in a red dress and carrying a knife in one hand. She floated through the air gracefully yet her eyes were fixed firmly on Miwako as if she didn't even notice the two of us in the room. Again there was a dark aura around her. When she spoke her voice seemed ethereal and distant yet contained great power. She declared that she had fulfilled her side of the agreement and demanded that Miwako fulfil hers. At first I thought that Miwako was going to panic and grab for the nearby paper and pen but to her credit she held her ground and slowly shook her head declaring that Hocho-san was released from their agreement and that she didn't need anything from her. It was exactly as Shiho had taught her yet the spirit's expression turned to one of vague annoyance mixed with amusement. It declared that was fine and that Miwako's soul was free however it still demanded payment in this life. This wasn't something that Shiho had taught Miwako to deal with and as she turned to her I heard Shiho apologise and say it was the best she could do. Before I could really comprehend what was going on Hocho-san crossed the distance between herself and Miwako and plunged her knife into the girl's heart. The spirit laughed with glee as it set about its work, stabbing Miwako over and over whilst Shiho and I looked away.

When the laughter stopped we looked up but the spirit had gone. We were left alone with the bloodied corpse of Miwako, her dress already staining a blood red colour. I looked at Shiho horrified, for the second time in two days we'd stood back and let an attack happen but she simply looked away and stated it was the best we could hope for. She said that Hocho-san always gets payment, there is no way to avoid that. If you enter an agreement with her then eventually she will kill you. At least by calling off the agreement we had apparently saved Miwako's spirit in the next life and for that Shiho was pleased. She also said that now that Miwako was no more, the spirit would vanish, waiting until she is next called upon by another unwitting victim.

Before we could leave the room however, something ghoulish happened. The corpse of Miwako slowly picked itself up, stared at us and grinned, her short dark hair rapidly growing in length and turning a blood red until she was virtually unrecognisable. With blood red hair and a blood stained dress she looked exactly like Hocho-san. That was how Shiho greeted her too declaring that we had no need of her. Hocho-san merely laughed and then spoke in her ethereal voice telling us that if we ever want to enter into an agreement with her then we only had to summon her. With that said she vanished leaving no trace of herself or Miwako and the room instantly became brighter. I asked Shiho what had just happened and she explained that the stories of Hocho-san say this is possible. Apparently she likes to take the bodies of those she's been in agreement with so that she can continue to torment them after death. At least, she says, that fate hasn't befallen Miwako yet with so many dead and Hocho-san still out there waiting for someone to summon her I can't help but feel like this wasn't the conclusion anybody wanted.

We told the police that the deaths would stop and the killer was gone. They didn't ask questions. It was clear from Shiho's face that she wasn't prepared to answer them anyway. I think this one has weighed heavily on her. Threatening school girls, letting children die before our eyes and a yōkai unlike anything she'd encountered before. Truthfully I think that stuff would weigh heavily on anybody. It might take her some time to get over the last few days.

We aren't staying in Kyoto long. Shiho is keen to get back to Tokyo. The incident with Hocho-san has her worried, really worried. She spends hours brooding over snippets of information sent to her about various mythical beings. She's clearly worried that they all might be real. If that's the case then Hocho-san might just be the least of our worries. It also begs the question, why now? If these things existed long enough ago to be thought of as myths then why did Hocho-san appear now? Has she always been active, killing people every night without us knowing or did something, or someone, bring her here right now? Shiho doesn't have the answers.

She did however come to one swift conclusion. Everything that happened with Hocho-san started when Miwako was targeted by that internet advert. Shiho is determined to prevent that from happening again. She wants to know if Hocho-san herself was behind the advert or, more worryingly, if someone out there has been trying to get people to summon her. I was certain that it had to be the spirit but Shiho warned me that I was too trusting and that there were plenty of odd groups out there wanting to see yōkai cause chaos. Releasing Hocho-san could simply be a test to see if yōkai are real or an attempt to reach something much darker. Our investigation into the advert will require some hacking capabilities and fortunately Sakura has that in abundance. We'll head to Tokyo tomorrow and see if we can find out where it came from.

Sakura has had some luck finding the website detailing Hocho-san. It's taken her a number of days to find a trace of it, even then it was using the hard drive of Miwako's PC. The actual site has been scrubbed from the internet but she was able to construct a snapshot. The website does exactly what Miwako told us. It contains full instructions of how to summon Hocho-san yet makes no mention of the cost of doing so.

It's unclear whether Hocho-san herself created the website. I certainly wouldn't put that past her abilities but Shiho is clearly unsatisfied. Sakura has set up an alert to scour the internet for any sign the website returns so that she can counter it but truthfully I don't know if we'll ever be able to stop Hocho-san returning. One thing is for certain, even Sakura is showing concern. She claims that her discussions with the Hachishakusama about it suggest that it at least believes Hocho-san and others to be real. I don't trust it but its words have spooked Sakura and I thought she didn't get scared by any yōkai.

Shiho is still obsessing over Hocho-san and her existence. I hear her talking to Sakura late into the night about various spirits that I don't recognise. Some are clearly not native to Japan and I've noticed that she's pulled out maps of all of Asia with various pins planted across multiple countries. I even saw her copy of the Gozu which she has skimmed through hoping for answers. I haven't touched the book but I caught Sakura taking a look. Maybe it doesn't affect her like humans.

Shiho plans to travel early next year to the points on her map, examining ancient ruins and following up on various reports of other legendary beings. She's asked me to join her and frankly how could I say no. I'm in the process of getting my visas sorted. It could well be the trip of a lifetime. I'll admit the yōkai she speaks of terrify me but I can't let her face them alone.

More positively, we've received an invite for New Year's Eve. Mika is having a little get together to celebrate the fact that she's finally got someone to share it with. She invited both myself and Shiho although was quick to extend that to Sakura when Fuku mentioned her. Shiho is a little nervous about Sakura going but the little demon insists claiming that she wants to protect us from Fuku. Apparently their little encounter did nothing to make Sakura trust her. I think she just wants another adventure.

For the third time this year I found myself heading for the Minami Alps in Yamanashi and Mika's wondrous home. As expected she welcomed us with great enthusiasm, even Sakura who was appalled that we were in league with such creatures. Takeyuki was in good spirits too informing us that Mika had spoken of nothing but our arrival for days. They have been getting on well with Fuku who has now fully settled into her new life and has actually improved her speech massively. No doubt due to the hard work of Mika who obsesses over her ability to talk.

It's funny watching them all interact. Sakura doesn't trust Fuku or Takeyuki yet seems to be developing a fondness for Mika as all who meet her do. Shiho was initially cautious around Fuku but now appears to have let up and poor Takeyuki seems totally bewildered about the fact that he now has a third yōkai in his house, probably one that's more dangerous than the other two. I know Mika's been lonely for decades but I don't think even she expected this much commotion. It's nice in its own way although Mika is worried about what we've said of Hocho-san.

New Year's Eve. What a year! I still can't believe most of what I've seen but I have a feeling this is only the start. Shiho and I set off on the hunt next week but for one night it's good to reflect on what a crazy year it's been.

A year ago I spent New Year alone in Kyoto struggling to get any articles published and not believing in yōkai. A year later I've had my eyes opened to a whole new world. I've also become a writer for supernatural publications and perhaps more importantly than any of that I have others to share the New Year with.

Sure, I'm surrounded by giant spider-human and cat-human hybrids as well as what can only be described as a demon that could easily kill us all without hesitation but we're sort of family now and central to it all was the woman I spent my year with. The yōkai hunter called Shiho.

I have a feeling that next year will be something special indeed.